The Shadows of Time

Joseph McCloskey

About the Author

Joseph McCloskey has been writing for over a decade. In addition to publishing several short stories in magazines and journals, he has published 'Chasing Dragons' and 'Anna' on Amazon. This is his third book.

He has lived in the Northwest of Ireland all his life, but travels as often and as far as his budget allows, crafting his stories around the places and people he has encountered. His love of history and all thing old shines through all his books.

Joseph can be contacted on josephmccloskey99@gmail.com.

Acknowledgements

I would like to start by thanking my wife for her patience and for encouraging me to go on; books don't flow readily from me, it is a labour of love, but it is still a labour.

I want to thank my mother for passing on her sense of humour, to thank my father for instilling in me a love of all things mechanical and for trying to pass on his distrust of everything that is not.

And to thank them both for making me understand the importance of history and tradition.

I am grateful to all my friends for their wonderful Irish way of using the English language, they have been a great source of inspiration and I have to thank Orla Kelly Publishing for putting it all together and making the book so presentable, and Jean Sullivan at Red Pen Edits for an honest proofreading that did not strip the story of my voice.

To Kevin, the most honest human being I know. He has weathered all that the ocean has thrown at him and still stands tall.

The Shadows of Time

Chapter 1

A shaft of light poured through the little sash window; it penetrated the glutinous black of the night to find a solitary pear tree at the bottom of the walled garden. The fruit hung heavy, glistening on its branches. A scavenging fox scurried across the grass; she froze, captured momentarily in the light. The vixen raised her haunches and looked around her, staring hard into the shadows. She took off at a trot when there was no sign of danger.

The near perfect silence of the night was shattered by the metallic ring of steel on steel. The sharp noise followed immediately by the flutter of wings taking flight and the scratching sound of tiny feet fighting for traction in the long grass. Crickets fell silent, stunned by the interruption. Other creatures paused to consider if there was a threat to be faced, frozen mid-stride as if caught in a game of musical chairs. A few moments passed, the night held its breath, then exhaled. God's creatures were free to carry on as before, the ebb and flow of life and death could continue.

The whitewashed walls of the two-storey farmhouse and the walls of the courtyard stood tall and incongruous against the lush green landscape of the farm and the surrounding hills. The house was visible from the far corners of the valley, its light and the warmth of its walls acted like a beacon to draw all manner of creatures to its bosom on the long winter nights.

The little garage, my haven, was nestled in a corner of the courtyard to the rear of the house. It was rarely in darkness, long fingers of light escaped through gaps where the top of the stone walls met the roof, they reached into the night sky like the searchlights that probed the sky over London during the blitz. Yet where light escaped, cold air could come in. Though the work often warmed us, we still felt the chill on those frosty nights when the windows glazed over with a thin sheen of ice.

We toiled away in our little sanctuary as if we were the only people left in the world, oblivious to the nightly life and death struggle that went on in the grass, the garden and the world beyond.

A black oily hand passed me a spanner. I looked at him and laughed.

'Your Mam will kill you if you go into the house with those hands.'

Michael turned his hands palms upward to the light, proudly examining his workman like hands. I threw him a rag.

'Wipe your hands and be off for your supper. Tell her I'll be up shortly.'

He took off for the house at a run. The darkness swallowed him up when he crossed the courtyard, then he re-appeared into the glow of the light that shone from the kitchen window. I heard the muffled sounds of herself lecturing him when he went inside, and I smiled. Still scolding the boy, she stepped outside. There under the glow of the outside light she stood, legs apart, a dishcloth clasped in her hand, her floral-patterned apron eternally soiled with a splattering of flour.

Her figure was considerably fuller than it had been when we first met all those years ago. She'd been the belle of the valley, with a shock of unruly brown hair that refused to stay in place, dark brown eyes that would have made her look sad if it were not for a broad smile that rarely left her face. She was the apple of my eye. I have no idea what possessed her to choose me. We'd grown old together, and yet when I looked at her I only ever saw that same young girl.

She shook her head as she stared in my direction, a strand of hair fell and frustrated her face. She brushed it aside with a quick swipe of her hand, she laughed and wagged a finger at me. I was late, again.

I spent a few minutes gathering the tools that were strewn around the floor. There was very little order in the garage. I was not tidy in my work. When I took hold of a job, I attacked it with enthusiasm; tools were discarded as I went, thrown at my feet as the job went on. It was only when I stopped to take a breather, that I would look back on the carnage around me and wonder how that had happened. There are those who would condemn my ways, and there is a lot of merit in their argument. I must concede it is indeed much easier to find a spanner carefully returned to its proper place than to spend an hour searching the floor and cursing. It confounded me, since I almost always worked alone, that the spanner I dropped at my feet the night before was not there on the floor the next evening, laying where I could have sworn I dropped it. Fairies are at it again, was my father's explanation. I had followed his example in this and other things. A tidy workshop, is a quiet workshop he'd say, and so I was cursed to follow his habits.

My old armchair in the corner beckoned to me. It was late. I should have gone in but I found it hard to pass up on my ritual, a cold beer and a smoke before I called it day. I dropped the spanner in my hand. I grinned as the metallic clang echoed around the walls. I took a beer from the freezer, popped the cap off on the corner of the workbench and slumped into the chair.

'Too late to change now,' I said aloud, and raised the bottle in a toast to the old man.

I sighed. It wasn't a tired, fatigued sigh. It was a sigh of satisfaction. It had been a long day and I was not a young man anymore. I should have been happy to retire to a chair by the fire in front of the telly for the evening, but my son, Michael, had brought in a car he hoped to bring back to life. I was not as optimistic. I hated to dampen his enthusiasm, but I found it hard to find a positive word to say about the rusty wreck I helped him push through the garage doors.

'It's her last chance,' he'd laughed awkwardly. 'The old girl will be for the breakers if we can't bring her around,' he'd pleaded, patting the roof affectionately like it was a faithful hound he was talking about.

'More like last rites for her, son,' I laughed. 'But we'll see what we can do.'

In truth, I was glad of the opportunity to spend a few precious hours with him. I hoped we could salvage the car. It would give him a bit of independence, but in the meantime, I would savour our time together.

He was young, he was full of energy and I could not discourage that. I tried to remember how it felt to be young and full of hope, but it was too hard, and too long ago. I was old and we had little to bind us together but blood. I had felt the gap between us widen these past years, his teenage years. Difficult times for us both, an aging father and a confused teenager. Yet in this turmoil we struck on a common ground. We both had a passion for cars.

I wondered if this passion for cars could be genetically passed from one generation to another? My father was forever tinkering with machines. I had been too, and I saw it in Michael, a love of all things mechanical. However, the intuition that comes with this understanding of mechanical things had left us lacking in some basic social skills. When brains, looks and talents were being handed out he must have stood in the same queue that I had, because we shared the same failure to understand the social etiquette that seemed to smooth the way for others.

At seventeen Michael's hormones were going off like fireworks inside a body that was battling with the transition from boyhood to manhood. He was also awakening to the attentions of the fairer sex. Spending time tinkering in a garage with his old man was nowhere near as appealing as a chance to spend a few hours with his friends, especially the young girls.

I knew what this renewed interest in the garage had stemmed from. This car would give him the freedom to pursue those same young ladies from the parish that were coming of age. He and his goals were no different to those of every young man that went before him. The circle of life continued.

I took a deep breath and turned my attentions away from Michael's car. I exhaled slowly as I looked towards her, to the grey form at the back of the garage, resting under a dusty cover. The contours of her bodywork flowed like the curved lines of a fifties movie star.

'Soon baby,' I whispered. 'He's almost ready. Soon we will begin again.'

Chapter 2

The two-storey farmhouse stood at the end of a long winding gravel lane. A long row of cypress trees stood tall and to attention all the way up to the house. A great courtyard with outlying buildings stretched away from the house at the back. The Bluestacks, a mountain range that ran along the northwest coast of Ireland, rose high above the valley surrounding it on three sides. The Eany river spilled into the valley from the mountains above, it rushed angrily through the foothills, but by the time it reached the valley below it had mellowed. It was tame. It meandered slowly through the fertile plains and flowed all the way to the sea. The river ran right through the middle of the estate, dissecting it into two equal halves. The farmhouse sat in the centre of this valley, like a great pearl resting in the palm of a giant hand.

The house had been built in the early eighteen hundreds. Though it was a great house at the time compared to the pathetic thatched structures that littered the valley, it was not as grand as it is now. Over time each owner stamped their mark on the property, extending the house upward and outward. In a few weeks, we would enter the twenty first century, a new millennium. The house would be almost two hundred years old.

The courtyard and surrounding buildings had changed a lot over those two hundred years, as did the countryside. Yet the stone walls that surrounded the estate remained unchanged; this perimeter, the boundary of the original estate could be traced back to the time of the plantation.

The estate had neither grown nor diminished in that time. It was one of the few constants in an area that had experienced dramatic changes over those same years.

The estate had once belonged to a great landlord who claimed direct lineage to the crown. His family had reigned here for several generations. My father used to say the house was held captive by the British until his family set it free.

The truth was the last owner, William Moore, was a benevolent soul. He had been good to his tenants, unlike a lot of his ilk. They fared well under his reign as landlord. Unfortunately, his only son, George, did not have the same love of the land his father had. His head was filled with wild notions of what went on in the world beyond the valley. William blamed his mother's love of books. There was an extensive library on the second floor and just like the house it too had grown with each new owner. The shelves were filled almost exclusively with romantic tales of adventurers and explorers, colourful and exciting stories that were destined to turn the head of the young man.

Young George had been educated at home. His governess used to sit him on her knee and read to him from the thick volumes that lined the shelves of this great library. Awestruck by their exploits, he dreamed of following in the footsteps of the great explorers, Shackleton and Scott. The daily grind of running an estate or tending to the farm held no appeal for him. There was nothing glamorous about dunging out manure from the stables or helping with a cow at calf, there was no glory in digging a ditch; his sights were set higher.

It was unfortunate for his father, and inevitably for George, that he turned sixteen in the summer of 1914, a few weeks before Gavrilo Princip assassinated Archduke Franz Ferdinand on the streets of Sarajevo. It was the spark that ignited the powder keg that was Europe at the time. Princip's actions and those of the Kaiser dragged all of Europe into a bloody conflict.

William knew what to expect. Unlike his wife, he was quick to see that life on the farm was not for George. The boy had itchy feet. The newspapers were filled with stories of the young of men of England enlisting to fight the rising evil in Europe. Young George began reading the excerpts aloud at the breakfast table. He had never taken an interest in current affairs before. His father knew he was planting the seed. He tried to dissuade the boy as best he could, discounting the reports as patriotic propaganda. Despite his pleas, George would not be distracted.

Some weeks later, dressed in his Sunday best, young George made his way to the market town of Strabane for market day. There, with a host of young farm boys he enlisted. He took the King's half crown, and added his name to a long list of volunteers for the 36th Ulster's.

His father could do nothing more than use what influence he had to ensure he was fast-tracked to an officer. This it turned out was not hard to do, coming from an upper class family with ties, however thin, to the Royal family. He was promoted to Lance Corporal even before they set foot on French soil. George's enthusiasm continued to ease him through the ranks. He was popular with the men, he was bold, confident, and like-able. The soldiers under his command would have followed him to hell, and that is exactly what they did.

After just a few weeks in the trenches he was promoted to the rank of captain. George had joined the army to travel, to see the world, to become a hero. His eagerness to prove himself worthy of his boyhood heroes bordered on recklessness, he took foolish chances. His dream was to return a decorated hero, have his name in the local newspaper.

Hundreds of thousands of young men just like George boarded ships, excited at the prospect of going to war to rid the world of the savage Hun. They went forth to change the world. Not enough of them returned. Those that did would never be the same. The world they rushed off to change, to mould to their ideals of right and wrong, had spat them back onto their home shores, though not in one piece. Almost all of them came home broken in one way or another.

Three years at the front had aged the young man. He was changed in every aspect. The effects of the unspeakable horrors he'd witnessed were etched on his face.

Chapter 3

The train rolled gently through the countryside like a meandering river, a thin black line snaking through a green landscape. The clickety-clack of the train on the tracks had lulled him into a pleasant slumber. The smell of turf fires and freshly cut grass filtered into the carriage through the open window. The old familiar smells filled his nostrils as he closed his eyes and nodded off. It had been days, maybe even weeks since he'd slept so peacefully.

The sharp toot of the train's whistle woke him with a start. He sprung from his seat, eyes wide open, staring and filled with fear. An older man, probably in his early fifties, sat across from him. He'd been watching George while he slept. He was still wearing his great coat, the army issue that was meant to protect them from the elements; it barely kept out the rain but became like a lead blanket when wet. He jumped up when George bolted upright. He laid a hand firmly on his shoulder to steady the boy.

'Easy son, you're safe here.' he said, in a hoarse voice. An ugly raised scar ran from the corner of his mouth to his ear, it twitched when he spoke. 'I know what it's like to be afraid, son.' he added. George tried not to look at him, or the ugliness of his wound. He made to say something but stopped himself, then turned his face to look at the kaleidoscope of green fields that passed the window. They sat back into their seats without another word.

The train rounded a long sweeping corner. George knew where they were. He popped his head out of the open window as the station came into view. He was not looking forward to this. He craned his neck to see if there was a welcoming committee on the platform, almost certain his mother would have organised something; she was forever on one committee or another. She would have revelled in the task of preparing a grand welcome for her son.

He sighed, relief written across on his face. The platform was bare. No fanfare, no marching band. While relieved, he was inwardly disappointed, curious that no-one had come to meet him.

The train came to an abrupt halt, the jolt shook the passengers onto their feet. Hurriedly they tugged their bags from overhead shelves, pushed and jostled each other as they rushed to get their things and get off the train. George however, was in no hurry to leave, he stepped out of their way and let them all leave before he made to go. When the carriage was empty, he stood and tugged at his bag to free it from the overhead shelf. He lost his balance and fell backwards onto the older man who had also waited behind. They helped each other to their feet and exchanged a smile. George opened his mouth to speak, he wanted to say something, to share something with this stranger. He might be the last person he would see in a while who understood how he felt, to say something about his experiences, what he had seen and done, but no words would come. They exchanged a knowing look and stepped away from each other. George had one foot out the carriage door when the older man took him by the arm.

'In time, we will forget all about it,' he said, he looked hard at George as he spoke. It was more a question than a statement. He waited for a reply, a reassurance from George that this would happen. George shrugged his shoulders, gave him a weak smile and turned away. He was not so sure he could ever forget.

It was two miles to the estate from the train station. The road to the village turned off sharply to the right just a few hundred yards from the platform and threaded its way through a pine forest that ran all the way to the walls of the estate. George relished the thought of the walk alone. It would give him time to acclimatize himself to his old world. He was well practiced at long marches. Over the course of his three years at the front he had marched several hundred miles, if he added it all up. Yet the two miles took him almost an hour. His pace was slow, he dallied, postponing the inevitable, a re-union he was not sure how to handle. He paused regularly to look on a scene that brought back a memory, a familiar wooded hill, a first glimpse of the river that dissected the valley.

He enjoyed the walk, he felt his mood lighten as he went. His comrades had complained tirelessly about the long marches to and from the front. He could not admit it to anyone but he'd enjoyed the marches. It was a form of therapy in the madness, and of course, time spent marching was better than time spent in the trench. He stared down at his boots as he walked. He allowed his mind to wander, kicking the round gravel stones from the road as he went. When he raised his head, he found he'd arrived at the entrance to the estate sooner than he'd expected. The lane to the house looked longer than he'd remembered, he hesitated and for an instant, considered turning, walking away before anyone knew he was there; though he had no idea where he would go. He dreaded the questions that would come, questions he did not want to answer. But it was too late, he had been seen.

'George?' his father shouted his name aloud when he saw him, then rushed to greet his son. He was older and slower than George remembered the old man. This was not the homecoming he had dreamed of as a young man. His father hugged him and pulled him close. The old man was overjoyed to have his son back in one piece. With an arm around the boy he led him up the road, firing question after question at the boy, not waiting for an answer. They turned into the courtyard, a brass band burst into life when they came into view. Tears flowed openly down his mother's face as she rushed up to him and taking his face in both her hands, she kissed him on the forehead.

Faces that he should have known came up to him. They shook his hand, patted him on the back and complimented him on how well he looked in his uniform. George cringed at their remarks, he did not stand proudly in his uniform like he had done on those first days on the parade ground. His shoulders sagged, he slouched, as if weighed down by the great burden of guilt he felt was resting on him. He was overcome, overwhelmed. It was all too much and too soon. He was not ready. He could not meet the eyes of the farm hands he'd grown up with.

His mother was riding the crest of the wave of euphoria that filled everyone in the courtyard. Barrels of ale were laid out. Rations that had been saved for a splash out on this occasion were being enjoyed by everyone, well almost everyone. Old William was not oblivious to the sad languor his son seemed loath to shake off. He couldn't understand why; the boy was returning a hero, and in one piece.

The evil that rose its head to overpower the world, had been quashed by young men like their George. The church heralded their bravery and their achievements, but none knew the horrors they'd endured. The press had failed to inform the world of the savagery that had passed and the toll it had taken on the young men who witnessed it. And so, they were misunderstood. Most struggled and failed to return to normality, George was no different.

His father was sure that time, home comforts and his mother's pampering would bring him back to life, but his father was wrong. Daily, he walked the farm like a ghost, barely acknowledging the workers he met. His mother was heartbroken. His father, desperate to draw out the spirited boy he brought into the world, tried anxiously to spoil him with anything he thought might bring him around.

George, now affectionately known to everyone as the Captain, brought one thing back from France that helped him through to the end of his days, a passion for the new-fangled horse-less carriages.

The old coach-house was quickly transformed into the garage I now sit in. I twisted awkwardly in the chair to look up at the pressed tin poster of the 1930 Alfa Romeo 6C. I have a faded photo of the Captain posing beside it right here in this garage. It occurred to me that I hadn't seen it in some time but I was sure it was lurking somewhere in the house. The car must have looked as out of this world to the stable boys that worked here as an alien spacecraft would if it were parked in the back of the garage today.

Chapter 4

I looked at the covered shape again. 'Your pedigree is just as illustrious, old girl,' I assured her.

Just then a gust of wind swirled along the floor, raising eddies of dust as it went. The cover fluttered and fell still again. I urged myself from the seat, crossed the floor to her side and dropped onto one knee to tuck in the edges of the cover that were disturbed by the breeze. I raised the cover a little, just enough to get a glimpse underneath. A tin, used as a weight to hold the cover in place fell to the ground with a crash, catching my hand as it passed. I sprang back clutching my hand. It felt like it had been slapped.

'Sorry,' I said aloud, talking a step back from her. 'Won't happen again.' I felt a twinge of embarrassment as if I'd just been caught trying to peep up a lady's skirt.

I rose to my feet, groaning involuntarily with the effort. I don't know when I started doing this but it angered me. I was once a supple young man and could spring to my feet like a young lamb, surely that was just a few years ago, or was it decades?

I threw open the rickety wooden double doors that kept the world at bay and welcomed in the dark. It was a beautiful night, the air was warm, the silence overpowering. The full moon perched on the rim of the Bluestacks was as reluctant to bid goodbye to the day as I was. I drew a deep breath, the crisp cold air filled my lungs. From the bottom drawer of a tool-box I drew out my pipe and tobacco. Settling back into the old chair I began the ritual. I tapped the contents of the pipe into the palm of my hand then blew the ash into the air, it swirled before me for a moment before it was sucked into the blackness. I struck a match. I held the lit match over the pipe and sucked hard, drawing the flame onto the fresh tobacco. The dried leaves glowed red in the near dark and the pipe came to life. The smoke climbed in long sinewy strands towards the roof and gathered to form shapes, like ghosts of those who'd sat here before me.

A movement caught the corner of my eye. The light in the kitchen had just gone out. I smiled as I imagined herself shuffling off to bed without me, scolding me for staying out so late as she went. I took some time to enjoy my smoke, mulling over all I'd done for the day and what I hoped to get done the next day. I liked this time, my time, an opportunity to take stock of things without interruption. When I was done, I eased myself from the chair, took a quick look around to make sure I hadn't left any fire hazards behind and paused at the door, my finger on the light switch.

'Goodnight,' I said, to no-one in particular and plunged the garage into darkness. The loud crunch of the gravel under my feet stopped the creatures of the night in their path again, they paused until I made my way to the farmhouse and my bed.

The stone walls of the old house that separated the rooms were thicker than a man, and yet they did little to stifle any sounds. The floorboards sang out as I tiptoed down the hall. Each step drew a whispered curse from me. The brass knob felt cold against my hand. I turned it slowly, already aware that it would squeak as it always did. Every night I swore I would oil it, and every morning I forgot.

'You'll get your death of cold in that shed,' she said, as I undressed and tried to slip quietly into our bed.

I smiled at the pair of eyes and a nose the peeped over the covers.

'I know you're always here to warm me,' I chuckled.

'What happened to your leg?' she asked.

'What?'

'You were limping coming down the hall.'

'How would you know that?' I asked, my voice raised.

She giggled under the covers. 'I can tell everything from those few steps coming down the hallway. I can even tell your mood.'

'Hah!' I laughed, making light of her claim, but secretly suspected it was true.

'If your feet are cold, you can bloody well go back out there.' she said, changing the subject.

Wrapped in each other we fell fast asleep.

Chapter 5

The night had barely cleared when I eased myself away from the warmth of Mary's side. I gathered the work clothes that were strewn around the floor where I'd stepped out of them and tiptoed down the hall towards the kitchen.

I was fully dressed when the kettle sang its familiar tune. Pulling back the curtains I looked out over the fields that stretched away from the house to the river. The dew lay heavy on the grass in a silvery web. I threw open the back door to look out on another fine morning. The warbles of the dawn chorus greeted me as I looked around. I shrugged as the cold bit and drew a long sigh as I looked towards the garage.

The clock above the stove chimed on the half hour. Six thirty, there was no sensible reason to be standing in the doorway at this hour with nowhere pressing to go. But my old bones were conditioned to the early morning start. I did try to sleep late once, but a foolish guilt drove me from the comfort of my bed. My father's voice rang in my head. His shouting still haunted me years after his passing. Bed was for the lazy and the sick once the sun was up, he used to say. I was still a prisoner of his doctrine.

Truth was, I liked this part of the day. When I walked through the courtyard I felt like the world belonged to me, I was the only man alive. Not a sound to break the silence but the crunch of the gravel beneath my feet and the song of the thrush.

'Those walls are going to need a coat of white-wash this summer,' I muttered as I ran my hand over the stones of the wall that enclosed the courtyard. The remains of the last coat of paint fell away under my hand like confetti. The thought didn't concern me, in fact I felt myself look forward to the task. 'A few will need pointing too,' I added, as I felt some of the stones loose to touch.

I finished my morning ritual of the walk around the grounds, and returned to the kitchen to find Mary standing over the stove pouring herself a cup of tea.

'You're early,' I said, looking again at the clock to make sure I was right about the time. She smiled sheepishly at me and took her cup to the table. It wasn't like her, she enjoyed her sleep in.

'Couldn't sleep,' she said finally.

'Are you alright?' We knew each other so well, I could tell from just those two words that something was troubling her.

'It's nothing,' she said with a wave of her hand, as if she was trying to swat away the discussion like it was a summer fly that buzzed around her head to annoy her.

'A foolish dream that keeps waking me.'

'A nightmare?' I asked.

'Not really,' she said, but did not sound convincing.

'In the dream, I wake in the middle of the night and you're gone from our bed. I get up and go to the kitchen and you're not here. I look to the garage but it's in darkness. I don't feel scared, more confused. Where could you be? Then you come up behind me and ask why I'm not in bed. We hug and I laugh. You shuffle back to bed and I'm about to turn off the kitchen light and join you when I glance back to the garage and the light just pops on.' Mary was staring into her mug as she told me all this. 'It always gives me a fright,' she said, as she looked up at me.

I pulled her close and laughed. 'Are you trying to tell me something? Am I spending too much time out there,' I nodded in the direction of the courtyard and the garage beyond.

'Heavens, no,' she assured me. 'You know nothing pleases me more than to know you are close.'

'You know that if you want, I can abandon the garage and spend every minute of every day following you around the house just so we can be together.'

'How long do you think an old woman of my age would get for murdering her husband?' she asked, pushing me playfully away. 'Off with you,' she said, still laughing. 'And get something done,' she was still shaking her head and laughing as she disappeared down the hallway to our bedroom clasping a steaming hot cup of tea in her hands.

God, I love that woman, I thought. An ache of longing filled me when I considered that sometime soon one of us would no longer be here.

I stopped in the middle of the courtyard on my way to the garage, I threw back my head and looked up to the sky. 'Forgive my selfishness, Lord, but please let me be first to go,' I shouted this at the top of my lungs, there was no reason my mad plea could not be heard at the far reaches of the valley, but I had reached that wonderful point in my life where I no longer cared. I was past caring about political correctness, or saying the wrong thing at the wrong time and offending some oversensitive sod. Those who knew me understood my ways, and I had no desire to make new friends.

I held my eyes shut for a time, then opened them, one eye at a time to look up at a clear cobalt blue sky. There was not a single cloud to interfere with the reception, a perfectly clear signal on a perfectly clear day. No reason why God would not hear my plea. The irony was I had lost my faith many years ago. I had no idea who it was I thought I was shouting at that morning. I laughed at my foolishness and continued to the garage.

I made a mental note that day to tidy up. I looked around the courtyard, every corner was filled with bits of old cars I'd repaired or salvaged. Getting to the back of the garage was tantamount to crossing an obstacle course.

Jimmy O'Donnell's van was parked by the garage door waiting for me. I had promised him I would service it. He was an old friend and I would do this one thing for him. I had long since given up on committing to any serious work, that was all behind me, forty years of it. This was to be my time. My chance to do the things I wanted to do, to get a chance to smell the roses. I threw open the flimsy doors. The smell of oil and petrol met me. Smell the roses indeed! I laughed, wrinkling my nose.

'Morning,' I said, as I stepped in, continuing my father's ritual. The first rays of sunlight peered over the ridge of the house and traced a line on the garage floor before me.

'Good morning to you too,' I nodded my head to greet

the sun on what looked to be another fine spring morning. I drew a deep breath and began.

'Sure, you still remember where everything is supposed to go?' The voice startled me. I looked up. Jimmy was silhouetted against the light of the door.

'Better than you know where everything goes.' I said, then stopped myself before we went down a too well trodden line of banter. 'Wait,' I laughed. 'Let's not go there, we're too old for all that innuendo.'

We laughed together, two old fools that knew each other's ways. Then I returned to work while Jimmy wandered around.

'If these walls could talk, Jack,' he said, reaching up and tugging at an old horse's harness that was draped over a rafter. I was leaning over the engine. I stood up, stretched and groaned, then joined him in looking from wall to rafter. Just then Mary arrived with two steaming mugs.

'Thought I heard voices,' she laughed. 'Wouldn't be the first time I caught him talking to himself.'

Jimmy smiled and took a mug.

'Two mugs for two mugs,' she called back as she went. We settled ourselves onto a corner of the workbench to finish our tea. Neither of us spoke for a time. Each considered our surroundings and all the things that had passed under this old roof. We were drawn to the poster of the 1930 Alfa Romeo 6C.

'What would one of those have cost back then?' Jimmy asked.

'The price of several small cottages, I imagine,' I said.

'Are there any photographs of the Captain in the house anywhere?'

'Very few,' I said. 'My grandfather threw out everything that reminded him of the British. When he and his brothers bought this house at the auction it was like he had taken something back from them. He wanted to purge the house of their presence.'

'Is it true he was in the IRA?' Jimmy turned to face me when he asked this.

I didn't hesitate. 'I'm sure he was; at that time, lots of men his age were. He and his kind drove the British out,' I paused to sip my tea. 'I wish I'd know the man.'

'Would you not consider selling some of those?' he pointed with his cup to the bridles and saddles that were draped over a rafter by the door.

'Wouldn't seem right,' I said, without hesitation. 'They belong here, always have.'

I looked around the strange mix of paraphernalia that was strewn along the top of the walls and over the rafters. Each piece attached to a character or an event that linked it to the estate. I often thought it would have made for a great field trip for history students. The farm implements from past to present were all here somewhere, in part or in whole. The changes in transport could be tracked, from the remains of a cart wheel above the door to the frame of a 1919 Crossley tender used by the Black and Tans, several old steering wheels, mementos from cars owned by the estate, and last but not least the poster of the Captain's old Alfa Romeo 6C, and above it the wood-rimmed steering wheel from it.

Images flooded my head, my youth, my father, growing up around the estate. This was happening to me more and more of late. I wondered if it was an age thing? I gave myself a fright for a moment when I pondered if it was the onset of Alzheimer's. I quickly dispensed with the notion, not because I was confident it could not be me, but because I was not going to allow myself to worry about something I had no power to prevent. I suspected it was more of a nostalgic thing, now that my life was nearing its last lap, I was taking more time to ponder where it had gone and how I had spent it.

'Will you get this finished today?' Jimmy asked, waking me from my daydreaming.

'I could leave it to you if you like,' I said, extending an oily spanner to him, a sharper edge to my voice than I intended.

'Smart-ass.' he laughed.

It took most of the day to do a job I would once have managed in a couple of hours. It wasn't easy to come to terms with having so much time on my hands that I didn't have to rush along, or watch the clock as I went.

Chapter 6

'Michael is washing up before dinner,' she said, plonking a piping hot plate on the table in front of me. I was starving. I pulled my chair into the table, picked up a knife and fork and was poised to dig in when she prodded me with her finger.

'Are you going to eat your dinner with those hands?'

'Aye,' I said, a look of mock disbelief on my face. 'Aren't they the only hands I have!'

She clipped me around the head with the tea towel, 'Off with you and wash up.'

I paused at the door. 'I'm going to tell him tonight.'

'Tell him what?' she called after me, in a voice louder than a whisper but not loud enough for Michael to hear.

'You know fine well what,' I turned back into the doorway. 'The '69. It's time. If I leave it much longer he might not be here to finish it.'

'Don't go putting pressure on the boy,' she wagged a finger at me. 'He might not have the same interest you have. What if he doesn't want to bother?'

'Jesus woman, have you any idea what you're saying. Of course, he'll be interested. I caught him staring longingly at her in the corner a few times already. What red-blooded boy wouldn't kill for the chance?'

She shook her head and frowned.

'He's not gay, is he?' I asked, readying myself for my escape.

The wet towel she threw met Michael in the face as he entered the kitchen.

'What's gotten into you two?'

We smiled at each other. 'Have your dinner,' I said. 'I've a surprise for you.'

We sat in silence at the table for quite a while. Michael pushed his food around the plate waiting for me to speak. I deliberately ignored him. I finished Mary's excellent stew, carefully mopping the plate clean.

'It's the car, isn't it? It has to be. You've decided to finish her, right?'

Mary smiled at me, she knew all along the boy would be overjoyed.

'It'll have to be done right,' I warned. 'I won't accept shoddy work. There'll be no cutting corners,' I said, waving the fork in my hand at him.

'Yes!' he shouted. Springing to his feet he threw his chair back noisily and punched the air. We were close he and I, but not in a touchy-feely way, but that night he threw his arms around me and hugged me at the table.

'You won't regret it, Dad. It will be stunning. I have a set of bling wheels picked out for it already.'

I was off the chair in an instant, words of protest on the tip of my tongue when he laughed.

'Gotcha!'

Dinner was over and the dishes were done, all three of us set off for the garage. The rain that had been beating down on the tin roof fell silent as I threw open the doors, crossed the garage and reached for the hem of the cover.

'Wait!' Mary shouted. 'We need more light.'

She turned on all the lights she could find, focusing those she could on the darkened corner where I stood.

'Don't just stand there on ceremony, let's see it,' Mary scolded. 'You're not going to make a speech, are you?'

I wanted to laugh but I refrained. Mary and Michael were excited at the prospect of seeing what was under the cover. It had been here as long as they could remember. But they had no idea of the importance of this moment. My father was the last man to see her in her entirety. I was no more than ten when I stood by his side, handing him spanners on demand, like an assistant to a great surgeon. Scalpel please, Jack he had joked, as we stood side by side. A rare moment of bonding for a young man and his father. Sadly, for me those moments were too few. He took ill shortly after that. I stood by his bedside, not fully understanding the extent of his illness.

'When I shake this flu, we'll have to get back to the car, son,' those were his last words to me. 'Don't you fret. You'll be the pride of the parish going off to the dance in the old girl.'

'Jack!' Mary called out. 'Are you okay?'

I shrugged and laughed it off. 'Ready, drum-roll if you please Michael.'

He turned over an empty oil drum, took two screwdrivers and beat a fast rhythm on the tin.

'Ladies and gentlemen, I give you, Esther,' I paused, and winked at Michael. 'The love of my life.'

Mary scoffed. 'Get on with it, you old fool,' she laughed.

'Esther Ryan would have nothing to do with you. Love of your life indeed, hah! In your dreams.'

I whisked off the grotty canvas cover with as much pomp and ceremony as my uncouth mechanic's hands could muster. Neither of them spoke for a long moment. Michael stepped closer, walked along her length and looked to me for approval before he set a hand along her contoured body.

'That's it?' Mary couldn't help herself. She was dumbfounded. 'It's a wreck!'

Michael and I looked at each other and smiled. I knew then that he had the vision. He could see her for what she would become. He could see past the crumbling wreck she was now.

'Glad you named her Esther,' Mary laughed, 'If you'd named that ugly wreck after me, I'd have your head. Esther indeed!' she shrugged her shoulders and laughed aloud.

I threw an arm around Michael, 'What do you think son? It's going to be a lot of work, but it will be worth it in the end.'

'Argh, I'll leave you two old fools to your ramblings.' Mary left us behind and made her way back to the house.

It was dark and late again when we went in. We were at the table plotting and planning when she came up from the bedroom.

'You'll both get your death of cold, the fire's gone out.'

We didn't respond. We were lost to her in the depths of reconstruction plans. 'I'll make tea,' she said, feeling a little left out and regretting her earlier negative remarks. She saw now the intensity of the discussions and knew this was important to us for so many reasons.

'This is so good for you both,' she said from under the covers. I was undressing when she spoke. 'Aye it'll be good for the boy. It will help him understand the importance of committing to something and seeing it through.'

'You need this, Jack,' she said in a softer tone. 'Michael will be gone from us soon. To college or off to make his way in the world. This time will be precious.'

I sat on the edge of the bed, silent for a long while when I considered what it would be like without him here.

'You miss him, don't you?' Mary whispered.

'What are you talking about woman? He's still here, and will be for a long time yet. He's just a boy.'

'You know what I mean. Your father. You miss him.'

Her words took the wind out of me. 'Yes Mary, I do. I miss him.' I slumped onto the end of our bed, my shirt half off and half on. 'He was taken far too young. Long before I had a chance to know him. I wanted to make him proud of me, but I never got the chance.'

'You're a good man, Jack. He would have been proud of you, as proud as I am.'

I shuffled under the cover and held her close.

'You're lucky I didn't see Esther Ryan first.' I said.

Mary threw back her head and laughed as she belted me with her pillow. I threw my arms around her and held her tight, her body rocking with laughter.

'You were never the sweetest of my beau's Jack, but you were the only one I knew would always make me laugh.'

Wrapped in each other we fell fast asleep again.

Chapter 7

A week went past before we began in earnest.

'Even a journey of a thousand miles, begins with a single step,' Michael quoted the much-abused Tibetan phrase.

'A thousand miles, eh!' I slapped him on the shoulder. 'It may feel just like that by the time we're done.'

The garage was tidied, every unnecessary item was thrown out. We pushed her out of the dark corner where she had rested for far too long and into the light. There was little left of her once lustrous red paint to shine. We stepped back from her to consider her lines. For most of an hour we walked around her, surveying her strengths and her weaknesses. The silence interrupted by the occasional intake of breath at an unfortunate discovery or an ooh and an aah at a pleasant surprise. A solid panel, a part that moved freely, not frozen and seized with rust. We exchanged a few concerned looks. He's getting cold feet, I thought. I knew it was a daunting task. My father and I had barely begun when he took ill.

'It's going to be a lot of work, Dad.'

I held back from offering encouragement. I would not guide him. He needed to thrash this out in his own head, decide if he was up to the challenge. I was nervous, afraid even. I knew I would respect his decision either way, but I could not deny that I would be disappointed if he got cold feet. It was a daunting task for anyone, even I had a moment of weakness, of indecision. But it was different for me, I had years to think it over, to consider what was involved and decide if it was worth all the work. Every day since my father's death I looked at her mangled form and wondered if one day I would be able to put her back together. Was it an impossible task? When Humpty Dumpty fell off the wall it was the wisest course of action to accept that he couldn't be put back together. After all there was just me, maybe Michael for a while, but there would be no King's horses and no King's men to help us out.

I knew what I would do either way. The '69, my father's heritage would have to be finished, there was no other way this would end. It was now a question of whether Michael wanted to be a part of that. I was more afraid that I would think less of him if he felt it was too much, than I was afraid of not having his help. While I always considered it important that a son should look up to and think well of his father, I also considered it important that a father be proud of his son. A lot was hanging on his next few words.

A long silence passed, the gravity of the moment weighed heavy on us both. The importance of it, this decision, weighed heavy on him. I felt guilty and was about to speak, to ease his burden and give him a soft way out. This was foolish. Mary would be angry with me for putting this much pressure on our son.

'What about all the parts we're going to need? Are they hard to find, or expensive?'

I smiled a rueful smile, but inwardly I felt like jumping up and down, hugging the boy and dancing. It was like there was fireworks going off around me, bursting in mad colours under the tin roof, filling the garage with bright bubbly colours.

Outwardly I remained composed. I was anticipating this question. He had a grasp of what was involved. He was working through what we'd need, if it could be had and if we could afford it. But most importantly he was in, he wanted to do this.

I turned away from him as I walked around the car, squeezing my eyes tight I mouthed the words, 'Yes!' then faced him with a grin.

'Sorted, son,' I said, with a smug air of confidence.

'Really?' he replied, surprised.

'EBay,' was all I needed to say.

He threw his head back. 'You're kidding?' he laughed, 'And you said you had no time for those new-fangled computers.'

'Had no choice, son. I could move with the times or be left behind like the old fossil I am.' He pulled up to me and reached out a hand. I could have laughed, cried or just plain burst with pride. I took his hand and shook it firmly, a solid handshake, one man to another. A pivotal moment, that was all I could think. I would be proud of him no matter what, but when he was willing to rise to this challenge he felt more like a son of mine than I could ever hope for.

'Tell me about her, Dad. Tell me again how she came to be here.'

'Hold on then,' I said. 'I'll have to get into the chair to get this right' I crossed the floor, slumped into the chair and made myself comfortable. I took a moment to gather the events in an orderly fashion in my head and began.

'Enzo Ferrari described them as the most beautiful cars ever made.' I looked past Michael to the '69. He crossed the floor to the car and ran a hand along the long sleek bonnet and over the flowing curve of the roof.

'The Jaguar E-Type, a Series II fixed head coupe, the '69 model.' I said beaming with pride. I'm sure my face was flushed.

'When Captain Moore vanished in the fifties the estate was bankrupt,' I paused. I hadn't thought about him in a long time. My father spoke highly of him, even though they'd never met. I think in a way he envied him and his flamboyant lifestyle. Racing sports cars at a time when most struggled to put bread on the table. I too felt an affinity with the man. I felt I could relate to his pain even though I had no first-hand experiences like his.

'He tried his hand at racing in the Phoenix Park,' I continued. 'But it didn't work out. He blew his inheritance trying to compete with richer men. In the end, he crashed his beloved Alfa Romeo, the 6C, like the poster there,' I pointed to the tin poster on the wall.

'The estate agent auctioned the farm to clear the family debts. My grandfather and his family pooled together their savings and bought the estate. The money would just about cover the Captain's debts. Without his father's guidance, the Captain lost his way after the war.' I looked up at Michael, he was staring at the old sign. 'My Grandfather and his brothers had no interest in cars of course. They were farmers, it was only ever about the land. But my father was fascinated with that poster.' I nodded at the tin likeness of the Alfa Romeo on the wall again. 'When my father learned that Captain Moore had raced cars in Phoenix Park he became fixated on the Captain and his life. He wanted to know everything about him. He was saddened to know that it ended so badly, a nasty crash, his beloved Alfa in tatters and his money all but gone. That's all that was left of the car after they sold the remainder to the scrap yard.' I pointed to a broad wood-rimmed steering wheel that hung from a rusty nail on the wall. 'The Captain was lucky to survive the accident. He had some broken bones and a few nasty cuts, but he had to rely on a crutch to walk afterwards.' I was surprised at how much of this I could recall. It was all second-hand information, the story told to me by father. Not unlike what I was doing right now.

'Movie legends like James Deane with their shiny sports cars were my father's idols. He drooled over them on the covers of glossy magazines. It was like porn to my him,' I laughed, and Michael smiled back at me. I knew he had no interest in the reminiscences of an old man, but he had the good manners to let me ramble on.

Talking about the Captain always brought me down, his was a sad story. But when I spoke of my father and our times together my voice rose an octave, and I became upbeat as thinking of him always cheered me up.

'My father befriended Patrick O'Dwyer, the son of a neighbouring farmer. This did not go down too well with our grandfather.' I paused to explain the significance of this. 'Patrick had served with the British army, the Royal Engineers in France from 1942 to 1945. The British were not very long gone from the Irish countryside. We fought a bloody war to wrestle free from them, so for many the wounds were still too raw. Anything British was tainted. Patrick and my father dabbled together at old cars and tractors.' I looked over to see if I still had Michael's attention. Mary told me I had a tendency to ramble on when I had an audience. I wasn't sure he was listening to me anymore, he was staring at the car.

I coughed into my hand loudly. 'It was a particularly wet summer, and that's saying something. Things were still tough in the countryside. There was always more money floating about in the cities, but just like now, country life was a struggle. More cars were appearing on the roads, if you could call the pot-holed horse and cart tracks roads. It was a school-day. I was rushing through my homework, hurrying to get it done so I could get outside to play. The sound of a crash gave me a start. My bedroom window looked out over the farm.' I leaned over and pointed to the window just under the eaves. Michael knew the window, it was now his room. 'You could see the road to the village in the distance back then. The sycamores are much taller now, you can't see the road anymore, can you?' I asked. Michael just nodded his head in agreement. 'A cloud of white smoke was rising from the hedgerows. I took off at a sprint to investigate.'

I lowered my voice. 'Life was so different then, so little happened. Something that broke the routine was a treat.' Michael smiled, to humour me I imagine. 'The narrow stone bridge out of town had already claimed a few victims that year, a few over eager young men and a few older men under the influence. Though on this day, she claimed quite a scalp.'

I paused and closed my eyes for a moment as I

remembered that day. I've always felt that the things that happened, these memories, were still out there somewhere, not in the past but in a faraway place I haven't visited in a while. They were still there, and one day when I had time I could make the journey and see them again. It was just a way of denying the sad truth. The past was gone forever, only ever to exist in our memories.

'Dad?' Michael was staring at me fondly, a grin on his face. 'Where did you go just then?' he asked.

I sniggered, the boy could read me as well as his mother.

'I was there at the bridge,' I said closing my eyes tight again. 'I was standing to the left of them, listening to all that was being said. The entire village had gathered to look at the crash.' I opened my eyes and smiled at Michael. 'I think that annoyed the American more than the damage to the car. His pride was hurt. He had made a stupid mistake. He'd taken the bridge too fast on a wet road. Send for Patrick, he'll know what to do – Danny from the grocery shop was the first to speak out. Several voices mumbled in agreement. I looked up at my father. I knew he felt left out that they hadn't called for him. He stood in the background, looking on in awe at this beautiful machine now wrapped around the stone of the hundred-year-old bridge. He was holding my hand but he paid me no attention.' I looked at my hand, the calloused hand of an old man, not the little boy's hand that had held onto his father that day.

'The American,' I laughed. 'He was busy fussing over his young bride. She was moaning and complaining, horrified at the thought that they might be stuck in this god-forsaken village in the middle of nowhere. We have theatre tickets for tonight! she screamed at him. The villagers looked at each other in bewilderment. This expensive looking motorcar was entangled in the stone bridge and she had theatre tickets!

Patrick arrived and was trying to assess the damage and hazard a guess as to what it would take to fix it. The American wasn't interested in costs, he wanted a time. He paced back and forth, the villagers stepped out of his way, sure that at any moment he would shake off this apathy and realise what he'd done. The American stopped pacing and turned to Patrick. Well? he asked. When can you have it fixed enough to drive?

Patrick stared at him in disbelief, then looked around to see if anyone else had heard the insane question. Weeks, maybe months! Patrick told him. It was an honest assessment of the damage. The American paced the road in disbelief. He had to be back in New York in five days, he said. He walked right up to Patrick, Surely, we can come to an arrangement? If it's money I don't mind paying. Patrick looked past him and past everyone else there. He was looking for my father's face in the crowd. Then he caught sight of him, he raised his eyebrows and shrugged his shoulders. He had no idea what he could do. My father shook his head and frowned, he had no idea what could be done either.'

I took a deep breath and looked at Michael again, 'You know son, my father told me he never knew what came over him that day, or where the idea came from. I'll give you a car to finish your holiday right now and five hundred pounds, he said out of the blue. The crowd fell silent and parted to leave my father facing the American. He was still clutching my hand.'

I threw my head against the back of the chair and squeezed my eyes shut again. 'I remember it so well. He looked down at me and winked, walked slowly to the car, took his time looking around it and walked up the American. Patrick was staring at him. The rest of the village were silent. The American stood by his bride, his mouth open, as if he was trying to catch flies. She sat on the wall of the bridge looking off into the distance. He stood picking at the moss that grew from the cracks in the masonry. I remember feeling sorry for him in that moment. He had no idea what to do next. My father looked at him, at the young lady and then slowly back at the car, shaking his head as he did. The American looked to the crowd. I guess he was wondering what they made of my father and his offer. Wondering if my father was the town idiot, wasting his time. But nobody was laughing. His bride stared up at him. Duckie let's just get out of here, please, she begged.

I was still holding his hand, though I think he'd forgotten I was there.

Well? my father asked.

She tugged hard at the tail of her husband's jacket again. Slowly and reluctantly the American held out a hand. Done, he said.

My father reached out a hand to shake his. He almost yanked me off the ground, I was still attached to the hand he was offering to the American.

Now, where the hell is this car? the American asked.

I watched him walk away with my father, his young bride in tow. He never stopped to look back. I couldn't believe it. He just walked away. I was sure he would look over his shoulder, get one last look at the car, at this fabulous looking machine.'

'Well,' Michael said loudly. 'She's all ours now, for better or for worse.' He rose from the tin drum he'd been sitting on, taking a long look in the direction of the Jag, the '69. He blew loudly through pursed lips.

I struggled from the chair and onto my feet. I stood by his side and threw an arm around him. 'C'mon, let's call it a day,' I said. 'We won't finish her tonight.'

Chapter 8

School commitments for Michael and odd jobs I'd promised to sort for old friends kept both of us away from her for another week. We were both frustrated, eager to get started. It was a damp wet Sunday. I had helped Mary with the dishes after dinner, Michael was lounging on the sofa channel hopping on the TV. He would normally vanish with a friend on a Sunday afternoon. The toot of a car horn would beckon. Mary would excuse him from washing up and he'd be gone for the day, but today he was deliberately loitering.

Our lives had fallen into a familiar pattern, a routine that was repeated every day. I did not stop to dwell on this, if I had, I would have been disappointed. Very few of us like to be considered predictable. We like to think of ourselves as spontaneous creatures, but very few of us are, and as we get older we find a comfort in routines. Somehow, it's nice to know what will be ahead of us each day.

We were slumped onto the couch, all three of us. Mary perused the Sunday papers for the latest celebrity gossip. I snatched the remote for the TV from Michael and took up changing channels where he left off.

I caught his eye. 'Well,' I asked. 'You free?'

He was off the couch like a bullet. When I caught up with him in the kitchen he was already struggling to get into his overalls. 'Did I just fire the starting gun?' I laughed as I raced to catch up.

'What's gotten into you two fools?' Mary called after us.

It would take a little time to develop a plan, a strategy, but that day was all about energy; we attacked the car with gusto. Sparks from the angle grinder flew into the air. The clang of metal on metal echoed around the garage. It was important just to make a start, to take that first step.

I was breathless when Mary arrived late that afternoon with tea.

'You're mad, the pair of you,' she laughed as she reached up and mopped the sweat that glistened on my brow. She sounded cross, but I knew she was delighted to see us together; father and son, happy in our work.

I don't know what time it was when we finally stopped. I hadn't noticed the sun go down or noticed when it had gotten dark and Michael had switched the lights on.

I stopped mid-task and stepped back. 'That's a damn good start,' I said, much louder than I intended. Michael acknowledged me with a low grunt. I smiled contently, wiping my hands on a rag and turned for the house. He did not follow me. He could not be pried away. He had to finish what he was doing before he called it a day.

'Is Michael with you?' Mary asked, craning her neck to glance over my shoulder as I came through the door.

'He'll be in shortly,' I said and moved to the table.

'Don't over-do it, Jack. He's just a boy,' her voice broke just a little, and she scurried about the kitchen busying herself as she always did when she was worried about something. I took her hand as she poured my tea.

'Don't fret Mary, he'll be fine. And he's not a boy anymore. I don't know how or when it happened but Michael is a man.'

I passed the best summer of my life with him in that garage. Progress on the car, the '69, was slow, but I was conscious that we were also working to an end goal. When we were done, he would be ready to leave. It would be our last time together. I sensed he knew it too. We were co-workers, father and son, but we also became friends. It was a wonderful time, too wonderful to last.

Chapter 9

I first felt it a week before I unveiled the car to Michael. Truth is, this was what prompted me to act sooner rather than later. Something wasn't right. I knew it and I didn't need a doctor to tell me this. Yet I did not allow myself to be negative about it. It was a twinge, a faint pain. Lots of people live for years with aches, pains and illnesses, I told myself. Whatever was ahead of me I was not going to be robbed of the opportunity to share the time with Michael that I was denied with my own father.

Mary though, was more astute than I gave her credit for. I noticed her watching me. I forced a smile whenever I caught her looking me over.

'You're tired, Jack. I can see it in you,' she said. 'Don't push yourself so hard.' She was standing over my feet that protruded from under the car.

'Nonsense woman, I'm fine. I'm having the time of my life.'

'Well just you remember that you're not as young as he is.'

'Are you doubting me?' I said, sliding out from under the car. I pulled myself out a little too fast, catching my head on a jagged edge. The gash was not deep but it bled like mad.

'Jesus!' she exclaimed.

'Tis but a scratch,' I joked, quoting from one of my favourite movies, Monty Python's Holy Grail.

'That's deep. It will need stitches,' she fussed. 'Are you okay?'

'It could kill an ordinary man, but not me,' I laughed, then stood up a little too fast and felt weak. I had to lean on Mary for support.

'Come with me, you big fool,' she scolded, 'Ordinary man indeed!'

'There's some duct tape here that would more than do,' Michael called after us.

'Don't encourage him.' she called back. 'He's going to be as big a fool as you are,' she whispered to me. She pretended she was disappointed by this but I knew her better.

'Hope so,' I replied. 'I really hope so.'

The summer flew past. The '69 was not even close to being done. We had been ambitious in our expectations. There was still too much to do, but we were both adamant it was best done slowly and done right.

It was time for him to go. Michael had to prepare for college. It had been a wonderful summer, too good to last. Long nights together working and laughing in the garage. The more I got to know the boy, the prouder I became of him, but more than that, I saw familiar traits in him; characteristics and habits that were not mine, but I remembered them in my father. A realisation struck me, Michael was more like my father than I was. How was that even possible?

There was something else too, there was a few times I found myself alone in the garage late at night, I couldn't put my finger on it, but I felt uncomfortable, uneasy. I turned away from my work at these times to check if I'd left the door open as if there was a draft when I felt a chill. The more I worked on the car, dealt with work my father and I had touched the more he came into my thoughts, how he behaved, all his little quirky habits. I began to remember things he did, phrases and expressions he used. This garage had been such a big part of his life, it was where he was at his best. Where he was happiest. My mother knew this, that was why she let him be when he was down here. When I looked around the walls I thought, this is also true for me, this is where I too have been at my happiest.

I began to see him in everything I touched, and now I saw him in my son. It was little things, the way Michael would approach a task, not hurried like me, but methodical and with a plan and a vision of how it would turn out. My father would have loved to work with him. Sometimes Michael would say something that would make me stop in my tracks. Once he caught his knuckle on a sharp edge, 'Hells bells!' he cried out. I stopped and stared at him.

'Where did you hear that?' I laughed. I'd heard him curse loudly and wildly several times when he got a painful knock but this was new.

'What?' he asked sucking on the wounded digit. 'I've never heard you say that before in your life.' I replied.

'Are you getting Alzheimer's, Dad? I hear it from you, you say it all the time. I don't think you even know you do it.' he laughed again.

I let it go, I was sure I never used the expression. Or did I? Yet I knew who did. My father was ordered to substitute it for the curses he bellowed when he banged a finger or

47

dropped a spanner. My mother insisted I would not be allowed into the garage if I was going to be subjected to foul language, and so 'Hells bells' accompanied every mistake or injury for as long as I could remember. I felt my father's presence so much stronger when Michael was working by my side.

I missed my father so much at times it hurt, having Michael here was a great consolation. He would be gone soon and I knew I would miss him terribly in our home in the evenings, but especially here in our little haven, the garage.

Chapter 10

Armed with a sharp wit, a clever mind and a good sense of humour, Michael was ready to leave the nest and face the big bad world. I was out of sorts for two whole days before he left. The house felt like a wake-house. Yet the weather was particularly good for those few days. The sun shone bright. Mary drew the curtains all the way back to let as much light as possible into the house. Even she could sense the grey gloom that was creeping into the house, probing every room and corner, preparing to make a home here when Michael would go. It was the perfect environment for gloom to thrive, I knew this, but did not have the energy or the will to fend it off. We were sad and afraid of the loneliness that was to come.

Michael was indifferent to it all. He buzzed around, gathering what he needed, excited at the prospect of college and moving on to a new chapter of his life. Neither Mary or I closed an eye to sleep on the night before he left. We even struggled to make conversation. We knew what his leaving meant and how it would change our world forever, but we also knew it was important that we put our best faces forward so that he could be encouraged to go, to see how happy we were for him to get an opportunity to make something of his life.

It was still dark when we heard him tip-toeing around the house. 'He can't sleep either,' Mary whispered.

'C'mon, let's join him,' I said.

The singing of the kettle brought Michael into the kitchen. He looked to the clock, about to speak.

'We can't sleep either,' Mary laughed, handing him a fresh cuppa. We sat at the table and talked, mostly about what college life might be like, careful to avoid the mention of leaving home or any other catch phrases that might start the waterworks with his mother. When he was done talking, we watched him go over his bag for the umpteenth time. He stuffed what he needed into a battered rucksack that he'd become quite attached to. It was all he wanted to take with him. His mother was horrified. She had saved the vouchers from the supermarket to buy matching luggage. They were set out on the kitchen floor as a surprise. Michael was careful to show his gratitude, but firm enough to make it clear he would not be taking them to college.

Mary couldn't help herself, it was how she was raised. A good impression on his first day was essential and it mattered to her that his fellow students know he came from a good house. The tatty old rucksack would reflect on his upbringing.

'What kind of mother will they think I am, to let him off to college with that?' she argued.

'It okay, Mam,' he consoled her. 'Nobody looks and nobody cares. Who I am and what I do will define me, not my luggage.' He threw an arm around her and pulled her close.

'Young people today,' she said, shaking her head. 'You are so much wiser than we ever were.'

I could see his logic, he was making a statement of sorts; this was who he was, someone who did not care for material things, was not image conscious and had a mind to do whatever he saw fit.

College must be such a tribal affair, I thought. Neither Mary or I had any first-hand knowledge of such places, but I tried to imagine what it would be like to throw so many eager young men into one great big melting pot. All meeting for the first time, trying to establish their place, make their presence felt and most of all be accepted by others. Surely this is an education in itself, a first step to prepare them for what lay ahead; for isn't all of life like this, a battle to get a foothold?

I wasn't afraid or nervous for him. I was confident he would do well and fit in quite nicely.

'You'll make a great engineer someday, son,' I said, ruffling his hair as if he were still the little boy that ran around my feet in the kitchen.

Mary gave him a great big bear hug and kissed him on the top of his forehead. 'You be careful, and remember your studies. Don't get distracted by the girls, alright?'

'Girls! There are girls in this college too?' He ducked and missed her hand as she made to give him a playful clip on the head.

'I'm not leaving the country. I expect I'll be back at the weekend,' he said, gathering his bag.

I reached for Mary's hand, she squeezed mine even tighter when we heard the car door open. His friends were howling and hooting at him to come on. Tommy, his lifelong buddy stepped out of the car and called to us. 'Don't worry, I'll take care of him.'

'That's what I'm worried about,' I called back, then laughed.

He squeezed into the crowded car and waved back at his mother as he went. I stepped behind Mary, wrapped both arms around her and gave her a squeeze as they vanished from sight.

'He's right you know, he will be back at the weekend,' she said. 'You're making more of this than it is, he's just going to college.'

'I know love, but he will never really ever be back here again. He's gone from us now, this will only ever be a stopping off point between his travels.'

'Don't be so melodramatic, you old fool.' She elbowed me in the ribs and made for the kitchen again.

'We did good, Mary. He's turned out well.' I called after her.

Chapter 11

I was tempted to set the work aside until the winter when he would be free again to join me, but there was so much to do. My father and I had barely started when he took ill. We had to strip her back to bare metal, straighten all the twisted bodywork and begin from scratch. I would hold off on the final work until he was here, we would do this together. I would not fire her up until he was here.

And so, it was just me and the '69 again. The work brought back so many memories. I had patiently anticipated this for so long. I was so afraid it would all be a great anti-climax; the work would be another chore and the glamour of it would quickly wear off. I need not have worried, I was happy in my work, as happy as I could ask to be.

Almost every day I stumbled on old tools of my fathers, trapped in hard to get at corners where they'd been dropped and were never found. I saw his handy-work in so many things.

'Tidy bit of work, Dad,' I said aloud, admiring a section he had welded into an inner panel. I could remember the day and the hour we were both together at this piece. The clarity of the memories that popped up out of the blue took me by surprise. I had no idea I remembered so much. It was like being taken back to revisit my own life; this garage, my father and that precious time we had, seemed embedded in my mind so solidly that the mere disturbance of anything close to those memories forced them out of the shadows and into the limelight – like bats in a cave disturbed by an intruder.

What I did miss, apart from Michael's company, was the extra pair of hands for the heavier tasks. Fool that I am, I tackled tasks that needed three men, not alone two. The bodywork and suspension were not too bad, but it was dealing with the great hulking mass of an engine block that worried me. The great cast iron lump was over-designed and engineered, being heavier and stronger than was required. Yet this stood to it, for this same block had been used in several models with little modification well into the eighties. I stripped it down, hoping it would not need an expensive rebuild. I was not so lucky, and given that I had emphasised to Michael that everything would have to be done as best we could, this was no place to cut corners. And so, the great lump, the heart of the beast was shipped off to a professional engine builder. It was an expensive piece of work, but I knew all along it was likely this would have to be done so I had budgeted for this. Mary the ever-diligent housewife kept a close watch on my spending. It was just as well, I would have been reckless. The '69 would have gotten anything and everything it needed regardless of the expense. As with most things in life it was a compromise, what I argued I needed and what Mary convinced me would do.

Michael was true to his word, for the first few weeks anyway. Every Friday night he got off the bus at the bottom of our road. Mary would have a piping hot dinner ready for him when he came through the door. She was of course convinced he was not taking care of himself properly, and was certainly not eating well enough. He courteously cleaned his plate for her every time and complained enthusiastically about the awful college canteen food, though I suspected it troubled him much less than he made out to his mother, but it was important that she felt she was still taking care of her little boy. When the establishment failed him, she would make sure he was well fed and would always have a good supply of warm socks and clean underwear. I suppose a mother never stops being a mother, just like a father never stops being a father. I listened to his stories of college life, reading as much as I could into the information. I was glad that he was mixing well, had friends and had a healthy social life alongside his studies.

We were delighted that he was willing to share his stories with us, but were not naive enough to believe that his time was split equally between sleep and study. A young man had other needs, and Michael was a good-looking boy. His stories were sprinkled with girls' names; Patricia said, Paula did, Yvonne helped me. Mary's ears perked up at the mention of every name. She discreetly asked if they were in his class, were they friends, were they in his company when he went out? Michael smiled and laughed it off.

His time was always too short, Sunday afternoon and the bus back to college came around too fast. I didn't drag him into the garage to help, but I was happy to see he still had an interest. He popped in once or twice over a weekend visit to have a look over the work. I showed him my progress, parts I'd sourced, work I'd done.

I was pleased to note his jealousy. I could see he would have liked to be part of the work. He was torn between his passion for engineering, his love of college life and a desire to be here with me working on the '69.

What I had not realised was that he could not remember a time when the '69 was not here. I hadn't considered this. I could remember the day my father bought the car, but I was a grown boy by then. To Michael it was an ever-present shape in the corner, something he was forbidden to touch or play near. I had just turned eight when the American had his fortuitous crash and my father took that leap of faith and bought the wrecked car. I know my father had a hard time for some years afterwards, it was a laughing point among his friends. He'd given away his car and his savings for a smashed wreck. But he took it on the chin. He had the vision to see what she could become and the hands to make it so. Fate however had dealt him a cruel blow and robbed him of the chance and of course, myself too. This was a second chance for us both, the '69 and I.

The first Friday night that Michael was not on the bus was a bit of a disappointment, but we both understood. By the time he'd missed the third weekend, I was low. We did get a brief message, swamped with studies, assignments to hand in and so on.

'I hope he isn't working too hard,' Mary said, without conviction.

I wasn't upset with the boy, it was just selfishness on my part. I looked forward to his company more than his help, but I knew this was how it would be, the great circle of life. So, I threw my energy into the work. Though I didn't say it to Mary or allow the thought to take root in my own mind, I had a growing fear that Michael might be absorbed in his new life and lose interest in our little project. Long distance relationships they say are hard to sustain, and it was reasonable to expect that life with his friends, girls, music and excitement would win over cold nights in a draughty garage with his old man.

Chapter 12

There was good news to cheer me. The great heart of the machine, the rebuilt engine had returned. It sat on a pallet in the centre of the courtyard all polished and painted like a peacock with its colourful feathers spread for all to admire.

It would have made sense to wait for help, a few friends, or Michael at the weekend, but I was impatient. I couldn't wait to see it back where it belonged. It must have weighed a ton, so it took considerable planning to set it up so that I could manoeuvre it into place without help. I borrowed a good block and tackle, winched the iron lump off the floor, high enough that I could push the car under it and then lowered it ever so slowly into place. It was a long and frustrating stop and start process without a second pair of hands or eyes to guide me, it was almost there. I just needed to move the car a little forward. I was already sweating profusely, partly from the effort but also from the stress and frustration of it all. I was so close but one wrong slip and I could set myself back months.

It was a tight fit to ease it into the transmission tunnel. I took a break, flopped down into my old chair and mopped my forehead with a reasonably clean rag.

'Okay baby, take a breather. One more big push will see it through. Deep breaths,' I laughed. 'Should have gotten the doctor to organise an epidural for you, although I don't know if it works when you're trying to put the baby back in!' I laughed again and began to cough.

It was an effort to get out of that chair again. I would gladly have sat there for an hour. I was exhausted, more than I know I should have been. 'Maybe it's me that should ask for an epidural. I'm getting too old for this, old girl?' I patted her on the wing.

I took a wide stance and braced myself, took a long deep breath and gave it my all for one big push. At first nothing happened. Then a slight movement, no more than a few millimetres but it was going. Encouraged I put everything into it. There was a harsh scraping sound of steel on steel as the gearbox squeezed past the mounts and then it swung with a lurch that caught me off guard. I fell onto the engine block panting and laughing at the same time.

I stepped away and slumped onto the corner of the workbench to catch my breath. Beads of sweat dripped off my nose onto the floor at my feet. 'Phew!' I gasped, 'that was tough.' I exhaled loudly. It had been a while since I'd been tested so. 'Getting old.' I said between breaths. I was smiling, regaining my composure when the first jolt hit me. I knew right away it was not good. A charge like an electric shock rocked the left side of my body, right up my arm and down my side. Even before I had time to react to it, I knew what it had to be. I'd heard it all before. I'd seen enough movies to know the tell tales signs. And yet I was strangely calm, even though I was well aware that this might not end well. I considered calling out to her, but stopped myself. Maybe it would be better this way, if she couldn't help why would I torment her by having her sit and watch me go. Taking slow deep breaths, I shuffled into the driver's seat of the car.

'You're going to see us all out before you're done, old girl,' I said, patting the dash with my right hand, my left arm hung limp and lifeless at my side.

A terrible fatigue overcame me. I tried to gather my thoughts. Were these to be my last moments? My son, Michael, I won't see him again. Will he be okay, what if he needs my help? Then of course there was Mary, I'd promised to stay by her side for always. She would be mad as hell and heartbroken.

A movement caught my attention, a shape in the corner, a blurring in the shadows, a distortion of the blackness. I looked hard into the darkness, curious to know what was there, but I could feel myself losing substance, drifting, melting away. My old bones, the carcass that housed the being that was Jack Doyle was being left behind. It was then that I saw him, the blackness pooled together to take his form and he stepped towards me, towards the car. He was walking with a purpose, a younger man than I remembered, a spanner swinging loosely in his hand. He didn't see me.

Then he stopped and stared hard into the car, as hard as I had stared into the shadows to see him. His face scrunched up in concentration, or concern, he was looking for me, trying to see me. Then that smile I had long since forgotten spread across his oil-stained face. It was just for an instant because he then frowned, a worried frown. I saw him open his mouth to speak but it was too late. I was slipping away. He turned away from me and stared back into the shadows from whence he came, was he calling to someone else? He was angry with them. I'd rarely seen the man shout. I looked past him. I could see nothing, but I felt it, an overpowering feeling of anguish and distress, and something else... I was not sure but it felt like anger. And then I was gone.

'Jack!' her shouts woke me. 'What are you doing? Do you know what time it is?'

I didn't answer. I struggled to move from the car seat, the pain in my arm gone. The weight on my chest eased, my breathing relaxed and normal.

She leaned into the car and drew up close, 'Are you alright? What are you doing sitting in here, you old fool?' she laughed, unable to mask her concern and her relief at finding me well.

'Sorry, love,' I said, planting a big kiss on her forehead. Had I just fallen asleep, was it all a dream? Yet the spanner my father had been carrying was sitting on the bonnet just below the windscreen.

I took a deep breath and exhaled loudly.

'Come on, you'll get your death out here alone.' she said, reaching a hand to help me out.

I tried to smile, my face blanched, but Mary missed it. She sat me down in our kitchen. I was shivering. The cold had leeched into my old bones. I was exhausted. I'd almost nodded off in the heat when the whistle of the kettle on the stove perked me up.

'Here, get that into you,' she said, pressing a mug into my hand. 'Then come down to bed. I'm off, it's freezing up here.'

I took my time finishing the tea. I tried to recall what I thought had happened. It was all a bit blurry, vague images.

Then I remembered his voice, his image standing there, speaking to me. My heart began to race again. I braced myself, ready to call for Mary. I held a finger to the pulse on my wrist, tried counting the beats. I watched the clock and counted, was that eighty something or ninety something beats. Too fast I knew. Closing my eyes, I leaned back and drew in deep slow breaths. I cleared my mind of everything that I was fretting over, Mary, Michael, the car. The kitchen was still, not a sound but the slow cadence of the old clock. Tick-tock. Sixty times every minute it sounded. I listened to it for a long time, counting the seconds I felt my pulse slow. My beating heart and my father's old clock fell in step with each other. My pulse slowed and beat in harmony with the clock. Sixty beats a minute was good rate for an old man.

Chapter 13

In the light of day, and with a clear head, I stood looking into the gaping mouth of the garage door and wondered if I was just a foolish old man who'd put too much sentimental importance in repairing an old wreck. Why had it become so important? Had it been nothing more than a means to share time with my son. A symbol of a lost opportunity with my own father. When I looked around these same walls where he too had delved, I felt sad again that I never had the time with him that I'd already had with my own son.

There were times, late at night, when I was in the throes of a difficult task, that I was sure I felt my father near me, heard his words of direction in my ear. I'd spring up and look around, half expecting, hoping he'd be there but even before I turned around I knew it was a foolishness, yet there always lingered that fine little thread of hope.

I strolled to the back of the garage, cautiously watching for a sign, some indication that I had not dreamed it all. Had he really stepped from the shadows the night before, just at the exact moment when I was tottering on the edge, about to lose my balance and fall from this world? He had looked anxious, was he trying to say something, was it the surprise of seeing me, or had I imagined it all in that near-death moment. People talk of their life passing before them in these moments, was that it? I could believe that. My father had been the largest most powerful presence in my life.

I kept the whole episode to myself, my attack and everything that came after. Mary would have panicked if she knew, she would have insisted on a hospital check-up. She would have stood over my every action for good. I'd never have a minute's peace in the garage on my own again.

I slipped away one afternoon, made an excuse that I had parts to pick up in town. I called to see Doc Brown. I never thought about making an appointment, didn't know it would be busy. I took one look around the waiting room; there wasn't a spare stool in sight. Without a word to the young girl behind the reception desk who eyed me curiously I turned to go.

'Jack, is that you?' the doctor had his head bowed and was staring out over the rim of his glasses. He looked old, the thought struck me as I looked back, mouth open and lost for an explanation. I was thinking of how he used to be such a great goalkeeper at school, even then he was larger than the average boy. He was a year older than me. We'd gone to the same school.

'You're busy, Doc. I'll call again.'

He gestured to me to follow him, then waved his hands in a placating manner at the receptionist who was already scowling. 'Personal matter,' he directed the remark at her and then at the waiting crowd. None of them seemed put out except the young and stern looking receptionist.

'What seems to be the trouble, Jack? We don't see you in here too often.' He foraged through the drawers of his desk as if he already knew what he was about to prescribe for me. He hummed as he did this, a habit I felt sure he was unaware of.

I gave him a brief description of what happened, making light of it all and emphasising that I was only here to satisfy Mary. I myself felt sure it was my own fault, a little over-exertion that was all.

'Have you looked at your birth certificate recently, Jack?' He looked at me over the rim of his glasses again. It had the effect of making me feel he did not believe me, as if he could tell I was holding back vital information.

'They didn't teach you to be a smart-ass at medical college, Doc,' I snapped. 'That's self-taught.'

'College is a long time ago, Jack. Just like breaking your back in that run-down old garage should be. Go home and keep Mary company.'

'You leave Mary out of this,' I snapped again, even louder. 'She wanted nothing to do with you then and she has nothing to do with you now.'

The doctor flinched, he stared at me for a long time, clearly smarting from the remark. He turned his attention to the monitor. 'Your heart's beating a little faster than it should, and your blood pressure is elevated,' he read aloud with no hint of emotion in his voice, even though I knew I had offended him. 'I'd like to send you for some more checks,' he continued. He did not look up from the monitor or attempt to make eye contact with me. 'Theresa at reception will make the appointments for you.' He turned his back on me and began fumbling for something in a glass cabinet that stood behind his desk.

I pulled on my shirt and turned to go. 'I'm sorry, Doc. I shouldn't have said that,' I was ashamed of myself. I had no idea why I said it, or why I would snap at the doctor of all people. 'You know it's not true,' I said, 'Mary thinks the world of you. I'm sorry, Doc. I think this gave me more of a fright than I realised.'

He stopped what he was doing but didn't turn around. 'Make sure you keep those appointments,' he said, as I walked out the door. I felt rotten for the rest of the day. It wasn't like me to be so sharp. The doctor was a good man. I intended to take his advice, I really did, but there was a lot to do, and what if they told me I had a dodgy heart? What could I do about it at this stage of my life anyway? So, I soldiered on, mildly aware that not everything was as it should be, but making no effort to investigate any further for fear I would not like the answers I got back.

Chapter 14

Once, and only once, I called out to him. I laughed at my foolishness afterwards.

'Dad, are you there?' my voice broke as I asked the question. I was more than a little choked up with emotion. I waited hard for an answer, closed my eyes and turned my ear to one side to focus on the echo of my voice, it seemed to linger abnormally long in the rafters before the sound was swallowed up by the night. No reply came back of course, but there was a moment in that silence when I was waiting, that void, that vacuum, when everything grew still. A moment when I thought I heard him sigh, as he often did when he was about to speak.

My attention was drawn to the metal sign. The old Alfa Romeo glistened as the single bulb over my head swung gently to and fro in the draught. I dropped my tools and crossed the floor to stand beside it. The air around me felt charged. I had very few photographs of my father. Any I had, had been taken here in this garage, himself clad in an oily overall. I smiled when I recalled that in my memories he was always wearing the same oil-stained overalls. This one physical thing I had, a greasy handprint on the corner of the sign. I made sure it was never wiped or cleaned. It was precious, as if some of his DNA was still trapped in the greasy stain.

He'd been moving the sign, lining it up. His old friend Patrick directing him.

'That's fine,' Patrick had said, 'No point making it perfect, nothing in here ever is.'

My father threw a rag at him. He ducked, laughing, then threw it back.

'Wipe that oily paw print off, will you,' Patrick called to my father.

My father had the rag poised over the sign, but he stopped. 'No, that's just about right. This old lady deserves to have a greasy handprint on her, not a collector's signature.'

And so it was that my father's handprint had never been touched. Though it was now so faded it was barely visible.

I raised my hand and spread my fingers wide, holding them in the air above the imprint of his. I had done this so many times over the years. Watching as my hand grew from the small soft hands of a boy to the calloused hands I now held over the sign, hands that now matched his own.

A breeze caught the wooden doors and threw them open with a loud crash. I didn't flinch, my hand remained poised over the sign. If I was being warned away there was no point, I was at home here. The Captain might have been the master of the estate once. I would like to think I was now master of the house, but I'd willingly give up that title to Mary. Yet there was no doubt that I was the master in my little haven.

'What do you think of the work so far, Dad?' I asked, my hand still raised and hovering over his own handprint. If I was asked if I believed he was there, or could hear me, I'd have laughed at the notion, but secretly I was never so sure, perhaps it was nothing more than wishful thinking. I spoke to him more and more often after that, asked questions, suggested solutions to problems I met with the work. I had a habit of talking to myself when I was working anyway, but it was never anything more than thinking aloud. The remarks were never directed at anyone else. I guess it was a symptom of spending so much time alone. But now those conversations ended with Dad. There was nothing unhealthy or eerie about it I told myself, however, I never told Mary.

Chapter 15

Michael stepped off the bus and strolled up the lane to the house. His rucksack hung loosely from his shoulder. He looked at his feet as he went, kicking the round stones that were carted from the gravel shore of the river decades before to make the road, just as he did as a schoolboy walking home from the local school. He passed the entrance to the courtyard and saw the light in the garage. It was late. The clock Mary had given me to place over the workbench had stopped again several weeks ago. She got tired of asking the same question night after night. 'Do you have any idea what time it is?' so she bought me that clock, but the batteries ran out and I hadn't replaced them. I pleaded complacency but the truth was even sadder. Call it morbid if you like but the constant ticking of the clock reminded me that every second that passed was one I would never get to experience again, taking me closer and closer to an inevitable end.

I was sitting in my old chair, lost in foolish thoughts when I heard the crunch of gravel under foot. I stirred and peered into the darkness. Since my heart attack episode and the encounter I think I had with my father, I was jittery, unsure if I was completely alone.

'Dad,' Michael called out, a little sheepishly.

'Michael!' I exclaimed with great enthusiasm. I was delighted to see him and relieved that it was not another apparition.

'Missed the early bus,' he explained, feeling the need to explain why he was so late on the road. He was surprised at such a hearty welcome. He crossed the courtyard to join me. 'Didn't want to miss another weekend at home.' he added.

'You know you're not obligated to come home every weekend son, you have a lot to do and you can't waste time. That's a long journey up and down to Galway every weekend.'

I rose to meet him, gave him a friendly punch on the shoulder. I felt the occasion did not warrant a father-son hug after such a short break.

He dropped his bag inside the door and walked to the car. Glancing around the garage as he went. I felt compelled to explain that I was going to do a general tidy up at the weekend. He was walking away from me, but I could tell he was smiling.

He took a turn around the car. 'She's really taking shape, Dad,' he nodded his head approvingly.

'It's slow,' I conceded with a sigh.' But we knew it would be.'

'Listen Dad, I'm sorry I didn't make it these past few weeks...'

I raised my hand and cut him off. 'Son, please don't. You know that we both understand. You have to focus on your studies. The car will wait. Won't you, old girl?' I said, turning towards her. 'She always has. She was beautiful once, and hopefully will be again. But it's not life or death, it's just a car. It was never meant to be this commitment that would hold you back from getting on with your life. I enjoy our time together. When you have time, feel free to join me, but I don't want it to be a burden, something you feel obliged to do.'

He went to speak and I stopped him again. 'We love to see you home, but you have your life, your friends, your studies. Come when you can.' I threw an arm around him and led him to the house.

I had grown so used to the smell of her baking, the kitchen always smelled of fresh scones. Michael had forgotten. I smiled as he threw his head back and inhaled.

'Always good to be home,' he said. He moved to warm himself by the stove. I heard her scurrying down the hall at the sound of voices in the kitchen.

'Look who I found loitering around outside.' I said.

Mary snatched the glasses from her nose, Michael had never seen her wearing glasses. She was embarrassed. I couldn't help but smile. The coy teenager I fell in love with was still there. She hugged him and slapped him playfully on the arm.

I noted how tall he'd grown, he towered over Mary. Clinging onto him she looked so small and so old. I felt a pang of longing for her.

'Why didn't you let us know you were coming this weekend? I would have had a dinner ready for you.' she scolded.

'Didn't come home just for the dinners, Mam,' he laughed. 'Although I do have a bit of laundry!' he grimaced. 'Sorry,' then threw his bags onto the floor.

Mary, as was her way, conjured a feast. 'Miracle of the loaves and the fishes, hah!'

I said, 'Your Mam can outdo them every time.'

'Stop with that blasphemy,' Mary snapped her head around to stare me down.

'Now Mary you know...' I began, but she stopped me mid-sentence with a raised finger. I knew the boundaries, and the lines it was wiser not to cross.

It was past midnight when we moved from the table to three chairs by the stove. Mary threw question after question at him. I think it was Michael's third yawn that did it, she relented, beginning to wilt herself.

'I have something for you, Dad.' Michael said, as I was about to get up and join her.

I looked to Mary and shrugged. He drew a bottle wrapped in brown paper from his rucksack.

'Have you become a wino in college?' Mary frowned at the paper bag.

'I have a college friend from Scotland. He brought me a bottle from a wee brewery beside him. He assured me you'd like it.'

I rubbed my hands together, 'Glasses, Mary.'

'I'll have one glass with you both then I'm off to bed. Remember your last hangover?' She pointed a warning finger at me.

Michael pulled three chairs closer to the great Aga, the colossus, a giant cast iron stove that dominated the kitchen. We had no idea how long it had been there. I sometimes imagined it being there even before the house, and the stone masons had built this great house around it. The fire had gone out hours before but it still radiated a wonderful heat.

A good whiskey, I always say, is like the company you

are in. Sometimes it is tolerable, sometimes you just don't feel like finishing your glass and then there are times like that night when it flowed like a nectar from the gods. I felt like I could have drunk all night as I listened to Michael speak about the wonders of engineering. I felt a pang of regret. I wished I'd had the opportunity to go to college. It passed quickly, regret was a foolish waste of time. Nothing could be gained by wondering what if. Besides, any regrets I had were quickly forgotten when I considered that the choices I made resulted in this fine young man that was sharing a drink with me.

I was leaning back, savouring the whiskey when the portrait above the stove caught my eye. William, the last great landlord, was looking down on me with a disapproving glare. I raised my glass and toasted him.

'Maybe I should get one of those done, Mary,' I said.

She looked up. The canvas and the broad ornately decorated frame around it, were discoloured and blackened. Decades suffering from the smoke and soot that billowed from the great Aga had stripped the painting of its colour.

'Lord Jack,' she said, as she sloshed the whiskey around in her glass. 'Doesn't sound quite right, does it?' I chuckled under my breath.

'Maybe I should be the one to get the portrait,' she hesitated waiting for an interruption. 'After all, I am lord of the house.'

'Fair point,' I conceded. 'and after all you look more like him than I do.'

Again, the dreaded tea towel.

Mary took this as her cue to leave us to our ramblings. She knew the conversation was heading downhill.

I pulled the wet tea towel from my face. 'Wyatt Earp wouldn't stand a chance against that woman.' I laughed, and Michael laughed with me. A silly half drunken laugh.

Despite her warning, we over indulged; the whiskey was a little too smooth. When I sat up the next morning I knew that, despite what I'd felt the night before, I was not invincible, and no matter how much I enjoyed the amber nectar I was mortal and there would be consequences.

'How's that head feel?' she asked, a grin on her face that told me she would be quick to gloat if I complained.

'I feel like a king,' I lied.

To my dismay, Michael was chirpy at breakfast, offering to get a few hours in at the garage with me before he attacked his assignments.

Youth, I cursed. 'Sure, there's plenty to do and lots that will need a second pair of hands.'

After an unusually large, unwelcome, and punitive fried breakfast from Mary, we faced the garage together.

'Close those doors behind you, Dad,' he said. I did, and when I turned there he was slumped onto his hands and knees, gasping like a runner who'd crossed the line after a marathon. I dropped to my knees to laugh by his side.

'Don't ever let her know. We'll never hear the end of it.' he stammered between breaths. We shared a few laughs, grabbed a little sleep and occasionally banged a hammer a few times to give the impression of activity. By late afternoon we both had come around enough to face Mary and the kitchen again.

When he boarded his bus on Sunday evening we were all so much better for the visit. We all understood our roles. Michael had a new life to forge, and Mary and I had to prepare for a life alone. This last thought was not an unpleasant one. We were good together. I made her laugh and she kept me sane, a match made in heaven.

Chapter 16

As with most things in life, things did not go as I'd planned. Running a house and keeping a son in college with no income and a poor pension was not easy. The '69 was not a priority anymore. I dabbled as best I could, saved and picked up bits and pieces here and there at auto jumbles and on eBay, and even though it was slow, there was progress.

Michael was curious that I was not forging ahead. I blamed my age and fatigue. He was proud, he wouldn't like to think that paying his way through college was in any way a burden on us.

'Your father has been very clever, believe it or not,' Mary assured him. 'We have a very nice pension that will keep us comfortable to the end of our days.'

He never spoke with me about it, but he probed his mother for answers. How were we managing, could we afford the fees, the bills? I was sure she could convince him that we had everything well in hand. The boy was shrewd, just like his mother, but Mary had a way with her. Without raising her voice or over-emphasising her point, she was able to make the whitest of lies palatable. With a look of pure innocence, she could dish out the most unfathomable lies and still face church on Sunday with a clear conscience. She could convince me it was day when it was night if she put her mind to it, but then I was an easy mark for her.

The college years flew by, Mary and I weathered the years well. Other than a few winter colds and flus, we both stayed healthy. I had no recurrence of the episode in the garage and chalked it down to my own stubborn stupidity, trying to do too much on my own.

Michael entered his fourth and last year of college. It was a challenging year for him. We arranged all the extra tutorials we could, he was a strong student, he studied hard and could retain information easily, but we wanted to give him every advantage we could.

With financial constraints keeping me away from the car, I found I had time on my hands. For the first time in ages we made the effort to do more things together. We went off on picnics on summer evenings, went for long walks through the woods.

My favourite spot was by the river where we had played as children. The great cycle of life kept on throwing up surprises. I thought we were too old for all that romantic nonsense. We sat in the long grass along the riverbank where we first courted, talking and reminiscing on all that had passed in the decades since we first lay there. Life had drawn us closer together again. When we found ourselves away from familiar surroundings – the garage for me, the kitchen for her, we felt freer to chat about our regrets and concerns. It was not that we became different people, it was that we became ourselves again. Two people who had met, laughed and made promises all those years ago, had time to be themselves again. The challenges that we had faced tried to mould us, to change us, but we held on to our true selves, and now that we had endured and overcome all those challenges we could allow those people to come forward again. It was like we were emerging from a long tunnel. We walked together into the light. It was like meeting an old friend after a long time apart. I felt like my battery was being recharged. I felt invigorated.

Though we did not speak of it, there was an awareness that life's clock was ticking towards an end. Greedily we mopped up all the simple pleasures life had to offer us while we were still able to enjoy them.

Mary took to watching me when she thought I wasn't looking. I was not that old a man, but I hadn't taken care of myself. She often argued that I was quicker to investigate a knock or a rattle in one of our cars than I was to check out an ache or a sudden twinge.

'It's a man thing,' I argued, as we walked hand in hand back to the house. 'We've been slower to let go our links to the cave than you women have been.' This was my defence mechanism, to crack a joke and change the subject.

She stopped and turned, took my hand and held it up to the light that broke through the branches and examined it.

'Yes, I see,' she said, dropping my hands from her grip. 'You're knuckles are grazed. You've been dragging them on the ground again, haven't you?' she took off at a faster pace, leaving me to catch up.

'Esther Ryan would never have said that to me,' I called after her. Though she was a long way ahead of me I could still hear her giggling and see her shoulders rock as she laughed.

There was a fresh pot of tea on the table when I entered the kitchen.

'We'll have to work out a handicap for our walks,' she said, pouring me a cup. 'Isn't that how golfers do it?'

'Do what?' I asked.

'Help those who can't keep up in the game.'

She pointed to the table. I was meant to sit. She'd pulled up a chair beside me and set two portions of piping hot apple pie on the table. I took a generous helping. 'Oh my,' I mumbled. 'That's almost as sweet as yourself, Mary.'

'Humph!' she snorted.

'You won't get another man at your age, you know,' I said.

'How do you know I haven't found one already? You spend so much time in that garage I could easily satisfy another man and you'd never know.' Her mouth was full as she spoke. I burst out laughing and so did she, spraying me with crumbs.

'You're stuck with me Mary, too late to change your mind now.' I leaned across and kissed her.

'Wouldn't want to,' she said. Her expression turned suddenly serious. 'Don't leave me alone here, Jack,' she took my hand. 'I can stand anything but loneliness.' I looked at the hand that held mine, it was cold and for the first time I noticed it was old and wrinkled. I gave a little shiver, to shrug off the notion.

'I promise you, Mary. I will never go farther away than that garage,' I took both her hands and pulled her close.

Chapter 17

College fees had all but drained our reserves. My meagre pension and savings were dwindling. We never let Michael know it was a problem, of course. I was hoping the '69 would be our retirement fund. The classic car market was on a high. Investors, used to speculating on the stock market had turned to the classic car market, the upper end of the market. Iconic marques like my E-Type Jaguar were fetching silly prices. Unfortunately, those college costs had absorbed our budget to finish the car and we were at a loss to find the money elsewhere to finish her. So, it was with great reluctance we agreed to sell off a portion of the farm. It was prime dairy farmland and was much sought after at that, so thankfully we had no problem finding a buyer. In hindsight, it was foolish of me. I should have sold it sooner, but I was reluctant to split up the farm.

'Farmer? You?' Mary laughed when I first protested. 'You were never a farmer. When was the last time you were out on any of those meadows? That land has been leased out for years to real farmers. It's only fair that they should have it. They will farm it, we never have, we never will.'

God, I hated it when she was right, and even though she was careful never to gloat, I knew she loved that it drove me mad.

But there's something about Irish people and the land. We have a strange bond with it. We don't want to let go, to sell or share it. Families have been torn apart in disputes over land up and down the length of the country. Maybe it goes back to the famine and our fight to own our own land. I don't know, but there it was. It was done, twenty acres down by the river, gone from the estate forever. I felt guilty, like I had betrayed someone. Sold out, surrendered to an old enemy. This feeling lasted no more than a few days. Mary told me to buck myself up. My hackles raised at the remark, and then as always, I saw the wisdom in her words.

Mary never understood my need to wallow in misery at times. She was always so pragmatic about things. I was just not like that. If something upset or bothered me I had to get right down and wade in that misery, absorb every morsel of it, soak it up and then when it got into every bone and sinew and was not able to overpower me, to defeat me, I would shake it off like a coat I had tried on and found did not fit to my liking. I could cast it off then with a shrug and move on.

Twenty acres was no more than a small fraction of the estate. It would not be missed, and it would have no impact on the value of the farm if Michael was to sell it all off sometime in the future, when Mary and I were long gone. It was a good decision, it was the right thing to do. The money appeared in our bank account a few days later and I found it even easier to shake off guilt. The financial pressure that had being growing these past months was gone.

Mary was scribbling on a sheet of paper. One of Michael's calculators lay unused on the table. I looked over her shoulder. 'Will I tell the sheriff to go away yet?' I joked.

'Aye well, you can, but I won't expect he'll be going too far before he's back again.'

'Really?' I asked, flabbergasted.

She handed me the sheet she was writing on, it was an indecipherable mess of numbers, written in no apparent order.

'Jesus, Mary. How am I supposed to make any sense of this?'

'Here,' she said snatching the page back. 'This is what we owe now,' she ran her finger over a number written in thick pencil. 'This is what I predict we will need to cover bills that will come in this month,' she moved her finger to another column of numbers, 'And that's what we will have left in the bank.'

'Christ woman, you nearly gave me a heart attack for nothing! That's more money than we've had in the bank in years.'

'Yes, but Michael still has this year at college. There's this big house to keep for just the two of us and then of course, there's that rusty monstrosity in the garage to finish.'

I clasped both hands around her and kissed her on the top of her head. 'I knew you wouldn't forget her, pet,' I said laughing loudly. 'I'll get out my shopping list right away and I can start ordering parts.'

'No, you bloody won't,' she spun around in her chair. 'I'll keep a tight rein on the purse and you can try and cut a few corners with that thing.'

I staggered and stumbled away from her. I grabbed the worktop to steady myself. 'Have you any idea what you've said?' I stammered. I took a knife from the kitchen drawer and held it against my chest as if it had been plunged into my heart.

'I know exactly what I'm saying, you old fool. Roll up your sleeves and get that thing finished so we can get it sold.'

'My God, you're a hard woman,' I laughed. I pretended to struggle with the knife and making a sweeping arc with my hand I pulled it from my chest, gasping in relief as I did.

The tea towel hit me on the cheek. I should have seen it coming, after all these years she was still quicker on the draw than me.

'Off with you and let me get some housework done.'

I crossed the room and planted a bit sloppy kiss on her forehead. 'Hard woman, my foot,' I laughed. 'putty in my hands.'

She was reaching for a second tea towel when I escaped through the door.

Chapter 18

That year winter dragged on longer than ever. It held the spring at bay, fending it off with hail showers and a sharp south-easterly wind that blew up the valley from the coast. There was hardly a bud on the trees. The birds chirped furiously, hungry and impatient. When the sun did finally shine, nature burst into bloom. Blossoms sprang from rosebuds overnight. Leaves appeared on trees that seemed barren just days before. It was like spring had been holding its breath but could hold it no longer. It exhaled with a desperate gasp, it's warm breath blowing life into the waiting flowers and trees.

I felt it myself, the winter had gone on far too long. I was waiting anxiously for the temperatures to rise. I found that my old bones felt the chill a lot more this year. I made a mental note to organise a decent heater for the garage for the next winter, if I was still here. I began to add that last comment to more and more of my remarks, it angered Mary when I said it. 'Next Xmas we'll get a bigger tree, if I'm still here. We'll change the car in the summer if I'm still here.'

'Don't you dare think of leaving without me,' she threatened.

The beginning of summer also brought Michael home to us. He was finished. It was over, his exams were done. It had been a hard slog and we were confident he'd be rewarded for his efforts. Michael had some time to kill as he waited for his exam results that would not come until early August. He had time to relax and forget his books for a while.

'Any plans for the summer?' I asked.

'Nothing definite,' he said with a rueful smile. One that suggested he had a different answer. He had something in mind, but was hesitant to tell.

'I wouldn't mind getting away for a bit,' he added sheepishly. 'Maybe somewhere in the US for a few months, while I wait for my results.'

We looked at each other for a moment, Mary and me, and then smiled.

'That sounds like just what the doctor ordered,' Mary said.

Michael drew a relieved sigh. I think he was reluctant to talk of leaving home again now that he had just finished college.

'Fingers crossed I'll get my exams,' he continued, relieved at our reaction to his America plans. 'Then I'll be able to start looking for a proper engineering position.'

'Of course, you'll get your exams,' Mary was crossing the kitchen to the stove, she stopped mid-stride. 'Don't be silly. After all that hard work!' she said it as if she had decided his results were going to be good and nobody was going to dare make it any different.

'Fresh cuppa anyone?' she continued, totally discounting any need for concern over exams.

'I'm okay, Mam.' Michael smiled at her. I shook my head and placed a hand over my cup.

'I know a man, who knows a man, who might be able to get you some summer work in Chicago?' I looked to Mary as I spoke, she stared at me. I saw the cracks in her brave facade. She would have liked to have him here at home, but that was not realistic, and it was not fair on the boy.

'Chicago,' Michael said in a low voice. 'I don't know anything about Chicago.' he pursed his lips as he considered the idea.

'All the more reason to go there,' I added. 'Find out what it's like, see a bit of the rest of the country when you have a few dollars saved. What do you think?'

He bowed his head, a long silence followed. Mary turned from the sink and smiled at me, we'd both seen this before.

Would you like chocolate or ice cream? The mountain bike or the racer? Every decision since he was a toddler was thought through, all options considered. He never made an impetuous decision.

'Could this man get work for two of us?'

The chink of dishes being washed stopped suddenly. 'Who is going with you?' Mary asked the question without turning around from her chores at the sink.

'The lecturer's wife is free for the summer, Mam. She offered to open my eyes and show me a bit of the world.'

Michael was quicker than I was. Ah, youth I thought. He was able to dodge the inevitable dishcloth. I got caught in the cross-fire, the sodden wet cloth left a wet stain on my shirt.

'Don't you be so smart with your old Mam,' she laughed.

'I've a classmate that might join me,' he said still chuckling. 'Be a bit of company, don't fancy going that far alone.'

'Chicago it is then. I'll make a call tomorrow.' I said. 'What's the time difference?'

'Not sure,' Michael said, getting up from the table. 'A real job with a pay-check!' he laughed.

Chapter 19

The tick of the clock on the mantle seemed louder than normal, was it even marking time slower than normal? Mary glared at it, stared it down, defying it to go on. She was waiting for the phone to ring at nine o'clock. Every second the clock counted after that hour made her more and more frustrated.

'We're going to have to buy a new kettle in the morning if you boil that one more time for tea?' I declared.

'I thought he would have called by now, Jack,' she said, sounding distraught. 'Why hasn't he called?' she fought back a sob. I rose from my chair, wrapped an arm around her and guided her to her seat by the stove. Michael was only gone a week but it was his first time calling home. He made the mistake of saying he'd call at nine. It was nine twenty now and Mary was panicking.

'Relax love, he will call. Just be patient. We have no idea what he is doing. There are any number of things that could hold him up and make him late, and for that matter he's just twenty minutes late, okay?'

She clasped her face in her hands. 'I hope he's getting on alright.'

'I have no doubt he is doing very well, Mary. He is a competent young man, you know he is. Have a bit more faith in him.'

'Hah! You have no idea what it's like to be a mother.' The shrill ring of the phone made her jump. I moved to reach the phone but she snatched it off the receiver before I had the chance to.

'Michael?' she asked, her hand pressed against her forehead and her eyes squeezed shut.

I watched her face for a reaction. Please let it be him, I thought. She'll explode if it's not him. A moments silence as she waited for a voice at the other end.

'How's the weather at home, Mam?'

Mary squealed aloud like a teenager. 'Don't you fret about the weather here, son. How are you? Are you well? Did you get settled in, what's work like?'

'Everything is good here, Mam. You don't have to worry. I have a great place to stay. The work is interesting. I've met a few Irish guys who are showing me around over the weekend.'

This was all she needed to hear, he was okay, everything else was cosmetic. They talked for a half hour before she handed me the phone, a tear in her eye. Mary called out a cheery goodnight to him and made her way to our bed. Content that he was safe and sound.

'Good to hear your voice, son,' I said. We made some small talk. He described Chicago.

'The buildings are unbelievably tall. The streets are wide and the people are very nice but so loud, and everyone is in a hurry.'

'Dear God, it sounds awful,' I joked. I'd never been to America. The images on the television gave me a good idea of what it was like, but there is nothing quite like being there.

'You'd be amazed at the size of some of the old sixties American motors. They go lumbering around the streets here, like great big dinosaurs.'

We yapped on for a while, eventually running out of things to say. 'It's getting late, getting close to bedtime over there,' he said. 'I forget about the time difference.'

'Night, son,' I said. 'Take care, and keep in touch. For your mother's sake.'

It was good to hear his voice. I was not as skittish as Mary but a few scary scenarios had popped into my head when he didn't call on time.

'He's doing well. I knew he would.' My voice was raised. The way people raise their voices when they are talking to the elderly. The garage, the walls, or anyone in here that was capable of listening would have to be old. I stood inside the garage door, thinking, of nothing in particular, just letting my mind wander. It was quiet, I drew comfort from this silence. This was the first time I had gone to the garage for no reason other than to talk to the ghosts, to relay to them my son's progress.

Back in the house Mary was getting ready for bed. Following lifelong habits. Each item of clothing folded on the same chair by the bed she had used since our wedding night. She brushed her hair with her mother's brush. Long even strokes, the way her mother had showed her.

I had stepped into the cold for no other reason than to go to the garage and speak aloud my fears for Michael, and for myself. What greater therapy could there be than to speak aloud the mad raving thoughts that come in and out of our heads, to ignore the codes of behaviour and social conduct and let it all go. Everyone should have somewhere like this. Somewhere to step out of their life, if only for a moment to take stock of things. 'Better than a fortune to a therapist,' I said aloud, defending my actions.

It had become second nature to me now, talking to myself, or secretly to my father. I was never sure which it was. It was easier to say I talked to myself, easier for anyone else to accept. One of those things that happens to people when they age, they would say.

Chapter 20

My goals for the car changed. I wanted to have each milestone tie in with Michael's plans. And so, the pressure was off for the summer with him gone.

It would have made more sense to finish all the mechanical work before I touched the paintwork, I knew I was putting the cart before the horse. Yet it was like an unwritten rule between us. I wouldn't fire up the engine until he was here. He'd committed so much time and effort he deserved to be here when I breathed life into the heart of the sleeping beast.

In my eyes, and in the eyes of enthusiasts, the '69, the E-Type Jaguar was more than just a car, it was a piece of art. Iron and steel moulded into elaborate shapes. And yet it was an inanimate object, and would remain so until its great heart, the great cast iron six-cylinder lump returned to life. Then, and only then would she be a real living thing to me. Her curved lines reflected the overhead lights of the garage. I stood back and admired her voluptuous form. Beautiful though she was, she was a sleeping beauty, she was awaiting the kiss of life. I wanted so much for Michael to be here for that iconic moment. When the engine would draw in its first breaths, when she would wake from her long slumber and take her first baby steps towards the garage door under her own steam.

I fell back into my chair and imagined what that moment would be like, a father and son completing a lifelong task. I closed my eyes and drifted off into foolish dreams of Mary and I driving through the countryside in the '69. In my dream, we were both young again. Mary wore that flowery dress she wore the first time we danced together. She set her hand on mine as we went, a soft, pale, unwrinkled hand.

An unwelcome apprehensiveness interrupted my fantasy. I'd lived long enough to learn that dreams rarely work out like we plan. I tossed and turned in the chair for a moment and woke with a start to find Mary was standing over me. That accusing look on her face.

'What?' I pleaded.

She turned her head to the clock on the wall. 'Will you for the love of God, please put a battery in that clock. Do you know what time it is?'

'Of course, I don't. The clock is stopped, Mary,' I said, aware that I was pushing my luck.

She didn't speak.

'I'm sorry, love. I nodded off. I'm coming up with you now.'

'I'll say you are. What if I hadn't wakened up? You could have been found here in the morning, dead from hypothermia.'

I peeled myself from the chair, it had engulfed me, taken my shape. 'You mean I could have woken up dead!' I scoffed.

'Don't you joke about this, Jack,' she said, prodding me on the shoulder as I walked beside her.

'When did you start talking in your sleep?' she asked.

'What?'

'You heard me. You were talking in your sleep. I never heard you do that before.'

'I didn't know I was, Mary. How would I? If I'm asleep I won't know, that's your job.'

'Don't you give me attitude at four in the morning.' she shoved me hard.

I laughed and walked closer to her, reaching for her hand.

'Get away with you, you old fool,' she laughed again even louder. 'We're not seventeen anymore.'

'Maybe we're not Mary, but can't we pretend we are? Who will know. I don't feel like an old man.' I said, stopping suddenly, taken by surprise by the thought that popped into my head to ambush me. 'Look at this shell that holds me up, Mary. It's the shell of an old man. But I don't feel like an old man. I may be a little wiser than I was when we first met,' Mary raised an eyebrow, about to interrupt, but I continued. 'But I don't feel old.'

She took my face in both her hands and kissed me, a big wet slobbery kiss. 'You're still my young man.' she said, her voice breaking ever so slightly. The light from the house showed in her face. I reached out and wiped the tear that had settled onto her cheek.

'I'm glad I chose you over Esther,' I whispered.

Mary shoved me away. She shook her head at me and laughed. 'Jack Doyle, you are a tonic to me.'

We were soon tucked up in bed snuggled up together, the duvet pulled up to our noses.

'Do you think of him often?' she asked.

'Michael?'

'No, your dad,' she said. 'You were talking to your dad in your sleep. I stood over you for a while, listening,' She took me by surprise, I couldn't answer right away. 'God knows, if there is any part of his soul left in this world, it would have to be in there, Jack. He put his heart into that place. Do you miss his company?'

'That's a silly question Mary. Of course, I miss him. He was my idol, my hero. No boy is as lucky as to have their own dad as their hero. It's such a pity I didn't have him around for a little longer.'

She sat up in bed, leaned over me and kissed me.

'Michael is a lucky boy Jack, you're his hero, his idol.'

I laughed and made light of it but I was chuffed. Every father needs the respect of his son, admiration is a bonus.

Chapter 21

Michael was a good son. He kept in touch, emails, texts and phone calls. It made the great distance between us smaller, and it made his mother happy.

I was in a particularly good mood that evening. Mary's words the night before had set me up for the day. Nothing could dampen the hum of contentment that had settled on me. I attacked each task that evening with a renewed vigour.

'Going well here now, Dad.' I talked as I worked. I could see an end to the work. I was excited and a little apprehensive. What would replace this task? Would this be my last work, would I have to settle back and take it easy afterwards?

My mind was elsewhere when I felt the car move. I was still speaking when I heard the creak. The axle stand had moved, or had I moved it by mistake? Holding my breath, I eased myself from under the car. It was perched tentatively on the corner of the chassis, the car dangerously close to falling to the floor. I brace myself and pressed my arms to the floor of the car. Taking a deep breath, and with all my strength I pushed, I saw a flicker of light between the stand and the chassis and pushed it back into place with my foot.

'Close call, Dad,' I gasped, exhausted at the effort. 'Think that's enough for one day, escape while you can,' I laughed. I was breathing heavy, winded by the effort. The chair beckoned to me. I was nestled snugly in place and stroking my pipe when the pain hit me like an electric charge. The pipe fell from my hand and landed on the floor at my feet as my arm fell limp.

'Aw shit, not now!' I pleaded.

Maybe it was my imagination, but I swear I heard a voice say 'Never a good time, son.' I chalked it down to the fright, but even if the voice was just in my head I knew who it was. It was him.

I was sure, just like the last time it would pass. I'd overdone it. If I could get a moment to sit and relax everything would be fine. But it hit me again, just to make its point, to remind me that this was no joke. This time it was serious. I was not in charge anymore. This time it took my breath away. My head flopped against my chest.

'Shit!' I shouted, angry, scared and struggling to catch a breath. The numbness that began as a dull ache in my left arm grew in intensity. I tried to deny it, to make light of it. It was a muscle spasm, it would pass. My heart helped me accept the truth. It took off, racing like an engine over-revving.

I looked to the distant light in the kitchen. She would be tidying before bed. She'd pause to look to the garage before she left. I saw her silhouette against the window and then she was gone. My mind raced, what could I do to attract her attention? While a part of me, the rational mind was reaching for ways to fix the problem another part of me was helping me to face the reality. There would be no help, this time I might not escape.

I tried to calm myself, hoping I could overcome this if I didn't panic. I closed my eyes and willed myself to slow my breathing, but my heart was having none of it. It was on full throttle and would not be placated. It didn't care how many kung-fu movies I'd seen where the hero could slow his heart rate at will.

Another jolt rocked me. 'Shit! I'm not going to get out of this,' I cried through clenched teeth. I was angry at the situation, my legs refused to help me up, my arms lay limp by my side. Panting, my breaths came in short burst like a woman enduring labour pains. I looked around me frantically, desperate but not knowing what to do. My eyes stopped on the '69.

I nodded my head in disbelief, the significance of this déja-vu moment struck me. 'Not again, first my dad, and now me.' I muttered. Was she going to be a witness to the death of another one of us?

A breeze blew the door in, shutting out the light from the house. I accepted this as a sign that my fate was sealed, nobody could help me.

I had no energy, I could not get up from the chair. An hour passed and then two. My eyes had glazed over, the garage around me became a blur. I could barely make out the '69. I think I fell in and out of consciousness a few times. In the end, I couldn't tell the difference.

'Someday she will be finished.' The voice came from nowhere in particular. My head was slumped forward as I answered. 'I wanted to finish it. Me and my son.' My voice rang angry in the silence.

Someone laughed. 'What makes you so special? You didn't think I wanted the same?'

I raised my head and looked around. I was alone, a voice in my head. I sat for what I thought was a long time, it may have been no more than a few minutes, but it felt like a lifetime. I wondered why Mary hadn't noticed me absent from our bed. Sometime in the middle of the night I resigned myself to the inevitable. It was not a shock. I wasn't afraid. It's not that I was brave. I always felt bravery was having the strength and courage to do something you were afraid to do. If you weren't afraid, it didn't take courage.

I won't say my life passed before me, but I did recall the faces that had passed through this garage over the years, friends and foes alike. They came and went around me, laughing and barking instructions at a figure in the distance, a familiar figure in a greasy overall. When they had all but passed, he turned to face me. I had forgotten his smile. It was so welcoming. I felt warmed by it. I felt at ease. I wasn't afraid. I had no pang of regret. I'd had a good life and then Michael stepped into the fray. 'You can't go. It's not finished. What about Mam? Who will look after her?'

I don't know why but until that point I was ready to let go. I did not want to fight it. It was my time. But my son was calling on me. I had responsibilities, things to do, jobs not yet finished, places Mary and I had not yet seen. I couldn't go. It wasn't fair, why me? Not yet. When I've finished the '69. Then I'll go.

'Jack? Jack, are you still down there?' I thought I heard her call out to me. The garage doors flapped in the wind and I thought I saw the light of our kitchen. I felt euphoric, Mary would come, rouse me from this and pull me into our bed.

But the door rattled again as if angry at her intrusion. A battle raged, the forces of nature called for me, my son demanded I honour my commitments, and then there was Mary, the most powerful spirit of all. She called for my return to her side. I was sure this would be the deciding vote; but the laws of nature have no regard for duties, responsibilities or loves.

The next jolt rocked me with a forced that made me spasm in the chair. As I drifted into unconsciousness I saw him through blurry eyes; standing over the engine, a spanner in his hand, looking back at me, his head tilted to one side as if he'd only just noticed me here. My mouth opened to speak but no words came. I wanted to rise and go to him, I wanted to rise and run to Mary, all warm and tucked up in our bed.

Chapter 22

Slowly they filed past. The old and the young, faces gnarled in despair; some genuine, some feigned. Strangers to Michael every one of them, and yet they shook his hand firmly and vigorously, eager to show the depth of their grief. Others laid a sympathetic hand on his shoulder and rhymed off the age-old mantra, sorry for your trouble.

But Michael was not grieving; he was in shock, he was numb. This procession of strangers, these mourners kept him from coming to terms with his pain.

Jack Doyle, me the man he wanted to grow up to be, the man he most admired in this world, had passed away. He was angry that there wasn't a fanfare to announce this monumental occasion. And yet somehow, he also understood that his father wasn't the god he thought him to be. He'd expected too much from him. He was just a man trying to do his best for his family, and he had. Michael was brought up well; he never wanted for anything.

As a boy, Michael had feared the day when the safety net his parents held discreetly in the background would no longer be there. Now that he was dipping his toe into the working world, he understood what responsibilities lay before him. He hoped he'd fare as well as I had.

Sitting at the end of the hallway in the old home he fought back feelings of anger and frustration at theses intruders in this time of personal loss. Why were they here? What compelled them to come? Tradition?

Jimmy, my old friend, threw an arm around him where

he was seated. 'How are you holding up?' he asked.

'Surprisingly well,' Michael replied, and it was true. 'When will all these strangers leave?' he asked, pulling himself up from his slouch. He tried to look at his father's old friend, eye to eye, but it was nigh impossible. Even with a back bent over from years of toil, Jimmy towered over Michael.

'You'll have the house and the shadows of the old man to yourself soon enough.' Jimmy paused and took a long look around him. 'They're strangers to you, but to your father they were his people. Men he's dealt and traded with. And some he fought with,' he added, with a wry smile. He turned to shake a hand, an old stooped figure years older than me. They leaned close and mumbled something. Jimmy patted him on the back with a loud whack, and the old man shuffled along.

'Men like old Doherty,' he gestured after the old man. 'An old adversary of your father, still respected him for what he was. There's no greater accolade for a man than to have friends and enemies come and show their respect.'

Michael nodded in agreement, but Jimmy wasn't convinced.

'What would you have us do? Turn them away? And leave me and you to sit here and wait for the morning to come so we could put him into the ground on our own,' he paused. 'You've been away too long. You've forgotten our ways.'

I could hear an anger rising in his voice.

'You're still too young to understand, when you've lived through as much as your old man has, you'll understand better.' Jimmy paused and took a long look in the direction of the bedroom where my coffin rested.

'Life's a bitch,' he said, 'an endless battle, and at the end you don't get a medal for completing the course. So, for your Dad, this here parade of strangers is his reward, an acknowledgment that he made it through to the end, and these old faces here are validating that. Well done Jack, you raised a family and saw to their needs.'

Michael felt guilty, even Jimmy could see the bitterness that he tried to hide.

'C'mon,' he said. 'Rise yourself and come with me.'

Michael followed him to the kitchen. Gathered around the table were a few old, craggy, but familiar faces. Men he'd seen come and go from this table since he was a boy. They nodded as he and his Jimmy entered. A chair was drawn back. Michael was expected to join them.

'Shush, the priest's starting the rosary,' came a whisper from the doorway.

'Arrgh, the auld man had no time for men of the collar,' a figure at the top of the table called out. 'We'll not mock him now with that foolishness.' His chest swelled in his shirt when he spoke.

A silence fell around the table.

'Sit with us, son,' he said, 'we'll have a drink to the auld fella.'

He shoved a glass along the table and it was promptly filled with an amber liquid. One of the women helping slammed a second bottle onto the table, then slammed the door on her way out.

Jackets were thrown off, a few sleeves were rolled up, and glasses were filled again.

'To the auld man!' a toast chanted loudly, with no regard for those on their knees in the hall. Thick forearms were raised and glasses clashed together.

'The priest will be up to yous,' Cathleen stood brazenly in the doorway a scowl on her face, one hand holding the open door, the other boldly on her hip.

'Send him in,' Jimmy growled back. 'I've a few questions for him.'

The door was slammed shut. A murmur of consensus ran around the table like a Mexican wave.

The whiskey burned Michael's throat on its way down, but he dared not flinch in this company. His glass had barely touched the table when it was filled up again.

Jimmy pressed himself onto the edge of Michael's seat. 'These are your father's people,' he whispered, as if they were a secret cult. Michael raised his head and took in the faces around him. Old men, all of them, but there was something in their attitude or their bearing that attested to a time when they were formidable men.

And still the drinking went on, though a few heads began to slump. Tall tales grew more unbelievable as the night wore on. Stories of rough men, hard times, and my exploits were exchanged with a mix of pride and humour.

'I'm sorry I didn't get to know him better.' Michael opened his mouth and shared this before he was aware the thought had entered my head.

The muttering fell away. 'It's your loss, young man,' the figure at the top of the table spoke again.

Bolstered by the whiskey Michael challenged him. 'What would you know of the man?' he demanded.

He threw back a chair and stood up, it scraped noisily across the tiled floor.

'He was the bane of my life,' he said, planting his knuckles loudly onto the table. He looked hard into the faces that stared back at him. 'Every man here knew him.' Heads nodded in agreement. 'He fought with each and every one of us at some time.' He slumped onto his chair again. 'This is a sad night for all of us. Do you know why, boy?'

Michael didn't know if he was expected to answer, but the faces around him remained still.

'This is not just the death of an old man, this is the death of an era. There are no more men like your father. Hard, mean, tough but honest men.'

A murmur rose around the table, glasses were raised and heads nodded.

'The mould was thrown away, there won't be another like him.' Jimmy added. 'Young man, you'd do well to follow his example.'

Somewhere deep down, aided by too much whiskey, a bitter truth raised its head. Michael was not like me. Yet here, wrapped in the warmth of their admiration for me, he saw me for the man I was and felt guilty for not realising it sooner. I had never forced ideals or standards on him. I had set a good example and invited him to follow it.

A curtain was drawn back suddenly, a shaft of light poured into a kitchen filled with cigarette smoke and the reek of whiskey. It was morning. A knock came to the door,

'It's nearly time,' a sheepish voice whispered, wary to enter.

When they carried me out through the kitchen door for the last time, Michael understood what he had lost.

Chapter 23

Mary stood on the doorstep of her kitchen, her head turned to slightly to catch the sounds on the breeze. 'The cuckoo's gone for another year,' she whispered. I always measured the year by the cry of nature, not by the calendar; when the cuckoo came and went, when the evenings grew long or short and when the corncrake left at the end of summer.

It was late evening, around about the time I would normally have slipped away to the garage after my dinner.

Michael laid a hand on her shoulder. 'Are you okay, Mam?' he asked, looking around to see what it was she was looking out on.

'I'm fine, son,' she lied.

It had been six months since the funeral and she missed me more with each passing day. She was lonely, but she didn't want just any company, she needed me.

'It's time you got back to your own life, son,' she said, turning into him and throwing an arm around him. Though many of her own friends had come to comfort and hug and hold her, she resented their pity, grew angry at their platitudes.

She loved to be held, to be comforted and to feel safe and protected. She missed this. Michael was of my flesh and blood. She tucked her nose into his chest and inhaled, breathing in his scent.

She shook her head and pushed him away. 'It's time Michael. You've been so good to stay so long.'

'I'm in no hurry, Mam,'

'I appreciate you taking the time, son. You did well in your exams, you are an engineer. Don't waste that. Go off and make him proud. It's what he would have wanted.'

She could see the turmoil in his face, he pined for adventure, but his feeling of duty to her held him back. This was the last thing she wanted. She had done her job... we had done our job, and had done it well. It was time for him to leave the nest.

It was a month later when the letter arrived. Michael had sent his C.V. to just about every engineering firm on the globe. He had no idea where he wanted to go, but he was anxious to put his newfound knowledge to work. Trancit International in Abu Dhabi, a prestigious engineering firm were the first to reply. They had a long list of questions and requirements. Michael smiled as he filled in the reply. He knew he had no difficulty meeting the criteria. His problem was his lack of experience, but he was confident he could present himself well at the interview.

'Get back in there and shave,' Mary demanded, pointing to the door. Even though he was a grown man she still felt he needed her direction.

'Mam!' he complained. 'Things have changed, they want me for my qualifications, not for my appearance.'

'Nonsense Michael,' she dismissed his complaints and turning him by the shoulder she marched him down the hall to the bathroom.

'Jesus Mam, I'll be late.'

'No, you won't, you have lots of time. A clean shave and a fresh shirt and tie.'

Michael closed the bathroom door. But Mary continued lecturing from outside the door. 'Appearance is everything Michael. Never forget that.' It was on the tip of her tongue to tell him that was what his father always said. She did offer him this one tit-bit.

'Shake their hands firmly and look them in the face when you introduce yourself.' The sound of sloshing from inside the bathroom fell away. 'Do you remember being told that Michael?' Mary continued.

The bathroom door opened, she could tell he was smiling even through the white beard of shaving foam that covered his face.

'College interviews,' he said. 'The father warned me, shake their hands, make sure it's a good stout handshake. No watery handshakes, son. Make sure they know you mean business.' He leaned out and kissed her on the cheek. Mary turned again to the kitchen, a tear in her eye and shaving foam on her cheek.

A panel of seven men, all middle-aged and stern looking, sat behind a long hardwood desk. They wore almost identical silvery grey, and very expensive looking suits. In the centre of the room, fifteen feet back from their table sat a solitary chair. Michael swallowed as he crossed the floor to sit. His footsteps echoed loud around the room, his confidence wavered, his courage was packing its bags and preparing to leave. He was bending down to sit when Mary's last words of advice rang in his ear. He stood up again and crossed the distance to the table. He reached across and shook each of their hands in turn, firmly, as advised. Then he took a seat.

The questions came thick and fast. It was not a problem, he knew he was up to the task. His qualifications were above what was required and he had nothing to hide. He was honest from the beginning. He made it clear he had no experience and could bring nothing but enthusiasm and his qualifications to the table.

'What does your father do?' The question came from the oldest of the group. The interview was almost over, some of the others were already stuffing their papers back into their briefcases. The mention of his father threw him, he lost his composure for a moment. It caught the others off guard too, they froze mid-action and turned their attention again to me, clearly curious to hear my answer.

'I'm afraid my father has passed away.'

The gentleman did not flinch or apologise for the question. He pursed his lips, nodded his head to acknowledge that he understood this, but was still awaiting an answer. Michael remained silent for rather too long, the older interviewer was about to move diplomatically to another question when Michael spoke.

'My father was the most capable engineer I know, but one without a formal education or a certificate to his name. I hope to make him proud one day.'

The older gentleman turned to the others and nodded his head. 'Family is everything.' he said, smiling for the first time as he scribbled some notes.

A few short questions later and they excused him with a promise to get in touch within the week to let him know if he was successful or not.

Barely three days passed when he had received the phone call. They wanted him in their Abu Dhabi branch at the start of the next week. The plane tickets would be in the post.

Mary was elated, and dejected, all at the same time. Michael would be successful, she knew he would, but he would also be gone and she would be alone. She went to the living room and sifted through the bookshelf. She was looking for an atlas, but almost every book she pulled out was a motoring manual, an automotive wiring guide or a classic car magazine. I was everywhere, there was just no escaping my presence in the house. Michael's old schoolbooks finally gave up an atlas. She had to search through the index inside the back cover, Mary had no idea where to start looking for Abu Dhabi, and there it was, sitting on the Persian Gulf. She traced a finger along the map, over Europe and the Mediterranean and over North Africa. Along the path an airplane might take, as if she was mentally making the journey. She flinched when her finger stopped over Abu Dhabi. It was a lot farther away than she had imagined, she drew a sharp intake of breath.

Michael looked over her shoulder. He knew what was going through her head. 'A few hours on a plane can take you anywhere, Mam,' he explained. 'Nowhere in the world is that far away anymore.'

Mary gave him a hug and a peck on the cheek. 'You must be so excited, son?'

'It's a great opportunity,' he said, watching her closely. It was clear she was trying to put on a brave face for his sake. She held it together well.

'Right, there's a lot to be done,' she shrugged off her worries. 'You'll need clothes to cope with the heat.' She was preparing to throw herself into the activity of planning; work always helped keep her mind occupied

'It gets very cold at night too, Mam.'

'Really!' she said, sounding exasperated. 'How can that be if it's so hot all day long?'

'In the desert, there is no cloud so...'

Mary cut him off with a raised finger. 'Forget I asked. I'll take your word for it.'

They discussed what he had, what they would need to buy, and where to buy it. I knew Michael, he would have easily taken care of all of this but he was being tactful. He knew she needed to be a mother, and he needed to be dependent on her, at least for now.

It was good for Mary that there was not too much time to wait before he left. Each hour that passed was an hour closer to him leaving and an hour closer to her being left alone.

Michael showed no sign of being nervous of this new venture, nor did he show any sign that he was excited by it either, but that was just his way.

'Just keep in touch, that's all I ask,' she said, as she helped him get his bags into the taxi. They held each other for a long time before she forced him away and held him at arm's length. She looked him up and down from head to toe. 'My baby,' she laughed, and shook her head. Michael laughed a nervous laugh with her and hurried into the taxi. The parting was as painful as he imagined it would be. He could not shake the feeling of guilt, he was abandoning his mother to a life alone in that great big empty house.

Mary watched him disappear down the road. The crunch of the gravel under the tyres grew fainter as he drove away. When the taxi turned onto the tarmac road the noise stopped. She caught sight of him one last time as he waved from the back window and then he was gone. Silence enveloped the estate. She wrapped her arms tighter around her chest, as if to fend off a chill, then turned and looked to the hills and to the meadows that stretched away from the house. There was no-one out there, no husband to return at the end of the day, no son in his room doing his homework, they were all gone and she was on her own. She was overcome with grief. She struggled for a breath. The once busy house was now quiet. We had all gone, abandoned her to live alone. She wrung her apron in her hands. She glanced up at Michael's bedroom window; the curtains were drawn. Then she turned her head to the garage, but fought back the urge to go there.

'Oh Jack,' she said, her voice breaking, pleading. 'It feels like just yesterday we drove up that road from the hospital with him. A small bundle on the seat between us. I watched him go off to school down that same road. And now he is gone... forever.' she was staring at the garage. There was an anger in her voice.

It had been the first time she spoke to me as if I were there, but it was not the last.

During everyday chores, she began to talk to me. 'I swear you must be sneaking in at night and stomping around the kitchen there's so much dirt,' she shouted at me above the din of the vacuum cleaner.

She had been despairing that her heart would never mend but she found solace in these conversations. It was a wonderful form of therapy. Mary knew only too well that it was not healthy to carry on talking to a dead man; but then it wasn't as if she expected an answer. Mary knew I was dead. It was strange that while she could easily accept that I was dead, she was reluctant to say that I was gone.

'Pity Jack is gone Mary, you could do with the company now that the boy is gone.' The postman was fumbling through his sack when he spoke; he was not known for his tact.

'Yes,' she replied, with a sharpness that was lost on him. 'It was inconsiderate of Jack to pass away so soon,' she said. The postman paused for a moment to consider the remark then continued relating the gossip of the day as he had done for years; even though Mary had never encouraged him to do so or offered him anything in the way of gossip to take with him from her house.

Mary looked to the garage, she felt compelled to look that way when it was in sight. She did not have the courage to go there yet, but it drew her to it like a powerful magnetic force that she found hard to resist. In moments of weakness she found herself under the arch, entering the courtyard almost sleep-walking. She would close her eyes and imagine she could hear the crunch of the gravel under my boots. She would snap out of her dream-like state with a jolt and hurry back to the comfort and security of her kitchen, sooth herself with a cup of strong tea and when she was satisfied the moment had passed she would draw back the curtains and look down at the garage again. She knew she would have to go there sometime soon, if only to put my ghost to rest, but only when she was ready.

She tried her best to get on with daily life now that both her men were gone. Good willed neighbours came and went, housework was done, and then she took to reading again, something she hadn't done in a while. It was good for her to get lost in fiction.

Chapter 24

The kitchen door was thrown open. Mary got quite a start in her seat by the stove. She had been knitting, a ball of wool popped off her knee and unwound itself as it rolled across the floor and came to a halt at the feet of the woman who had stormed into her kitchen. She hadn't knocked, hadn't waited to be invited in, and yet there she stood, two large and heavy looking bags weighing her down. She stood in centre of the kitchen floor looking around the room from floor to ceiling without even acknowledging that she had seen Mary. She was sopping wet, the rain trickled off a well-worn wax-oiled coat and formed two great pools of water at her feet. Mary stared at her over the rim of her glasses, and then at the puddle forming on her floor. The woman followed Mary's gaze down to the puddle and shrugged her shoulders. She opened her mouth wide to speak but Mary beat her to it.

'A bit late for the funeral,' Mary said, without rising from her seat.

'Yeah, sorry about that. I was going to come but then I hadn't visited in so long, it seemed a waste coming to see him when he was dead.'

Mary stiffened in the chair, the hairs on the back of her neck bristled. She was on the verge of lashing out, but Mary was a generous and a charitable woman, she knew Eileen's history. She was one of the few who understood her and her strange ways. Her remarks about the funeral would have sounded callous or offensive to many, but Mary knew there was no malice in her words. Eileen's social skills were crude, she spoke her mind honestly, but not always tactfully.

Eileen was my older sister, older by four years. Ours was not a close-knit family, so Eileen and I were never really that close. Even as a child Eileen held herself back from making friends. She was reluctant to interact with her classmates at school and was often found wandering off on her own. She refrained from showing any emotions from an early age. My father joked that she took after his wife's side of the family, a remark that always cost him a clout with whatever my mother had to hand. She was not a mean-spirited woman but she made no effort to conform to any form of social etiquette.

'Tea?' Mary asked, matter of factly.

'Why not.' Eileen replied.

'Why not indeed.' there was an edge to Mary's voice that Eileen noted, but showed no sign that she cared either way.

'Is my old room free for a few nights?' she asked, taking the cup and saucer from Mary.

Mary hesitated, long enough for Eileen to realise she would have to offer some explanation. 'Just for a few nights. I thought I'd pay my respects, take a walk around the old homestead and be on my way.'

Mary was tempted to turn her down, think up some excuse and turn her away, but it was not in her nature. Besides, she felt a little sorry for this old spinster that sat across from her at the table. Though she looked physically fit and healthy, there was a sadness that lingered around her like a foul odour. Everyone who met her could detect it, but not Eileen. She had become as accustomed to it as she was to the loneliness that was now part and parcel of her own existence.

Eileen had never married. Mary could not remember any boys in her life when she was young. The age difference between them was not considerable now, but four years was a big difference when they were both still teenagers. Eileen would have been of a courting age years before it was acceptable for Mary to have any dealings with boys. Yet when she thought on it there was that one unfortunate episode. It was so long ago, Mary could barely remember the details, she had taken little notice of the rumours that surrounded the event at the time. She did remember that I had been protective of Eileen.

She had been engaged to a young protestant boy, Wilfred, from an estate in the next parish. It was no more than ten miles away. My father had always joked that there was no point having a girlfriend farther away than you could cycle, and so it was that marriages were almost always kept within the neighbouring parishes.

Neither of their families were overjoyed at the arrangement. It was a long time ago, but old wounds were still raw. The British were still widely hated, and the protestant community still felt an entitlement, a sense of superiority that was soon to be taken from them. It made for a tense atmosphere between both communities, and many generations were needed to filter that tension away.

The young lovers were set on facing all obstacles together. They could not be ordered apart, they even went so far as to set a date. Eileen was a strong-willed woman; it was hard to see any of that iron will in the willowy figure that sat across from Mary now.

Wilfred, however, was not so brave, he succumbed to the pressure his family, friends and his community applied. What was worse, he lacked the courage to tell Eileen he could not go ahead with the wedding, instead he allowed his family to ship him off to wealthy Scottish relations. So, on her wedding day Eileen stood alone at the altar. Father Doherty stood before her for a full hour waiting, hoping something had gone wrong to delay the boy. He stood in solidarity with the lonely little figure who would not accept that the love of her life had abandoned her. The congregation slowly filtered away, making as little noise as possible. Each felt a pang of guilt as they left, as if they too were abandoning her.

To her credit, Eileen did not run away from the parish, she stayed around for a few years, braving the stares, the awkward conversations and the whispers, and then one day she was gone. She did keep in touch with me, a letter now and again and a Christmas card that usually didn't arrive until near Easter, but it made me happy to know that she was well and I hoped she had found happiness wherever she was.

Both ladies sat in silence once they had exhausted the customary niceties and small talk.

'I never liked them, you know,' Eileen said, out of the blue.

'What?' Mary asked, with no idea who she was talking about.

'Them,' she pointed at the portraits on the wall. 'They made me nervous, the way their eyes followed you when you passed through a room. It's like they are up there all the time watching us.'

'I never really thought about it like that before, but thanks Eileen, that will help on the long winter nights here on my own!'

Eileen shrugged and smiled. She stared up at the portraits. The images of the old lords of the house, blackened by years of smoke from the great Aga stove, were barely recognisable. Her eyes wandered to the ceiling and the crumbling cornices.

'Jesus, Eileen, if you hadn't pointed them out to me I would never have paid them any attention,' Mary cursed, still averting her eyes.

'The kitchen will need a coat of paint this summer,' Mary explained defensively.

'Waste of time Mary, doesn't matter how many times you paint that ceiling, the walls have absorbed so much smoke from that stove they will never stop leeching out the soot.' Eileen looked to the window. Mary stiffened, was this uninvited guest going to review her house?

'Roses are slow to bloom this year,' Eileen said, sitting up in her chair, stretching to look out the window. I could always tell the seasons by the flowers at the window. Mary looked to the thorny bramble that peered above the window sill from the garden outside.

'Spring is late this year,' Mary agreed, and remembered that this was Eileen's home. She had grown up in this kitchen.

She relaxed and lowered her hackles, her mood softened. This uninvited guest was coming back to reminisce, maybe to look back on her life and take stock of where she was and on where things went wrong.

The days passed and the ladies found a middle ground where they could make company for each other; though they had little in common other than age and some life experiences. They took long walks together around the farm. Eileen recounted tales of my exploits as a boy, it helped them to bond. They did of course have me in common. Several days passed before the garage was mentioned, they both knew its significance. After a week of avoiding the subject Eileen broke silence on the matter.

'The garage. Mary, would it be alright if I had a look around?' Eileen asked, coming to a sudden stop while they walked past the courtyard entrance. Mary was about to make light of it and encourage her to go and do whatever she wanted to do, but she knew the request warranted an honest reply.

'Of course, you can,' she said. Then hesitated for a long moment before she continued. Eileen waited, she saw Mary was struggling for words. 'You know Eileen, it was where his heart was. It was where he was at his happiest. You go ahead, but I hope you understand if I don't join you.'

Eileen reached out and took Mary's hand, she held it for a moment but said nothing. It was a rare display of affection. They both felt the weight of the moment.

Mary excused herself. 'Memories of himself are a bit too raw for me to venture in there just yet.' She turned and marched briskly towards the house, not daring to look back for fear she might catch a glimpse of the open door and see further inside.

It took a stout shove to open the doors, they had never been shut, or the garage starved of light for so long. Eileen stepped around the mess that I'd left behind me. The clack of her sandals echoed hollow around the walls.

'Still as untidy as ever,' she tutted aloud, then caught her breath suddenly. She froze, afraid to move for fear of making a sound that might mask what she thought she heard. Was it a creak of a rafter? It was faint and impossible to say for sure what it was, but it was a sound that did not belong in an empty building. Eileen didn't scare easily. She stood and stared hard into the dark corner, defying the shadows.

She spied the Captain's old uniform hanging from a beam, the steering wheel of his old car, her father's tattered Castrol oil beret and her grandfather's farm implements. She turned and took two steps to the wall, placing both hands on the stone wall she bowed her head and, as if she intended to push the stones from the wall, she braced herself, legs apart and leaned into the wall. Her breaths came out in long slow laments, her eyes shut tight in concentration. She held this position for several minutes, then stepped back suddenly, still staring at the wall.

'Oh my,' she whispered, 'Oh my...' She wrapped her arms tightly around her shoulders and exhaled loudly. She walked slowly around, not touching anything but sniffing the air and taking in all she saw. A pair of my overalls were still draped over my old chair. She leaned closer and put her nose to the chair. At her leisure and with no sign that fear was driving her she backed away from the chair.

The air stirred, something was unsettled in the shadows. Eileen took several cautious steps towards the back of the garage. The air grew still, the sounds from outside were no longer to be heard.

'Jack?' she asked, and waited, squinting and staring hard into the shadows. She sniffed the air again, closed her eyes and leaned her head back. Then she flinched suddenly. 'Jack?' she asked again and waited, as if for an answer. 'Are you alright?' she paused. 'Are you alone?' She kept her eyes closed and did not see the angry swirl of the shadows, the light from the window being absorbed and stirred into the blackness, being swallowed up, like the creamy head on a pint of Guinness slowly turning into an inky black.

She swallowed loudly and walked deeper into the garage. 'My word,' she exclaimed, 'Is this old piece of junk still here.' She laughed, as her hand touched the metal of the '69.

'Do you remember when father swore he would see it finished one day.' she laughed again, the hearty laugh of someone recalling a childhood memory. 'He was an optimistic old fool, but a kind one.' She looked to the rafters again as she spoke.

She turned to leave, paused at the door and looked towards the farmhouse. 'You were lucky you found Mary,' she said, maybe to herself, though loud enough for anyone else to hear. 'She's a good woman. I would like to stay and keep her company but I know we could not live together for long. Our honeymoon period is almost over, nobody can live with me for too long.' She began to walk. 'I miss you Jack,' she called back. 'I've always missed you. It was the one thing that made it hard for me to leave.' She shared these thoughts and then she was gone, back to join Mary at the house.

Chapter 25

Mary was clasping a mug of tea in both hands by the window when the phone rang. The mug that had warmed her hands had grown cold in the hour that she stood there. The phone gave her a start but she was slow to pick it up. She was fixated on the garage, barely visible in an early morning mist.

'How are you holding up this morning, Mam?'

'I'm good son, great to hear your voice. It's hard to believe you're so far away. You sound so clear, as if you were speaking to me from your room.'

Michael swallowed. He felt lonelier than he ever had. He wanted to be with her in their kitchen, to stand with her by the window. He knew she would be there. He struggled for words, something that would lift her and make her smile or laugh.

'I still think he's down there sometimes,' she said at last. 'Banging away in the dark.'

'Why don't you come visit me, Mam? I'll organise the tickets. It would be good for you to get away for a while.'

She didn't answer.

'A year today Michael, a full year,' she said.

'Are the neighbours still calling?' he asked, hoping to change from this morbid subject.

'Yes, they're being very good. Oh, and Eileen has come to spend a few days.' There was a long silence. 'Of course, you won't remember her,' Mary laughed. 'Eileen is the aunt you never met.'

'The company will be good for you, Mam.'

There was another awkward silence as each of them struggled for words.

'Bríd is taking me for dinner later, we're going to have a girl's day out. Eileen will come too of course,' she said, with a forced enthusiasm.

'That's good, Mam. It'll do you good to get out for a while.'

'Thanks for calling Michael. It was important to talk, especially this morning. Take care, son and we'll see you soon.'

They were both painfully aware of her slip. We'll see you, not I'll see you.

Bríd did manage to get Mary out of the house. They went to Doherty's, a little pub in the centre of the village. They were careful to avoid any familiar haunts of ours, but that was not a problem, we rarely frequented the pubs of the village, or any village for that matter. I enjoyed a whiskey at the end of the day but liked to savour it in the comfort of my own kitchen.

The ladies had a wonderful lunch. They laughed heartily and even managed to get in a bit of shopping after. It was late evening when they returned. Bríd felt guilty walking away from the house and leaving Mary, but Mary was content to be back in her comfort zone. Eileen quickly excused herself and went off to bed, her room door closed with a loud thud that echoed around the house. They had shared a bottle of wine over lunch. Mary felt a little lightheaded, it had been ages since she'd had a drink. The warm fog of alcohol still lingered, she tottered around the kitchen, a little unsteady on her feet.

'It's here somewhere,' she said, louder than she intended, and pressing a finger against her lips and shushed herself. She continued to rummage through a cupboard. 'I know you won't be needing it now,' she laughed. 'Aha!' she cried out, again too loud. There it was, a bottle of my favourite whiskey.

She pulled cup after cup, and mug after mug, out of the cupboard until she found it, my favourite mug. She poured a generous measure of whiskey for herself, too generous considering she was not a whiskey drinker. It stung her throat as it went down.

'Jesus!' she exclaimed. 'How do you drink this?' She cupped a hand over her mouth to stifle a cough and to silence her voice. She looked to the hallway, listening, hoping she hadn't wakened Eileen.

She looked out the window towards the garage and raised her mug. She didn't know what to toast. 'Can hardly say to your health, now can I?' she laughed. The sadness of it all was sobering, she steadied herself and stepped back from the window. 'God bless you, Jack.' she raised the glass to the ceiling, a defiant toast to the ghosts, to the portraits and to anyone that might take offense.

Emboldened by the whiskey, and wrapped in one of my old coats, she stomped off into the dark. She almost tripped on the gravel, and hesitated for an instant, but only an instant, before she flung them open. She hadn't set foot in there since my death. In a sense, she blamed this place, it was like the other woman, it had kept me away from her for years. She did a slow three sixty degree turn. She didn't know what to expect walking in here again after a year. She drew a deep breath and was about to leave again when she spied my old armchair.

She flopped into it with a groan, it was hard and knobbly, springs protruded into her backside. She wriggled about to make herself comfortable. There it was, the sweet spot, a comfortable position, no springs, no jabs. This was where I had sat, where I too had made myself comfortable. Closing her eyes, she threw her head back and imagined I was engulfing her like the chair was now. Her head lolled to one side against the grubby material of the chair and my old overall that was still draped over the back. She took a deep breath and it hit her; the smell of my tobacco. A smell she had always found offensive, but now it smelled like the essence of me. My clothes had stank of it, that and a heady mix of oil and petrol. Mary drew it into her lungs and held her breath. Holding onto the scent in her lungs like she was holding onto a piece of me. She closed her eyes, her muscles relaxed, melted into the lumpy form of the chair. She was exhausted after a long day, that and a generous helping of alcohol and the chairs old magic helped her nod off to sleep.

'I'm getting up now,' she shouted, in response to a prod she was sure she felt on her shoulder. She had been dreaming, she was sure it was myself urging her up for a fresh cup of tea in the morning.

Mary laughed when she opened her eyes and saw where she had been sleeping. She struggled from the chair and left, shaking her head as she went. Half way across the courtyard she stopped and turned to face the garage. She turned back and shut the doors tight.

'Bye, love.' was all she said. It had been an awakening. She could not go on like this. She would have to let me go and get on with whatever was left for her in her last years. She decided she would make a concerted effort not to talk to me aloud anymore, it would be hard and she'd miss the conversations, but it was for the better.

Eileen was packed and standing in the kitchen. She stared up at the portraits. 'Are you watching over them?' she asked in a whisper. 'And you, William, are you with him? Is that you down there?' William looked down at her, covered in soot, his best tweeds barely visible. 'Life never turns out the way we would like. Your boy is gone, let it go, be at peace.'

When Mary came into the kitchen Eileen was still speaking. She didn't ask to who or why. She herself knew it was acceptable at their age to talk to themselves, or to inanimate objects. The stove, the kitchen or even the house.

She looked at Eileen and got the impression she had been of two minds as to whether she should take off or should wait and say her farewell.

'It's time I left,' she declared matter of factly, as if her leaving needed to be explained.

'If you must,' Mary replied, pulling her dressing gown tighter around herself to fend off the morning chill. She turned to stoke the embers in the stove to generate a little heat.

'It's been good to see you again,' Mary said, then turned to Eileen, extended both arms inviting Eileen to move closer for a hug. Eileen a stranger to human contact or intimacy looked decidedly uncomfortable. Mary took the initiative, she moved closer and pulled Eileen to her.

'It really has been good to see you, Eileen. Please don't be a stranger. Your old room is always here for you.'

Eileen fought back a tear, shook her head acknowledging the generous offer. She took a long look around the kitchen, as if it were her last, and hurried through the door. Mary watched her go and felt a pang of sorrow for the sad looking hunched figure that was shuffling towards the road, two small bags, her worldly possessions under her arm. She stopped suddenly and turned. Mary snatched at the curtains, staring hard to see why she had stopped. Eileen set her bags down and with one hand held over her heart, she waved towards the garage with the other.

Mary stared at the garage, her heart beating fast in her chest. She swallowed hard, she knew what it was, even felt it herself. If there was any essence of me left in this world it would be bound to the old stones and the trivia contained inside those walls.

Chapter 26

Mary leaned over the oven, her hair covered in a light smattering of flour. She was baking again. It's a science, timing is everything. The bread needs to rise just the right amount, but not burn. The little secrets of how to get it just right were handed down from one generation to the next; no notes, no text-books, no recipes on paper. Everything by word of mouth, from mother to daughter, each lesson memorised by heart.

Mary found great solace in baking. She loved the homely smells that rushed out of the oven when she threw open the door. There was something comforting, therapeutic in kneading the dough. She drew great satisfaction from creating something from nothing more than seeds. More than anything she enjoyed the activity. A busy mind is a content mind, her mother had always said.

She was absorbed in her work, when the bang of a car door caught her attention. She looked to the clock above the stove. Ten thirty on a Monday morning. She wasn't expecting anyone. She pulled the curtains to one side ever so little, just enough to see out but not enough to draw the attention of whoever was there. She saw a long black car outside, muffled voices and the shuffling of feet heading to the door. For no apparent reason, she was frightened. She patted her apron to shake off the flour, a plume of white filled the kitchen.

'Fresh bread, Mam!' he exclaimed, 'I've timed it just right.'

Mary fought to free herself from the grubby apron to hug her son. Michael didn't wait. He wrapped his powerful arms around her and picked her off the floor.

'Michael look at your good suit,' she fussed as she laughed, at the same time fighting back the tears. He kissed her on the top of her head and led her to the table.

'Sit Mam, is there tea in that pot?' He pressed her into a chair. She nodded her head, breathing fast and lost for words. Her mouth opened to speak but not a single word would form there. He poured two cups of tea, gave her a moment to compose herself and braced himself for the questions.

'Why didn't you tell me you were coming,' She raised her hands to her head, distraught, surprised, excited, worried. 'Is everything okay?'

'Everything is just great Mam, couldn't be better. I thought I'd surprise you, that's all. I knew only too well if I gave you notice you'd make a fuss getting yourself and the house ready.' Mary took a quick look around the kitchen. The walls hadn't been painted in four years, the kitchen was a mess.

Michael followed her gaze. 'It's just like I remember it, home.' he said.

Springing from her chair she threw open the oven door. The room filled with smoke and the pleasant smell of overcooked bread. Mary pulled out the scorched scones and laughed.

'What's with all the baking?'

'The neighbours love it, they can't get enough of my baking,' she answered, defensively.

Michael tilted his head to one aside and smiled at her.

'Okay,' she laughed. 'I love it, it's kind of like a therapy.'

Michael joined her laughing, 'That's good, Mam. If it makes you happy, you keep baking.' He knew from her letters she was lonely and just getting by, the last thing she needed was a lecture.

They talked about his job in Dubai, his life there and the people he worked with. Mary listened carefully. There was no mention of any females. 'Are there any women working there?' she asked.

Michael suppressed a smile. 'Don't you watch the news Mam? It's the Middle East. There are no women in the Middle East. Muslims don't allow them in.'

She threw her tea towel at him. 'Don't you get smart with your old Mam.' she laughed.

She did note that he didn't answer the question.

'Flash car Michael, is it yours?'

'Company car. They had it waiting for me at the airport.'

'Ooh!' she mocked. 'Your father would have been impressed.'

An uncomfortable silence followed at the mention of me. The elephant in the room that they'd been reluctant to acknowledge.

'His hard work and your help got me where I am. I couldn't have done it without you both.'

Mary looked at him stunned, 'Son, that's our job! You're father always said we had to give you every chance we could, and so we did. The rest was up to you. Right,' she said, jumping from her seat. 'Have you eaten?'

'No, I've fasted since morning. I didn't eat at the airport. I was looking forward to some home cooking.'

'I'll make you something,' she said, uncertainty in her tone. She threw open a few cupboards and stared in. 'Not much in the house but provisions for one old lady.' she laughed.

'Anything home-cooked is good. The food out there is grand but it's still foreign food, Mam.'

'How about a big fry?'

Michael walked over to join her as she stared into the refrigerator. 'Sounds perfect. You can never go too far wrong with a greasy old fry.'

Mary cooked and fired questions at him. Michael answered as best he could, trying to glean something from her of what life was like here on her own. Mary was a true diplomat. She talked around his questions but answered none.

'Your old room is probably a mess,' she said, yawning. 'I can have it ready in a tick though.'

'Nonsense, Mam. It's fine as it is. I slept in worse in college.' They bade each other good night and went off to bed.

A week passed, Mary was reborn. A healthy colour returned to her cheeks, she hummed while she worked and more importantly she slept like a log, something she hadn't done in an age.

Michael had saved up his holidays. He had a month off and would spend every minute of it at home. He helped in the garden, trimmed the hedges, painted the stone walls around the courtyard, but was reluctant to enter the garage. He was afraid. He had coped surprisingly well with his father's death. He was afraid that grief was yet to come, it was waiting to ambush him and the most likely spot would be inside those doors.

Ten days into his holiday he mentioned he might have a friend calling. Mary perked up at the news. 'A friend?'

'Yes, Mam. Savita, she's Asian, a co-worker.'

Mary tried to hide her surprise – a girlfriend, an Arab, what religion was she, how would she greet her?

'It's okay Mam. She's been in America for years. She has no unusual beliefs or rituals. You'll like her.'

Mary smiled, her son could read her well. 'And do you like her?' she asked.

'I do Mam, I like her.'

'Good, then I'm sure I'll really like her.'

Mary was positively glowing after that news, glowing like an expecting mother would glow. The house too gained a new life, it felt warmer, homely again. Michael was set to work, gardens needed weeding, fences mended, crumbling stone walls straightened.

'She's just a friend, Mam. She won't be taking notes or judging anyone.'

'Humour me, Michael. I'd like things to be just right when your new bride – sorry, friend, comes.'

Michael snapped his head around to find his mother grinning from ear to ear.

'Gotcha,' she laughed, pointing a finger at him.

The truth was she did feel put under pressure by Savita's visit. It was decades since there was another woman in the house, she wouldn't count Eileen's visit. The last time would have been when she was carried over the threshold herself, to live in her new home with her husband and her mother-in-law. Not the perfect scenario, but it was the best that could be done in those times. It had been tense at first, but when neither woman saw the other as a threat they quickly became good friends.

'Don't worry Mam, she'll love you,' Michael assured her, as she did a last-minute check around the house on the morning Savita was due to arrive. Mary stood apprehensively in the kitchen as Michael went to greet Savita from the taxi. There was shouting and laughing, the scuffle of bags, the sound of car doors slamming, the taxi leaving, a moments silence and then the kitchen door flew open as Michael hurried in, weighed down by cases and shoulder bags.

Mary stepped back. She was frustrated that every dress she tried from her wardrobe that morning was too big. She had shrunk considerably since she'd last had need of a good dress. She was wearing, she professed to Michael, something she might be expected to wear to her own wake. She stood in anxious anticipation, her broad welcoming smile filling her flushed face. She wiped her sweating palms on her hips one last time before she extended her hand to greet Savita.

A whirlwind of colour and cloth blew into the kitchen. Mary was completely surprised by Savita, dressed in a flowing summer dress breezed in, gasping from the effort of carrying the bags and speaking at ninety miles an hour. It was like a firecracker filled with bright vibrant colours had been thrown into the room. Savita filled the room with a wonderful light and energy, it radiated from her, forcing Mary to instinctively take a step back. She spoke so fast Mary was unable to follow a word she was saying. She just stood there like a rabbit caught in the glare of a cars headlights. Mary was awestruck by this wonderful, beautiful, pint-sized creature so full of energy that had burst into her world. Her immediate reaction was she liked her, and Mary trusted her instincts beyond anything else. Savita launched herself at Mary, hugging her while still talking and laughing.

'I'm so pleased to meet you, Mrs Doyle. Michael has told me so much about you, and the house is just as he described. It's just fabulous. I live in the city. I can't believe how much open space there is here. Wow!'

Mary was speechless.

Savita, turned to Michael. 'This is just wonderful,' she said.

The girl was a breath of fresh air, but Mary did suspect she was fuelled by a nervous energy and was perhaps as apprehensive of their first meeting as she was. It was understandable, she was being introduced to a new world, a strange home and the landlady was your boyfriend's mother.

It had occurred to Mary to ask about sleeping arrangements, but since Michael kept referring to her as just a friend she decided to wait and let nature take its course if there was more to it. Michael took her bags off to her room, Savita followed still talking.

Mary felt there was a pure and genuine honesty about the girl. She was pleased, relieved too. It would have been hard work to deal with her if they could not get along.

Just like when Mary came into the house herself for the first time, it was a little tense at first, but she made every extra effort to make Savita feel at home.

As the days passed, guards were dropped, defences lowered, and they became friends. Savita was easy to like, she was bubbly and full of energy, but she was respectful of Mary's role as the head of the house.

Disappointed that there might be no chemistry between them, Mary was almost resigned to the fact that she was in fact no more than a co-worker. Then one night when she was helping herself to a cup of hot milk around four in the morning she heard giggling from Savita's room. She stood listening in the hall for a while and tiptoed away with a smile.

For the first time in an age, she felt the urge to speak to me again. To tell me our son was at home and well... and not alone.

She made no mention of it, but the next night when Michael went to his room his things were gone. He was on his way to the kitchen to ask what was up when Savita summoned him with an extended finger from the top of the hallway. There, in Savita's room were his things, nicely folded away and the single bed they'd shared late into the night replaced by a double bed from the spare room. They laughed and fell upon each other.

It was a happy house again. Mary had missed that, it had always been a happy house.

However, Mary was aware of the clock that was ticking towards the day they would leave. The thought of being alone again scared her.

Chapter 27

Life at the house settled into a familiar routine. Michael worked methodically through his list of things to be done, happily ticking each job off the list as he went. He tried to push thoughts of the garage to the back of his mind; he was reluctant to go there. He hoped something would change that would make it suddenly easier, otherwise he would have to walk through the garage, have a look around and see if there was anything that needed dealing with in there. Each time it entered his head he ignored it, moved on to something else but it was in his peripheral vision each time he passed the courtyard. It was demanding to be noticed; he had to force himself to look away. He had been to visit my grave, that was easy. This was the test, the garage was where we got to know each other, where we became friends, where he knew those memories were waiting patiently for him.

He had told Savita all about his life growing up on the farm and the garage was central to all his stories. When he was just a boy it was the castle he and his friends defended against an evil enemy, when they first experimented with alcohol it was here they shared their first beer. Growing up revolved around those whitewashed walls.

Savita was helping Mary prune the roses. They'd worked their way along the flower bed along the wall and along the perimeter of the walled garden.

Mary stood up. 'I'm getting too old for this,' she laughed, wincing as she stretched. Savita plucked a rose petal, held it to her nose and inhaled. She closed her eyes and spun around, her arms outstretched and her head tilted back to catch the sun.

Mary laughed with her as she watched. Savita came to a halt and opened her eyes. She was standing no more than ten feet from the door. Neither of them spoke for a moment. Savita gave Mary a long questioning look.

'Okay,' Mary said, feeling suddenly brave. 'I'll show you around.'

Savita was ecstatic, she had no idea what to expect. Michael's description of the place made her think of a wonderful expansive building like something from the Willy Wonka Factory. It needed to be to house the adventures that he'd described.

The rickety doors protested as Mary forced them open. Stale air rushed past her, tainted by a strong scent of oil, damp and petrol. The familiar smells induced powerful memories. Her heart lurched, her head grew light. She closed her eyes to compose herself but the image of my oily face forced its way into her head. With a gasp, she stepped back.

Savita missed this, she was already ahead of Mary, wandering around, staring into every corner. The garage was as always, a mess. It was almost how I left it. Savita had the corner of the cover in her hand about to draw it up when Mary yelled. 'No! Don't touch that!'

Savita stumbled, taken aback by the severity of Mary's tone. She didn't know how to react. Mary just stood there, silent and pale staring at the shape in the corner.

'I'm sorry, Mary. I didn't mean to...' she started to apologise, though she had no idea what for, when she turned and saw Mary's face, pale and drawn and staring past her. 'Are you alright Mary?' Savita asked, rushing to her side to steady her. Mary looked as if she might drop to the ground at any moment.

Clasping Savita's wrist tightly, Mary smiled at her. 'I'm sorry,' she said, in a softer tone. 'Forgive me, I didn't mean to give you a fright,' she turned her head and looked over Savita's shoulder to the back of the garage. 'She kept him from me,' she nodded towards the canvas covered lump.

Michael came running when he heard the shout. When he saw both ladies standing still by the open door he came to a noisy halt in the loose gravel. He ventured closer, laid a hand on his mother's shoulder and walked on in.

Savita glanced first at Mary and then at Michael. Neither of them offered an explanation. 'What's wrong? Who are you talking about?' she asked.

Michael walked tentatively to the back of the garage, like a horse trainer would do, so as not to frighten away a feisty stallion. He reached out and gently laid a hand on the canvas cover. 'Easy girl,' he whispered. 'Surely you remember me?' A metal oil can fell to the ground with a crash. Savita and Mary almost leaped out of their skin. Michael didn't flinch. He took a long look around the garage.

Savita looked to Mary. She squeezed the younger woman's hand tighter and pressed her finger against her lips to urge her to be silent, and patient. Whatever was happening in the garage, Savita understood it was important to them both.

Michael turned to face them and waved both hands palms downward in a gesture of assurance that all was okay.

He turned, fixed the cover back exactly as he found it and backed away from the car. Mary watched his every move. She had looked frightened, but now she just looked relieved. Michael threw an arm around them both and ushered them out. Savita struggled to look back but he ushered her on.

'Time for tea, Michael,' Mary wrestled free of his embrace to leave the young couple holding each other. 'Savita has something special prepared,' Mary added.

Mary had hoped he would not go into the garage. She was afraid. Their life had been near perfect these last weeks. She didn't want the garage to cast the same spell over her son she thought it had somehow cast a spell on me; but that was never true. I was a free agent. I came here because it was where I wanted to be.

Savita had prepared some traditional Indian food. Mary did her best to sample it but it was a little too spicy for her conservative Irish taste. She excused herself, bade them both good night and went off to bed, leaving them to finish their meal and the wine together.

Truth was she didn't feel altogether too well. The little fright in the garage had triggered a bout of palpitations that had drained her of energy. She threw herself onto her bed and tried to relax, to control her breathing. She woke with a start a few hours later, even though she could not remember falling asleep. A chill had gone through her lying on top of the bed fully clothed. She tiptoed to the kitchen. Made herself a cup of hot chocolate as quietly as she could. While she waited for it to cool, she drew back the curtains and looked out towards the garage. It was in darkness. In the dream she had moments before she woke, it had been fully lit, the doors were lying wide open and rattling in the breeze. She smiled at her foolishness and returned to her bed.

She'd barely left the kitchen when the glow of a dim light flickered in the garage.

Chapter 28

Mary sat up in her bed. She looked at the clock, it was earlier than she would normally awaken. A wave of nausea washed over her when the significance of the day dawned on her. This was the day Michael and Savita were leaving. She took a few long deep breaths and threw her feet onto the cold floor. She dressed and looked at her reflection in the mirror. The happy glowing face she had looked on these past weeks was gone. Fear of the loneliness to come was etched in the wrinkles on her brow and the crow's feet around her eyes. She steeled herself and put on her bravest face.

Michael and Savita were already in the kitchen. Savita was busying herself setting out recipes for the few traditional Indian dishes that Mary liked. The atmosphere was heavy, weighed down with the sadness of a difficult farewell that was looming. Savita looked even more dejected than Michael. She had grown incredibly fond of his mother; it was easy, Mary was a gem.

The clock chimed midday and as if on cue, the taxi rolled up the drive to the back door. Mary helped them to the door but would go no farther, she said her farewells from the security of her kitchen, her haven. Tears were streaming down Savita's cheeks. Mary hugged her warmly, kissed her on the top of the head and smiled at her as she ushered her away.

'Take care of yourself Mary, and thank you for being so kind,' she spun on her heel and left.

'I'm worried you'll be lonely here on your own, Mam.'

He held her at arm's length, peering into her face so she could not mask the lie.

'I've always been here on my own,' she laughed. 'Your father spent his days down there,' she pointed to the garage.

'I wish you would come with us. I have a huge apartment, you would have freedom to wander around, bake and tidy if you like.'

'I have my friends who call, my roses and of course, my lifelong friend – my stove.' she laughed, looking back at the cast iron black lump.

Michael kissed her on the forehead, hugged her and left. He made to close the door behind him, but she stopped him. 'Leave it open,' she said.

The burble of the engine and the thrum of the tyres on the gravel echoed off the stone walls around the house. The sound grew ever fainter, and then it was gone... and so was Michael.

That first day alone was one of the hardest for Mary since I left her. She wandered the grounds aimlessly. Several times she strolled in the direction of the garage. I felt sure she wanted to talk, to air her thoughts, but she knew it wasn't wise or healthy. She was alone and would have to come to terms with it again.

The house too seemed to mourn this return to silence. The patter of feet late at night, and the uplifting tinkle of laughter that echoed in every corner was gone. Corners that previously seemed brighter, grew ever darker. The light was gone from the house, and the light was slowly leaving Mary.

Michael had tried to familiarise Mary with the internet. He explained how she could keep a track of what he was doing, see for herself what was happening in the world; but it was a lost cause. Mary struggled to get to grips with the remote control for the TV. This new-fangled internet was too much.

Michael gave up and Mary resigned herself to writing letters. Snail mail, he called it, and she laughed at the term.

'I like waiting for the postman. It gives me something to look forward to.' she had said.

Michael had been about to protest, but changed his mind and gave up. He knew his mother, she was as stubborn as he was.

When the first letter arrived, Mary was both elated and disappointed. It was penned by her newfound friend and her son's lover. Savita told her all about their life in Dubai. She painted a wonderful picture. Mary saw through the ploy, she knew she was planting the seeds for an invite. If the mountain can't come to Mohamed, then Mohamed must come to the mountain. Michael and Savita led full and busy lives. They had exciting careers and could never realistically move home.

Mary had no sensible reason not to move out and stay with them, if only for a short while. She was flattered that her potential daughter-in-law genuinely wanted her to come. She knew she would be made welcome and pampered, but she knew there was no way she could ever leave her home. In her reply, she made it clear that while she would like to see Michael's new home and would indeed enjoy a visit she was too old for the journey. There was too much to do around the farm and it was impossible to leave the house empty for too long. In her search for an acceptable reason for not going, she realised that the real reason she would not go was because she would not leave me. This both frightened and saddened her. I was gone. I was not at work. I was not labouring in the garage. I was gone from her forever and would never return.

For the first time in a long time she fell to her knees and cried.

'You have my heart, you old fool. Come back and take this empty shell with you. I don't want to be here anymore.'

Mary fell asleep on the cold tiles of her kitchen floor. She had sobbed for a long time before fatigue won over. Night came and the house grew cold. She winced as the cold penetrated her bones and sitting up she began to shiver. Her left arm had fallen asleep where she lay on it. Pins and needles began in her hand and climbed up her arm as warm blood flowed through the constricted arteries. A dull light had filled the kitchen. Mary struggled to her feet and winced again. Her back ached, her hips were sore and her head throbbed. She looked at the clock, it had just turned six o'clock. Pulling back the net curtains on the window she stared at the glow of the rising sun through gritty eyes. The garage stood as a stark silhouette against its yellow light. It shone through the garage as if it were lit from inside. A dark cloud passed over and for an instant – just an instant, she thought the garage remained lit. The sun returned and it looked normal again.

'Tea,' she said. 'I need a hot cup of tea.'

Chapter 29

'There's nothing like a routine to keep the mind occupied,' Mary recited her mother's mantra. Then she began in earnest, baking, weeding and housekeeping. A rigorous itinerary, broken up by frequent rest stops and cups of tea. Tea was good, it gave Mary a chance to contemplate what she had left to do while she sipped, and how she would manage her time to get it done. She pushed aside a thought that kept popping into the back of her mind, soon these daily tasks would be beyond her ability. Denial was her best way of dealing with this potential problem. Mary felt it was as good a way as any to cope with an inevitability that she was powerless to change.

The calendar over the hearth had three dates circled. Michael's birthday, her wedding anniversary and the third escaped her. She knew it was circled for a reason and it would eventually pop into her head when she was least expecting it.

The following day was our wedding anniversary. It was always a hard day, I was hopeless with dates. I rarely bought a card, though I regretted it now, and never a gift, yet Mary always dragged me off somewhere to mark the occasion.

One last rally and she'd call it a day. She finished her tea and roused herself to make a start on a spring-clean of upstairs bedrooms. She marvelled at how dusty and dirty a house could get with just one resident. The spare room had become a convenient spot to throw all the unwanted items that were cluttering the house. She rolled up a grubby unwanted rug dragged it up the stairs and stood it against the door as she struggled to press the contents of the room back from the door far enough to get the rug squeezed in, then she struggled to press the door shut against the full room.

A faint tinkling sound caught her attention, she snapped her head around, the light flickered on something bobbing over the top of the stairs. She hurried to the top step and watched it bounce on each step on its way to the bottom. It spun around in a great circle and came to a halt against the kitchen door. Even before she reached down to pick it up Mary knew what it was. She turned the shiny object over in her hand and held it to the light, then closing her fingers tightly around it she drew a deep breath and exhaled slowly.

'Oh my… Oh Jack…' she lamented.

I had lost that wedding ring some twenty years before. Truth was I rarely wore it and never mourned its loss; but Mary had turned the house upside down in her search for it to no avail. How could it materialize now after all these years?

She picked her cardigan from the chair, threw it loosely over her shoulders and stormed off towards the garage. She was angry and scared, but also elated. This was just the kick in the ass she needed to make her get up and go down on her own, to shout out the questions she wanted answered, even if she would only be heard by those stone walls. It would be enough. She was content to direct her anger at the building, those stones that housed me and kept me enclosed and away from her.

It was late evening; the sun had set and it was dark outside. She stopped at the door, held her hand over the rusty door handle for a moment, there was no turning back now. She had to go in or she might never come back again. The courage she felt on leaving the house was deserting her, it had leaked away with every step she took. She was faltering and she knew it; it was now or never. With one great effort, she pushed the doors in and stepped inside, not far but far enough to satisfy herself that she was in, just in case she got cold feet and turned and ran. It would give her courage for the next time, to take a step farther knowing she had already been inside the door. She stood shaking nervously, her breath coming in short sharp gasps. She tried to speak, her mouth was dry, she swallowed and tried to whet her mouth enough so she could speak. 'Jack, are you here?' she heard her own voice and those foolish words, and though she knew it was madness she clung to a thread of hope that something would happen, some miraculous sign, to let her know I was there, in some form.

She took a few brave steps inside, slowly regaining her courage. There was never anything to fear in the garage, this was my space, but Mary was always welcome. There should have been nothing to fear here.

'Jack Doyle, you come back here right this minute and take me with you. I warned you not to leave me behind.' Her anger gave her strength, her voice broke, her eyes filled with tears.

She imagined my response, something smart, a witty quip that would melt her heart. She knew I didn't like conflict.

I was always quick to concede defeat, even apologise when I was not at fault. It drove her mad.

Silence...

A full moon passed in and out of the clouds, throwing the garage into light and then dipping it back into complete darkness. A light breeze raised eddies of dust along the courtyard and blew past her into the garage. She gathered her cardigan tighter around her shoulders to fend off the chill. She stood there waiting, listening for another ten minutes, then turned to go. She had barely taken a step when she smelled it again, the strong scent of my tobacco. She froze. 'Jack?' She was almost afraid to turn around - but she did. There was no-one there. She walked to my favourite chair, pressed her nose into the fabric and inhaled. It still stank of tobacco. She smiled again, the breeze must have stimulated the scent. It was nothing.

PART II

Chapter 30

I opened my eyes to familiar surroundings. All around me was a mess as usual. I hadn't tidied up before I sat down. The floor was an obstacle course of boxes and cables, as challenging as any army assault course. I smiled and braced myself for the effort to rise from the chair, for a change the springs didn't jab me when I moved and the effort didn't bring a twinge of pain. I felt pleased that the rest had done me good.

It was still dark out. I thought I had slept for hours and it would have been closer to first light. Yet Mary hadn't come calling, she must have fallen into a deep sleep. I glanced out of habit at the clock that no longer worked, still eleven thirty.

I pushed the doors out, fully open, into a clear moonlit night. A light breeze rustled the branches of the apple trees over the wall in the courtyard, the leaves fell to the ground like confetti. There was no chill in the air, and it struck me that it was early in the year for the trees to shed their leaves. I turned to go back into the garage, but the doors I'd thrown open only moments before were shut tight. My chest tightened, a feeling, a sense, a memory somewhere in the dark recesses of my mind showed me a glimpse of something amiss. My head felt like it was filled with cotton wool. I couldn't concentrate. I tried to make sense of it. My brain ran through every combination of possible explanations, before it allowed me to consider the irrational notion that occurred to me. I slapped myself, but felt nothing. Was I still asleep, dreaming?

I opened the doors and went back inside. I held an arm to the light, the sleeve of my overall was rolled up to my elbow but not a single goose-bump was raised against the obvious chill of the night.

'No, no, no!' I mumbled, as I closed my eyes and inhaled through my nose. This final act confirmed it. It was gone, the heady scent of old oil and petrol, nothing. I could smell nothing. I ran through the door again and made for the house. I woke with a jolt, back in the chair.

A light came on in the kitchen, Mary's shadow crossed in front of the window. 'Mary, Mary!' I screamed at the top of my lungs. I was easily within earshot of the house. My voice echoed in the silence of the night, and yet a bird that sat atop the wall did not stir.

'Sweet Jesus, no!' I cried, 'This cannot be! This nightmare cannot be...'

My attention turned to the back of the garage. The cover was draped over her again. Why would Mary throw the cover back over the car? I'd been working on it every night this week! Or had I? Was it this week, or a few weeks ago? Yet what have I done in the time since?

A cloud of dust rose into the air when I threw the cover off. Yet I felt no urge to cough. A thick layer of dust had covered the body of the car. I wanted to concentrate and make sense of this. Was I dreaming? Would I wake up any minute and feel the warmth of Mary by my side? I had no answers and no means to find any, my head offered no help.

'Jack, are you here?' her voice froze me. I felt a pang of longing, an unnatural longing for someone I should have been with that morning. I missed her. I realised that I missed her because I hadn't seen her in a long time.

'Jack Doyle, you come back here right this minute and take me with you. I warned you not to leave me behind.'

I hurried to greet her, I was sure she was looking straight at me but as I drew closer I saw she was still looking into the depth of the garage behind me.

'Mary, I'm here, right here.' I held out a hand to touch her but I withdrew it before I got the shock of seeing her ignore, or reject it.

'What kind of hell is this?' I pleaded, my head thrown back, eyes shut tight facing the rafters.

A breeze rose, whirling the dust around her feet. She pulled her cardigan around her and turned to go. I threw myself after her, but could get no farther than the courtyard.

She paused and drew something from her pocket. She rolled it in the palm of her hand, it flickered in the moonlight. I can't explain how, but I just knew what it was.

Mary read the inscription on the inside of the ring.

'Together forever,' I read it with her.

She fell to the ground as if struck from behind. 'Mary!' I shouted at the top of my lungs. I ran to her, this time my way was not barred. I dropped onto one knee and shouted her name again, hoping I could somehow rouse her. I wanted to hold her, to comfort her; but I had no substance. I was useless to her. It was like trying to hold and comfort the wind. She lay limp on the ground at my feet, her chest rising and falling, her breathing shallow and barely audible. I was powerless. I couldn't move her or raise the alarm. I couldn't comfort her or make her aware that I was here by her side. I ran to the garage again, looked wildly around me for something, I had no idea what. Then I saw it.

I summoned all my strength and dragged the blanket from my chair. I don't know how I did it. I remember hearing of people performing acts of super-human strength to save someone in a crisis, maybe it was that? It felt like I was pulling a great lead weight behind me. I managed to drape it over her. I hoped it would be enough to fend off the worst of the night chill. The blanket was old, hand-knit and very heavy, but it would not save her if she was to lay motionless here for the night. I looked to the crest of the hills to where the first light of the morning sun would show itself, but there was no amber glow, it would be hours before the sun rose high enough to bring her some warmth. I threw myself onto the gravel by her side. I lay there with her, trying to bestow whatever heat or energy I could, to protect her from the cold.

It was a long night. I counted each and every one of her heartbeats. My hand melted into her chest, lying there I cupped her struggling heart. It beat so faintly I had to concentrate to feel it pulse in my hand. Time seemed to slow right down to almost a halt. It seemed as if minutes passed between beats. It tortured me to think that each one could be her last.

A horrible, selfish thought took seed in my head. If she passed away here in my arms would we be together again? She still held my ring in her hand. Together forever – will that innocent pledge be enough to bind us together here and now? Together forever, alive or dead?

First light brought familiar rumblings. Frank, the busy body postman. As predictable as the seasons. I called out to him, but he could not hear me. His busy body nature came to her aid. Frank could never miss a chance to have a good nosy around before he moved on, and it was then that he saw the tiny little figure curled up on the gravel yard. He plucked Mary from the cold and carried her to the warmth of the house, and away from me. Her heart was at its weakest. It felt like a tiny robin cupped in my hand about to pass away.

I watched her go. She looked older, tired. How long had I been lost to her? Has it been months or years and why?

I felt weak, my head felt light. I retired to the chair where I could watch the house, but my eyes grew heavy and I slipped away.

Chapter 31

Michael and Savita were standing over Mary when she woke. Their faces, and the unfamiliar surroundings confused Mary. She stared at them, her mouth open searching for words.

'It's okay, Mam. We came as soon as we heard,' Michael laid a hand on her arm, she looked down at his hand and at the tubes and wires that were attached to her arm, and still she did not speak. The words stuck in her throat, a great traffic jam of questions so desperate to get out, like five lanes of traffic trying to squeeze through a narrow alley.

Michael saw the distress in her face. 'It's all okay, Mam. You had a bit of a scare, but the doctors are taking good care of you. Relax, be patient and we'll explain everything. You just need to rest now.'

The mention of doctors made her snap her head around to take in her surroundings. Just then a young woman with a clipboard appeared. She nodded and smiled at Mary to acknowledge her, then turned to talk with Savita and Michael. She paused half way through their whispering, they all turned to look at Mary and smiled at her reassuringly.

Mary was tired. She didn't have the energy to sit up and ask the questions she knew she should ask. She let her head fall back onto the pillow and drifted off to sleep again, even though she had been in and out of sleep for most of the past day. The doctors were happy to see her rest, and glad that her family were here to answer her questions when she could compose herself and feel up to talking.

After a good night's sleep Mary felt more like herself. She was tucking into a breakfast of tea and toast when Savita came in, followed closely by Michael with a worried frown on his face. Savita held Mary's hand firmly as she and Michael talked through the turn of events that had brought her here.

She was upset that she couldn't remember anything after she'd left the garage. They told her the postman had found her lying in the courtyard, a light blanket draped over her. She had a mild heart attack, there was no permanent damage but the doctors had warned her she would have to take it much easier.

Michael and Savita collected Mary that afternoon at the hospital and took her home. She apologised profusely for dragging them from their jobs and their lives. She felt awful and guilty - but also delighted to have them back with her while she tried to piece together what had happened.

It was three days before Savita would allow Mary to lift even a cup. Savita waited on her hand and foot, fussing and pampering her like she had never been pampered before. It was wonderful, but at times a little frustrating.

As they sat down to dinner on the third day the subject arose again. 'Mam, you should really come out and stay with us. You'd love it. It's warm sunny and the neighbourhood is great. It's not at all like you imagine.'

'You mean you don't live in a tent in the desert that you both share with a camel?'

'Very funny, Mam.'

Savita didn't interfere. She knew this would have to be between them.

'Maybe I could come for a short visit.' Mary eventually conceded.

Savita yelped like a teenager, 'It will be wonderful. I will show you all the sites and we can go shopping together...'

Michael raised an eyebrow and she smiled at him and sank back onto her seat. 'We will of course have to wait until you are well enough to travel.' Savita continued.

'What about your work? Won't you both have to get back soon?'

They exchanged a glance, and a smile. 'We have agreed that I should stop working.' Savita reached out and took hold of Michael's hand. 'We are trying for a baby.'

Mary cupped her hands over her heart, she was overcome with emotion. It had never come up and she never mentioned children, not even in jest, but it is every mother's wish to have grandchildren.

'I'm going to be a granny at last,' she said, with a hearty laugh. 'I've felt old and so like one for so long.'

The house came to life again. The shadows were banished from the corners, the roses blushed an even brighter red and all seemed good with the world.

Savita and Michael were gone to the shop. Mary was alone in the house for the first time in days. It felt different, she did not feel lonely knowing she would have company again in a few hours. She supped her tea loudly and sat contentedly by the window. 'It's not that bad being on my own. We're old friends,' she said, looking around her and up to the ceiling. 'You and I have been through a lot together.' She was talking to the house, the walls, her stove.

There was a loud rap at the door. It gave Mary a start. She looked to the clock, it had just gone noon. Savita and Michael couldn't possibly be back from the shops yet, she thought, besides why would they knock?

She roused herself from her chair in the corner where she was just beginning to nod off to sleep.

'Ah Mary, it's so good to see you up and around again,' Frank had been their postman for near twenty-five years now. He knew each family along his route; knew who was writing from Australia, who was expected home soon and who was leaving. Mary watched the clock around this time most days, waiting to see if he would stop with a letter from her son. A few days away from her routine and she'd forgotten all about him.

'Frank, I'm so sorry I wasn't able to see you sooner and thank you. If you hadn't found me that morning, I would never have survived.'

'I was only too glad, Mary. You're a strong woman, not everyone would survive a night out on the cold yard.' He turned back to his van. From the back seat, he withdrew a tartan patterned blanket. 'Here this is yours, it was thrown over you. I picked it up when the ambulance arrived and didn't know what to do with it since. You were lucky you had it to hand. That skimpy cardigan wouldn't have offered much protection from the cold.' He handed her two letters, bade her good day and was off.

Mary had not heard a word after he mentioned the blanket. She clutched it firmly with both hands and stared at it in disbelief. *It was the blanket from my chair.* She tried to remember. Did she take it with her when she left the garage? Maybe she felt the chill and took it in her hand, she was angry that she couldn't remember. She stepped out into the street and looked towards the garage. She would return it later. She stood there staring for a long time. The corners of her rosy lips turned ever so slightly upwards in an involuntary smile, an acceptance of something she suspected for a long time but wouldn't allow herself to acknowledge.

Chapter 32

A few weeks of pampering and Mary had regained her strength sufficiently to demand Michael and Savita return to their work and their other life. They had taken too much time out of their lives already, she insisted she would be fine. The neighbours would keep a good watch and in a week or two she would be back to her old self.

The doctors told a different story. Mary had a serious heart attack and would have to take it easy. Her days of hard work were over.

Resting in her chair, a blanket tucked around her feet and legs she watched them pack for the off again.

'I'll set things in place at work so that I can get more time off to visit. Savita, God willing, will be a mother soon and we think the best place for her to be during the pregnancy is back here. It's quiet, services are close to hand and you will be here to help her,' Michael's words were music to her ears. Mary was tempted to protest, but she knew there was an element of truth in his argument, but she was also fairly sure they had her best interests at heart.

Savita could tell Mary was not convinced, 'Mary, this is not our first time trying for a child. There have been complications. I was told I might have to resort to total bedrest for almost the entire duration of the pregnancy. If this happens, I will need your help. I will need to be here.' She kissed Mary on the cheek and they bade her farewell with a promise of a speedy return.

Michael hesitated at the door.

'I have a whole world full of good friends to take care of me. Off with you both, and I'll see you soon.' Mary said waving him away.

'When you get back on your feet you will come visit, Mam. You promised, remember?'

'Of course, I look forward to it – even though the journey scares me.'

'Don't fret, Savita can come back here and accompany you if you like.'

'That's kind of you, but it's not necessary.'

She waved them off and returned to her little haven, her kitchen. 'Just you and me again,' she said patting the stove. She tried not to look at the portraits that she knew would be looking down on her.

A season lapsed without incident. Mary felt reasonably good, although she found it hard to sleep. She waited anxiously but there was no news from Dubai. Her heart went out to them both. A child would bond them together, take them from a happy couple to a happy family. She wanted this so much for them both, but especially for Michael.

Staring out the window into the black of night, cupping a hot chocolate in both hands, she felt the first twinge. Then a tingling sensation in her left arm, followed by a heaviness in her chest. She knew the symptoms, she'd laid too many old friends to rest who'd gone the same way. Mary wasn't afraid, she smiled and welcomed it. The first jolt hit her like an electric shock, she rocked where she stood. Closing her eyes, she tried to relax and control her breathing. A wave of fear tried to overpower her, but she would have none of it. There was nothing to fear. She had lived long, and lived well. She felt a pang of regret that she might not see her grandson. Staring out the window she imagined how the rose bulbs she planted would look in the spring. She looked around her kitchen, her home. She looked up at the blackened portraits and held their gaze. 'How many of us have you seen come and go?' she asked. 'Will I be another ghost to join you lingering around this kitchen?'

She felt the next jolt like a physical blow, it came just as the garage burst into light. Beams of light flooded from every window illuminating the courtyard. Mary took a step towards the window and closed her eyes. She closed her eyes and tilted her head back to greet it, to invite it in. It was time. She was ready.

Frank was unfortunate enough to find Mary for a second time. This time she was sprawled on the floor, but this time there was no reviving her. Her body was stone cold and rigid. She didn't look as if she'd fallen, but as if she'd just taken a moment to lay down and rest. She looked perfectly at ease. Frank was surprised that he couldn't wake her up. She looked content, as if she was lost in a pleasant dream. There was even a faint glimmer of a smile on her face.

Chapter 33

I opened my eyes to unfamiliar surroundings. Pale brown cardboard boxes of all shapes and sizes were stacked around the floor, right up to my feet; there was hardly room to move. The windows were covered in a thick film of grime that blocked out almost all the light. I looked all around me, it took me a moment for my eyes to adjust to the darkness inside the garage. Dust motes floated in the air above my head. Cobwebs hung loosely over the rafters like fine silk scarves. I rose from the chair and picked my way through the carnage on the floor to find a space where I could stand and look around.

The garage was different somehow, it felt different. Maybe it was just the darkness. I took a rag and wiped the windows. Sunlight poured in, slowly at first, and then in a great flood. I was sure there was a moment when even the sunlight hesitated at the window, as if it was reluctant to try and force this darkness back. The sunlight was important. I felt at ease when it pooled around me and brightened the garage. I felt comforted by its warmth. There was a chill that accompanied the darkness that unnerved me. And there was something else. There was a strange density to the dark shadows that was not natural. I was sure if I reached into it, my hand would be lost in the darkness, like plunging a hand into pool of black oil.

My state of being, whatever that was, had made me more sensitive, receptive to changes, movements in the air, to the temperature around me and to energies I could feel but could not explain.

From my position of security, standing in a shaft of light, I looked into the shadows that were forced into the farther recesses of the garage. They seemed to cower there, angry at this unwanted intrusion of light.

There was more – there was a presence in those shadows. I was conscious of this, maybe more than one. I knew this, it was not an assumption, I was certain of it. However, I could not tell for sure if it was a presence I should be afraid of.

I could sense conflict in those shadows. There were energies and forces at odds with each other in the blackness that I could not understand and dared not consider. I was new to this world and as such had no idea who or what else inhabited it.

When I looked closer into the shadows I saw that they were not still, they swirled and swayed to an agenda of their own, like a thick primordial soup that would be impenetrable if I were to try and pass through. And yet I felt drawn to them, something wanted me nearer. There was frustration and anger there that wanted to be acknowledged. I felt the desire to step closer, to investigate, to step into the blackness. When I allowed myself to consider the thought I felt an excitement, but it was an excitement I knew I should not indulge in. Maybe it was just my stern Catholic upbringing but I felt guilty at the idea, as if it was a sinful pleasure I was considering. I shook myself and stepped quickly away from the back of the garage to rid myself of the idea. I had no understanding of the plane I existed in and I did not have the courage to take any chances until I knew more of my new world.

'What the hell!' I cried out. The dry screeching sound gave me a fright. I turned to find there was someone at the door. They were struggling to push it open. The hinges cried out as they were forced.

'Why were the hinges so stiff to open,' I was pondering this when I was distracted by a tall figure that stepped into the doorway, he was silhouetted against the sunlit background. He raised a hand to shield his eyes and peered into the garage. He was of a medium built, his back arched ever so slightly and though his shoulders sagged I suspected he had once been a fine fellow. He had a receding hairline, and a little paunch over the waist-band of his trousers that suggested he was suffering the onset of a middle-aged spread.

Tentatively he stepped into the garage, picking his step through the obstacle course. He threw a few boxes aside, all the while peering into the back as he did. He's looking for her. I thought. I know it, he wants to see the car. He picked up the boxes and set them one on top of the other at first but he grew anxious, impatient and in the end, he just threw them out of his way, and then he was there, standing over the contoured shape.

He paused for a long moment before he pulled back the covers. Yet he didn't yank them off in one rough tug, he eased them back slowly, exposing the car bit by bit. I walked around him. One of the advantages of being invisible to the world was I could stand six inches from someone, stare into their faces to see what I could see, watch them react to a question. There was no hiding from this kind of scrutiny.

He looked familiar, and yet I knew I had never seen him before. Who the hell was he and what did he think he was doing?

It was still quite dark in the garage, the light from the open door was slow to penetrate the shadows at the back of the garage.

A plume of dust rose from the cover when he pulled it back. It swirled around him in great eddies, hung in the air above him in a cloud magnetically drawn to him.

There was no way I was letting him take her out of there until I knew who he was and what he was doing. I had no idea how I would do that, but I was resigned to doing everything in my power to keep her here.

'Michael,' a voice bellowed from the direction of the house. 'Are you out there?' I turned at the sound of a woman's voice. Then snapped my head around to look at the stranger again as her words sunk in.

'No, no, no, it can't be!' I cried out stepping back, shaken by the revelation. I ran my hands forcefully through my hair, then walked right up to him again, so close I could feel his breath on my face. I scrutinized his features but struggled to accept the facts. I refused to accept what I was seeing. What was I recognising? Could this stranger, this grown man that stood before me be my son, my boy? Despair washed over me, engulfed me. He was a grown man, maybe in his forties. Where had, his life gone, how had I missed it? Where had I been? Was I asleep on that cursed chair while my son became a man just outside my door?

A woman entered the doorway, she pulled a shawl over her bare shoulders and shrugged.

'What are you doing in there?' she asked, almost scolding. There was a sharpness, a frustration in her tone. 'It's just a lot of old rubbish.'

'I'm just looking through some of our old stuff, love. I'll be right in.'

She hesitated, took a quick look around but did not come in. It was not that she did not come in, it was that I sensed her reluctance to come in. She pulled her shawl even tighter around her shoulders and turned to the house without another word.

He patted the car on the roof, just like one would pat the head of a faithful old hound. Then he left. As I watch him go I wondered what the hell it was that bound me to this world. Mary had departed, she was gone to a better place I hope, but why could I not follow her? Was she sitting somewhere watching and waiting for me to join her?

Chapter 34

'Why can't I get you out of my bloody head?' he shouted through gritted teeth. He was standing in the doorway, it was dark outside, night time again. His words woke me, or summoned me from wherever it was I went when I was not here and conscious. He moved quickly to the back of the garage, more aggressively this time. He was angry, I sensed it. He took no care as he pulled off her cover and threw it leaving her fully exposed. She sat there in all her nakedness before his anger.

He squeezed his eyes shut and threw his head back. 'I should have stayed here, Dad. Far away hills look green. Isn't that what they say? And it's true. For all the majesty of the wider world, there's never been anywhere I could call home like here. I should have come back and helped you finish her. We promised each other we would.' I knew he was talking to himself, but he was also talking to me.

'Oh Christ!' I exclaimed loudly, but no-one could hear. 'Is that it? Is this what binds me to this earth? A father and a son's foolish promise to each other? Surely not?'

Even as I questioned it, I felt sure it had to be true. What else would hold me here. I was not being punished, even though at times it felt like a punishment, like a kind of hell. Yet I knew I had not been a bad man. Why would I be punished?

Michael threw himself onto a stack of boxes. He sat with his head in his hands staring at the car.

It's been right here all the time. The'69, it had always

been my dream to finish what I started, what my father started, and what a father and a son had started.

'Do it now son, do it for me.' The words popped into my head and out of my mouth. I felt like somebody else had said the words. Michael didn't move, then his eyes darted to my old chair, but the sound of Savita coming through the door caught his attention.

'It's that car, isn't it?' she said., still reluctant to come in. 'Your mother was afraid of its influence on you and on your father. She told me it had taken him away from her.'

He hesitated, 'Yes, I think it is. I don't know why it's still playing on my mind after all these years.'

'Come with me,' she said, her voice suddenly soft, full of understanding and sympathy. 'We have too much on our plate to be fooling around with an old car.'

Michael didn't move. She turned to go, and was surprised that he had not gotten up to follow her.

'What is it?' she asked.

'I don't know,' he answered, still staring at the lump of metal.

'I'll put the kettle on,' she said, eager to coax him away from the garage.

'It might be good for me.' he said.

'What?' she exclaimed, not sure she heard him right.

He didn't answer her.

'But your health Michael, you need to watch your health. You know what you were told.'

'Yes, I do,' he snapped, 'But I will not sit and vegetate. I need to be active, this will keep my mind straight, keep me from going insane.' he paused. 'This could be good for me.' I could tell he was trying to convince himself as much as her. He needed to convince himself that it was a good thing to do.

Even though she disagreed with him she conceded this point; she knew how he could be when he was like this.

Michael stormed past her heading towards the house. She put out her hand to stop him. 'Wait, don't rush away from me.' I could tell he was still fuming. Angry at himself, angry at her, angry at the world. I wondered what it was that he needed to be concerned about. What did she mean when she said he should know what they told him?

I watched her take hold of his hand and not let go.

'Whatever you decide to do is always okay with me, love. I just worry, that's all.'

His anger melted, she held his gaze and would not let him look away. Her dark brown eyes were like great big muddy pools. I could see how Michael could get lost in those eyes, but I could also see that she was good for him. She was looking out for him, she did not want to control him.

He was still lost in thought when she reached up on her tip-toes and kissed him.

'Men and their toys,' she whispered, smiling up at him, but as she turned she looked apprehensively back into the garage, at what she knew would be a threat, something that could come between them.

'You're really going to do this, aren't you?' she asked, an air of incredulity in her voice.

'Yes, I am,' he said, sounding surprised that he had made the decision, a strange conviction in his voice.

Savita shook her head and sighed. 'Well you aren't going to start tonight, so come to bed. I'm getting cold.'

'Be right in.'

'Don't be too long. You'll get your death of cold in this shed.'

I smiled at her last words, a familiar warning from Mary when she lectured me on my late nights down here.

And so, it began. Slowly at first, an hour here and there, but more in earnest as the evenings drew long; just as it had been with me.

Michael approached the project like all things he did, carefully and methodically. He took stock of what he needed, parts, panels and tools, and the order he needed to approach the job. I was impressed. His education had served him well. He even had a clipboard with several lists attached.

It was while reading through one of these lists that he first spoke to us both, the '69 and myself.

'It's not as bad as I feared, old girl. It's not a mammoth task after all. You did well Dad, all the critical structural work is finished, and finished well.' I turned to face him and found him slumped in my old chair.

'Of course, it's finished well,' I walked closer to him. 'Don't forget I was your tutor long before any college lecturers.' Of course, he couldn't hear me, but oh how I wished he could. I was filled with pride and something else, a strange sensation somewhere deep down in my gut that I hadn't felt before. It was the beginning of something; or perhaps the end of something. When this was done, I would be gone from him forever. It was all about the car, the '69. She had been the common link between us all, all three generations. She needed to be finished and then it would be over for me. I was sure of it.

It made me angry that I had no control over when I came and went. I wanted to be here whenever he worked, but that was not how it was happening. I often woke in the chair to find the garage clean, clutter free and the '69 sitting centre stage on the floor. I was flicking in and out of his life, like a light switch switching off and on. I got to see fleeting glimpses of him and his work.

The rustle of tearing paper made me stir. There were empty boxes and ripped packaging thrown outside the door. Shiny chrome pieces glittered on the bench; door handles, window surrounds, bumpers. A wiring loom was laid out on the floor beside complex wiring diagrams.

'You're going to need help with this, son. That's just a chaotic mess.' I whispered, as I looked at the nest of wires on the floor.

'You sure that isn't one of your mother's knitting patterns you have there?' Savita stood in the doorway, her arms folded, struggling to suppress a wicked grin.

'Very bloody funny,' Michael threw a clump of bubble wrap in her direction.

'You sure you want to do this?' She asked again. 'We agreed we needed to come back here and spend some time away from it all after what happened. But is this really necessary?'

'Look love, maybe it's a kind of therapy for me. You

deal with it in your way. This is mine. I need to be occupied. I need to keep busy.'

'It would be better if we sat down and talked it through. No point ignoring it.'

Michael tossed a spanner from hand to hand then flung it at the wall. 'I'm tired of being told what I should feel and how I should deal with it, alright!'

Savita spun on her heels and marched back towards the house.

'Will one of you say what the hell this is all about so I can understand.' I screamed. 'What's wrong Michael, are you sick?'

Michael slumped into my chair and cupped his head in both hands. He had always had a temper, but he had a soft heart and I could see he regretted his outburst.

'It's not always easy, son. She means well,' I stood over him, laid a hand on his head and stroked his hair. I did this when he was a boy and he and his mother had argued. 'She's just worried about you, son. Your mother was like this sometimes.'

'Yeah, I know. I know.'

I reeled, was that a coincidence or did he just answer me? I drew my hand away.

'Michael,' I said, moving closer. 'Michael!' I shouted. He raised his head and looked slowly around him but it was not a reaction to me.

Chapter 35

It was an age before I returned. The days were growing longer. Another season had come and gone. How many since I passed away? I had no idea. Progress on the '69 was slow. Obviously, he was not here all that often. Was there something keeping him away, an illness, Savita? I could only guess. I was alone, I looked around but Michael had not arrived yet. I knew I would not be alone for long. There was always a reason for me being here. Michael or Savita would be here before me or would be on their way, their presence the catalyst to draw me back into a conscious state from wherever it was I slipped to when I was not there. I heard the familiar crunch of gravel under foot.

'Okay baby, let's get this over and done with.' There was a tiredness in his voice. Yet there was also something else, something different about him. I stared hard into his features. He looked content, that was it. He wasn't approaching his work here like it was a chore. He was enjoying this. He looked much better, the grey pallor had left his skin, there was a healthy glow in his cheeks. I caught him humming while he worked.

He arrived at around the same time of evening that I would have started my evening vigil alone here. I was happy to be summoned to watch again.

Several weeks passed and Michael maintained his schedule, it was the longest consistent spell of work the car had seen in its entire life. It felt good to see her coming together. Michael stumbled on small repairs we'd both done together all those years ago, when I was still a relatively young man and he was still a boy, and then there was my time with my father, these same roles reversed where I was the boy, an excited apprentice to my own father.

Michael stumbled on a section on the boot floor where we had cut out and welded in a repair panel. He ran his fingers over the weld, it looked like a raised welt, a scar on a wound. He stayed there, holding his fingers on the cold metal. I moved closer, eager to know what could be going through his mind, was he thinking of our time together?

'The bodywork is finished, the wiring loom in place, I've plumbed in the radiator.' He paused, his fork poised over his dinner, as if he'd forgotten something. Savita sat across from him at the table. She suppressed a smile as she listened intently to what he was saying. She had no idea what any of it meant, was this good news he was reporting or was he rhyming out a list of problems?

'The all-important moment is looming ever closer. The moment when that great big six-cylinder will hopefully belch into life.'

'I'm so excited,' she mocked.

'You should be,' he laughed. 'Wait until it's finished, you have no idea how beautiful it will be, a piece of living art. I know you appreciate art. You've dragged me through those god-awful galleries every time we holiday.'

Chapter 36

A sunbeam shone through the window and danced on the pressed tin image of the Captain's old Alfa Romeo. I rarely made my presence felt during daylight hours and never when it was empty. The doors were thrown open to allow the sunlight in. Tiny particles of dust suspended in the air were caught in the sunlight. I rose from my seat and looked around me expectantly, trying to see who or what it was that drew me here. I heard the faint rumble of voices from the farmhouse, but there was no sign of anyone heading this way. I ran a finger over the contours of the old sign. Above it, dangling from a rafter, was a rusty spoked wheel from God knows what. The other rafters and wall-plates held similar motoring memorabilia; most of it worthless. There was a powerful energy here, a heritage, the Captain, my father and my own passion for the art and beauty of these old cars. These old artefacts created a static energy that still lingered. I was still admiring this old rubbish when he walked past me.

'Okay then, here we go. This is it.' he tilted open the bonnet and stood back to survey the scene. I walk over to join him.

'Wow!' I said. I'm impressed; shiny new plugs, polished rocker covers and the sweet smell of petrol. 'You have fuel at the carbs?' I asked. Why hadn't I come back here to see all this? It had to have taken weeks upon weeks of long nights to get this work done.

'We have petrol, a spark and a strong battery,' he almost mimicked my remarks.

'Fingers crossed,' he said, as he stretched to the ignition key and turned it. Without hesitation, the old girl turned over, burbling and backfiring. It wasn't right but it was a start and it was close, we both knew this.

'Check ignition timing,' we said together. Repeating the mantra my father had repeated to me and I had repeated to Michael all those years ago, and he'd never forgotten.

'One more time before I go,' he said. This time she backfired once and stuttered into life for a second before she died.

A smug grin of self-satisfaction lit up his face. He was pleased with himself, and so he should have been. I imagine he would have been apprehensive, wary of that moment. The engine turning over, even if it hadn't started it was another milestone, another step closer to completion.

I felt it almost immediately, the instant she teetered on the edge of bubbling to life, I felt mine teeter on the edge of fading away. It felt like an icy hand reached into my chest, enclose my heart in a vice-like grip... and then let go as the engine stuttered and stalled.

So, this was how it would be. I should have known. The rebirth of the '69 would herald my own proper and complete death.

'Michael, please. It's getting late, you'll get your death of cold.'

'It's okay, I'm fine. You don't have to baby me all the time.'

'I'll have to baby you if you behave like one. You know well what they said. It's too much, you're doing too much.'

I heard her lecture him from time to time, but there was genuine concern and worry in her voice this time.

Michael set his tools aside and walked to where she stood. The worry that was etched on her face told of some great sadness. She looked tired, I hadn't noticed this before.

'I'm sorry, love. I was enjoying myself and lost track if time.' He engulfed her little bird-like frame in his arms.

'We agreed to do this. It's what you said you wanted, but there's no sense being reckless about it.' They were walking away from me as she spoke.

'Look at me, Savita.' they stopped and he stepped away from her. 'I feel better than I have in years,' he slapped his chest vigorously with his hands in a Tarzan-like gesture. 'I think I even look better.'

She smiled, 'I know, love. I have noticed, but it's still there, it won't go away just like that.' She raised a hand to his cheek and held it there, to comfort him, to console him.

I wanted to hear what they were saying but they were walking out of earshot.

'Time is precious to us, we need to spend what little we have of it well.' Her words echoed through my head as they disappeared into the house. Were they going to leave here soon? Why was time an issue?

I stood in the doorway for some time after they disappeared into the house. It struck me that I was there alone, was there something else? I usually slipped away after he left. I was never alone in the garage without a purpose. Was there something more to come today?

Whatever cruel puppet that pulled at my strings had a

plan, a purpose for me being here each time; and yet here I was staring out into courtyard alone. Was I being given a moment to contemplate what I was missing. The beauty of a country morning, the song of the birds, the wonderful changing light of the Irish landscape. Clouds passed between me and the sun, throwing shadows and then glorious sunshine on me in alternating waves. I did miss this. I closed my eyes and wished I could feel the warmth of the sun on my face, smell the country smells that were carried on the breeze.

Heavy rain on the mountain overnight was trickling down the gullies, coming together to swell the tributaries that converged to make the River Eany. I listened hard, imagining I could hear its thunderous roar as it passed along the edge of the estate, hurrying on its way to the ocean ten miles away.

I was staring hard into the distance to catch sight of the trees along its route, where I played as a boy, when I saw him. A tall sinewy figure lurking under the shade of a tree. He was a long way off, but when he raised his head our eyes met, his image was drawn closer to me as if through a magnifying glass. I could see the lines on his face, the neat cut of his tweed jacket and the ivory handle of the cane he swished at his feet to chop the tall grass. I felt my heart lurch. I had never seen this man before; and yet there was something familiar about him. He didn't look out of place, he didn't look like a stranger. He looked like he belonged there.

Chapter 37

I wasn't fully awake when I felt the jolt. It felt like I was getting an electric shock. Ironic that I should think that. Through gritty eyes I saw Michael standing over the '69, a set of jump leads stretched from the family car to the battery of the '69. Was my heart inextricably linked to the heart of the old girl, her engine? He turned the engine over again and I was no longer in my seat but standing at his shoulder. She did not start, but she was close.

'A little squirt of fuel into the carbs might give her a helping hand son,' I suggested. 'Give her a squirt of fuel right down her throat.'

He stood scratching his head, then reached down and pumped the throttle several times.

'Not quite the same son,' I muttered. 'But it could work.'

The bark of the engine rattled the tin roof of the old garage as she howled into life.

'Yeah baby,' Michael shouted above the din. He clenched his fists and punched the air. He looked around, then glanced towards the house. Savita was nowhere in sight. He sighed and smiled to himself.

I knew what he was thinking, it would have been nice to have someone to share this moment with, he was thinking of me. I was with him, he just didn't know it.

Michael blipped the throttle several times sharply then let the engine idle. It burbled smoothly under the bonnet, no frightening rattles or knocks. He shut it down, took three long steps back and settled onto the workbench to look over the car. She was seventy percent complete. He pursed his lips and looked wholly satisfied with his progress. And so he should be, he'd done well. I may have done the lion's share of the work, but even I was continuing the good work of my own father. And so here she was, almost done, three generations and some years later.

'What colour had you decided on, Dad?' he pondered, 'You never did say.'

It was true, there was so much to be done it seemed so far off into the future to consider. We never did discuss a colour. I would have like to see her finished in an old English white, to contrast with the red leather interior.

'British racing green, or maybe a nice glossy red,' he asked, reaching for the light switch.

Chapter 38

He looked the same but different. His hair was cropped real short, he had never worn his hair like this – for an instant I thought it was Jimmy, until Michael joined him.

'James, thanks for coming over.' Michael took his hand and welcomed him into the garage.

'Wow! Michael, she's a beauty.'

'Yes, she is, even if I do say so myself,' Michael laughed. 'Even if my father and his father had a hand in getting her this far.'

'When I told my dad where I was going, he couldn't believe it was still here. He said he called to your dad quite often when he was working from here.'

'So, you must be Jimmy's lad,' I said, as I walked around him. 'Fine looking boy, just like your father.'

James took a long look at the car. He surveyed her lines, ran his hands along the body, feeling for flaws or blemishes. He dropped to one knee and cast his eye along the bodywork to check that it was true.

Michael stood back and watched, so did I. James seemed to know what he was doing, he asked all the right questions. Looked at all the vulnerable spots for weaknesses and looked generally impressed with what he saw.

'The work is good Michael, really good.'

Michael seemed to grow an inch taller considering this praise.

'She won't need a lot of preparation for paint.' James continued.

'That's really good news James. I'm as far as my limited abilities can go. I need professional help from here on.'

'I wouldn't knock your work Michael. I've seen so-called professionals turn out poorer work than this.'

Michael walked away from him and settled himself into my chair.

'That's his chair, isn't it?' James asked, nodding at the chair.

'Yep, that's it,' Michael patted the armrests, plumes of dust rose into the air around him. 'What do you know of it?' Michael asked, gagging and coughing in the dust.

'My father spoke of it, laughed at how your dad ended his day chugging on his pipe in that chair. He even joked with your father that his ghost would be found in that chair.'

'Humph!' Michael snorted. 'When we came back here, back home, I felt lost. It had been so long since I'd lived in this house, I felt like a stranger. The same with this garage, I was reluctant to come in here. It was his haven, most of my memories are of him bent over some project or other, spattered in oil and smelling of petrol.'

James listened carefully, he knew he was listening to a man pouring out his heart to a stranger who knew nothing of his situation, someone he didn't care to impress or worry if he offended.

'It was her,' he gestured to the car. 'She drew me here. It was his last and his oldest project. He'd waited all his life for me to grow up so we could finish it together, and then he died.' Michael looked at James. 'You know I sometimes think that if there is a God up there, he is a comedian. Having a laugh at us and our foolish plans.'

James turned to the car again. This innocent lump of metal that had affected so many men in this house.

'Savita was reluctant to come here after what happened.' Michael hesitated, considering if he should say any more. 'We've been trying all our lives for a child. She was four months pregnant when she miscarried. It almost destroyed us both. We were like two zombies unable to communicate with each other. We needed to get away from there. Go somewhere where we could heal each other.' Michael spread both arms wide. 'Where else would we go. This was always a happy place, full of happy memories.'

James was reluctant to speak, to interrupt, but he felt compelled to contribute something. 'It looks like it's helped Michael, you seem content.'

'Ha-ha,' Michael laughed.

James didn't understand, had he said something wrong?

'We'd gone through every fertility clinic that would take us. I had more tests done than an astronaut. I felt like a pin cushion, I had so many blood tests. They were trying to find out if the problem was with me or with Savita. Nothing was conclusive, and yet after all those years of tests nothing showed up until we had all but given up and went for one last round of checks.' Michael looked towards the house to where he knew Savita was working hard, baking and cleaning.

'Aggressive and very advanced, the doctor said. I knew he was reluctant to speak out against his fellow doctors, but it has to have been a monumental blunder that it wasn't spotted sooner... or in time.'

James swallowed, he felt uncomfortable. This was the kind of news you share with a close friend, not someone you've met an hour before. What was he expected to say?

Michael struggled from the seat. 'Well, our prospects of a family were completely gone and my future looked pretty grim, so I came home with my tail between my legs.'

Michael walked past James as if he wasn't there. He stopped and stood over the car. 'This helped me escape it all, forget about all our misfortunes for a while, and most importantly, to remember again where I came from.' he nodded his head as if he were agreeing with someone. 'My father was not a quitter, and neither am I.'

'I'll do you proud, Michael,' James said, laying a hand on his shoulder.

Michael snapped his head around and looked at James as if he'd only just realised he was there. 'Good James, that would be good. The old man would like that.'

'Old English white,' Michael added. 'It will contrast perfectly with the red leather interior.' Michael looked to the seats that were still draped over a rafter.

James looked wide-eyed at the cobweb covered seat hanging upside down.

Michael smiled, 'They may not look like much but believe it or not they will clean up quite well. The leather shows its age but I've been told if it's still intact and the structure of the seat is good it's better for the car to retain as much of its original material as possible.'

'That's right,' James piped up, 'A lovely patina, that's how it's described. Though when a fine patina becomes a tatty seat is open to interpretation, I guess.'

Michael stared at James, listening to his first useful contribution. 'Very good point James, we'll have a look at that when we get that far. You okay to start this week?'

'Certainly,' James replied.

With that Michael took off for the house with James closely behind.

I stepped from the shadows. If I had tears to shed, I would have shed them there and then. I felt empty, like a dead tree, hollow and wizened inside. I could not summon a single emotion. I wanted to feel the pain of hurt, the ache of sadness. I should have felt heartbroken for my son, for his suffering, but I began to grow thin, to fade away. I tottered between both worlds for a moment, I was almost gone then was suddenly whisked back.

Savita was standing over the car. I could see she'd been crying. It angered me that I knew so little of what went on in my son's life. Imprisoned by those bricks and stones, I knew nothing of what was happening in the wider world, had days or years passed since Michael last stood here? How many seasons had come and gone since I died, since Mary had died?

'Mary was afraid of you; did you know that?' Savita had both hands planted firmly on the bonnet. She was staring into the cockpit of the car as if she was talking to someone in the driver's seat.

Why would Mary be afraid of the car? She knew I loved her and her alone. This was just a distraction, something for me to do when I wasn't with her. This revelation should have hurt me, to know that Mary could have been discontent, unhappy and that I had spent time here in the garage and not with her.

'You've cast your spell on my Michael now, haven't you?' There was no anger in her voice but an acceptance. 'He will not rest until you are done, finished. I know him, he won't be able to stop. That's good though, because then you will be gone from our lives and from this house. I will have peace, and I will have my husband back.' She smacked both hands loudly on the bonnet to drive her point home.

I watched her leave. I wasn't angry with her. I understood she was in pain. They had been through so much, and here he was, wasting precious time trying to finish this car. A foolish project an old man had begun years ago, and now burdened his son with a commitment to finish it.

'Fuck you!' I shouted at the top of my lungs. So much work, time energy and expense, for what? A lump of metal?

A sound made me spin around, it was barely audible but it was there. It might have been nothing more than a gust of wind through the timbers but it sounded like the old man's cough. The way he would cough when he was about to chastise me, but was reluctant to. I stared hard, daring him or whatever lurked there to come out, to challenge me, to tell me what the hell it was they wanted.

Chapter 39

The kitchen was in near darkness when Michael came in. A single candle sat on the centre of the table. A thin line of smoke rose into the air from the lick of flame, filling the air with an unusual but familiar scent. Michael reached for the light switch.

'Don't,' she whispered, her voice so low he barely heard her. He quickly withdrew his hand from the switch.

She was sitting at the table, a traditional Indian sari thrown loosely over her shoulders. He stared at her for a long time, he remembered the floral pattern, remembered the first time she wore it and he remembered that scent. He was about to speak when she rose slowly, crossed the room, bridging the distance between them in a fluent seamless movement and pressing a finger gently against his lips, she shook her head. She ushered him to his seat and began to serve him. She set a dish on the table between them. The aroma of herbs and spices rose to fill the kitchen. It smelled so good, and he was starving. She served him as her mother had taught her to. Yet she did not feel uncomfortable behaving subserviently to a man. She was his equal, just as qualified, but it was also part of her tradition. It was how she had been brought up. She had abandoned those old-world values when she left for college. She had no doubt that she was the equal of any man, but tonight she wanted to treat her man in the old ways. She would serve him, see to his every need and make sure she satisfied him in every sense.

Michael tried to speak a few times but she silenced him

on each occasion with a firm shake of her head and a frown. He did however, groan and moan as he tasted the food. He was enjoying every minute of this.

He knew of course, she was trying to replicate their first night together at her apartment. That was a long time ago, he was a much younger man and had performed like an Olympian that night. He was conscious that Savita may have forgotten his age or condition and was apprehensive. What if he let her down, disappointed her?

'Let's just enjoy the food,' she said, leaning in and kissing him on the top of his head.

'I'm as transparent to you as a glass bowl, love,' he whispered.

Savita sniggered and hugged him.

He'd lost count of how many courses she'd served him. The curry was hot, not too hot, just the way he liked it. Challenging, that was how he liked his curry. Not so mild as to be tasteless, or too fiery to tolerate, but just the way Savita had served it. Sweat began to form in great blooms on his forehead. She daubed it away with a towel. 'Are you okay, my love?' she asked with a smile. 'Was the curry too much for you?'

'Hah!' he laughed, 'bring it on. I can take anything you have there,' he pointed to the stove.

'Very well,' she said, turning again to the great Aga. He watched her as she stood at the stove with her back to him. She sprinkled something into a pot and stirred vigorously.

'A few moments, my love,' she said, and with a wicked grin she set a large pitcher of water on the table. Michael stared at it and swallowed.

'My life insurance policy doesn't cover death by curry,' he pointed out.

Her petite frame shook as she laughed. She returned from the kitchen dresser with a bottle.

'Whiskey?' he exclaimed. 'Where did you get this?'

'Single malt whiskey,' she corrected him. 'I had a friend source it for me, they said you and your father had enjoyed this once.'

He fought back a tear at the mention of my name.

'The old boy was partial to a wee dram.' he laughed, rubbing his hands together.

'You will join me?'

'Of course,' she said. 'I believe I can handle anything you can handle.'

'Careful, don't emasculate me before the night is done.' Michael tried to laugh off the awkward silence that followed his foolish comment. They hadn't had sex since her miscarriage.

Several large whiskeys later and they were both wilting. Savita rose to clear the table.

'Not tonight, it can wait until morning,' he said, grabbing her by the waist as she passed. They fell to the floor giggling and laughing. Pent up frustration and several months of mounting stress erupted from them both; two pressure cookers about to burst. They stumbled through the kitchen, knocking over dishes, cutlery, pans and chairs as they went, like a whirlwind they passed through the kitchen. The whiskey had done its work. Down through the hallway, peeling off layers they tripped and stumbled. They didn't make it to the bed. Halfway through the door they fell upon each other in their nakedness. They made angry love, angry not with each other, but angry at the world. A world that had placed obstacles in the way of their happiness, but they knew that night that they could overcome them. It was fun sex too, they laughed and frolicked together. They were themselves again. Not the people they had become because of what they'd encountered, but their old selves.

A beam of sunlight shone through a crack in the curtains and fell on Michael's face. He cringed and shied away from it, but the sudden movement awoke the drummer that was resting in his head; he was no longer resting. Michael recognised the beat, his head throbbed to the rhythm of O'Sullivan's march, a traditional Irish tune his father played repeatedly in the garage when he was working. It was too fast and too loud this morning. He dived under the cover to escape, but his wife was already hiding there.

'Oh boy,' he groaned.

'You said it,' she replied, snuggling up to him.

Suddenly the night's activities came back to him. He sprang upright and looked around the room.

'Did we do this?' he asked.

'We certainly did,' she cooed, a cheeky grin on her face. She pressed her body against him and was contemplating getting frisky again when the first wave of nausea washed over her. She gagged and bolted upright.

Michael laughed as he watched her dash for the bathroom, 'I'm ready for round two, love. What about you?'

'Fuck off and get me something to drink,' she yelled from inside the bathroom. 'I think I'm going to die!'

They tiptoed around the house for the rest of the day like two worn out war veterans. But by late evening they were starting to come around.

'Was that wise?' Michael asked, knowing the rebuke would come.

'It's natural, that's all. I don't expect anything will come of it, but we must move on.'

'We'll always have each other,' Michael was conscious as he said this, that this may not be true if things did not turn out well for him.

Savita frowned, the dark realisation crossed her own mind.

'Maybe you cured me last night,' he looked at her wide-eyed and smiled.

'How do you know I wasn't trying to kill you? Curry, whiskey and sex?' Savita replied, she stood facing him her hands braced on her hips, then winked at him wickedly as she turned and left the room.

Chapter 40

James began a few days after he met with Michael. He was happy to work alone, it was Michael who felt uncomfortable. He didn't like sitting in the house when James was working in the garage, and yet did not want James to think he was looking over his shoulder all the time.

The situation was resolved a few nights into the work. James knocked at the kitchen door. Michael was off the chair and answered the door before Savita had a chance to stir in her seat.

'I'm stuck for a second pair of hands, any chance you're free?' Michael was out the door and on his heels towards the garage. The ice was broken, they worked side by side from then on. They made small talk, laughed at mistakes they made and became comfortable in each other's company.

James looked forward to his evenings at the garage. Like Michael, he was not a drinker, had no hobbies and had few close friends, so it became more and more of a social occasion for the pair of them.

It became later and later each evening when they finished up. In fact, they managed to finish up their work reasonably early but their conversations dragged on longer and longer.

'You know, it's like trying to put a jigsaw together without the picture on the box,' James pointed out while wiping his hands.

'What do you mean?' Michael asked, confused by the remark.

'I've never seen an E-Type Jag in the flesh,' he said. 'I don't know what they look like finished.'

'What box are you talking about?'

'The cover,' James exclaimed. 'You must have had a jigsaw as a boy. You know how the picture on the cover of the box is supposed to look like the finished jigsaw? Well we don't have a box with a picture.'

Michael laughed heartily, 'We'll have to remedy that. Surely one of the girls can oblige us and dig up something on the internet that we can stick up on the wall here to help us along.'

And so, this was how Savita and Deirdre, James' wife, got roped into the project.

Several attempts were made to get a suitable image. The girls had difficulty grasping the importance of getting the model right.

'It's a Series II, 1969 FHC.'

'What the hell is a FHC?' Savita asked in confusion.

Michael looked at James and shook his head.

'A French Harlots Corset,' Michael uttered each syllable slowly, Savita jotted them down. She raised her head about to go.

'Wait!' James called her back. He turned to Michael. 'You can't do this! You'll regret it, Michael. Don't let her go!'

'Sorry, love. It's a fixed head coupe,' Michael apologised to Savita.

Savita stared at the notes she'd taken. His delivery was so deadpan she didn't take time to consider the words. She raised her eyebrows and scowled at him. 'That was a close call, darling! James may just have saved your life.'

I watched them with pride. They were having a good time. I felt the mood in the garage lighten when they laughed together. The shadows were even forced to recede farther back at these times. The power of positivity I thought, not to be underrated.

Chapter 41

I wished I had my sense of smell. I squeezed my eyes shut and tried to remember what it was like, that potent scent that made your eyes tears up, intoxicating, so strong you could taste it thick on your tongue. The fumes of fresh paint lingered in the air. Dangerous fumes that had melted the lungs of many old garage hands who took no precautions to protect themselves. Fools who took no heed of the warnings and advice given. Fools who spent their last days sucking on oxygen, sitting by their windows watching a world they could take no part in, counting the days to the end.

The garage was spotless, the floor was swept, the walls looked like they had been wiped clean, and the tools, for the first time ever were stowed away in their proper place. The place looked like an operating theatre. Covers were draped over the bench. There was a thin sheen of white on the floor and walls. It was an off-white. I smiled as I drew closer to the walls to look at the shade.

'Old English white,' I said aloud.

Under the gleam of the lights she sat. I would have said she looked proud if that was possible. James had done well, he was as good as his word. The paintwork was breathtaking. I leaned close and looked along her lines under the glow of the light. 'Flawless. Jimmy would have been proud of you, young man. That is a fine piece of work.'

I would have liked to have been there to see him practicing his trade, but someone, something, had not seen fit to allow me that treat.

I didn't know why, but there seemed to be no pattern to the frequency of my visits. Was I being punished, tortured like this? Shown snippets of my old world and what had become of it, given a chance to see my family, an opportunity to witness my son's pain and suffering without the ability to act, to step in and help. In life, it was my role, my duty as a father to do all within my power to ease his path through life, often without his knowing. And here I was a helpless, a useless witness to this drama that unfolded before me. I should have been distraught, but my emotions had been muted.

I felt a flush of anger; it took me by surprise. I was encouraged that it was still in me to feel an emotion. I tried to embrace it, to nurture it, like a flicker of flame that could grow into a raging fire. I fanned it as best I could, but it left me, it was just a taster of what I was missing... I was being tortured. I was sure of it. But why?

The sound of laughter made me turn to the door. I looked up to the house and there was Michael with an arm around James, guiding him into the house. 'That's a helluva paint job, James. You should be proud of it.' I heard him say.

James looked pleased. Savita added her praise to the conversation. James was basking in this attention when they vanished through the back door and into the kitchen. As I watched them, I realised they had become friends. This was good for Michael; a man should have some male companions. We are different. I don't mean women are from Venus and men are from Mars different. I mean we look at things differently. He needed someone with a common perspective, a man's perspective; especially when he needed to finish the car. James knew what it meant to see the '69 done and back on the road.

A few hours later the burble of raised voices drew my attention again to the house. Slurred voices broke the silence of the late evening. Under the glow of light from the kitchen they stumbled on unsteady legs, laughing and bidding each other good night. James shook Michael's hand, he held it a rather long time as he repeatedly pressed on his newfound friend how pleased he was with his work. James's wife burst into a fit of uncontrollably laughter at some innocuous comment Savita had made. Her laughter was infectious, Michael joined them laughing. All the while James held his hand firmly. Michael turned to face him.

'Thank you,' James said, suddenly serious.

'For what?' Michael asked, still laughing, the weight of James's seriousness starting to settle on him.

'I needed this,' James continued. 'We've had a tough time lately,' he looked at Michael and then towards the garage. 'This was good for me.'

Michael followed his gaze. 'I guess it was good for both of us.'

A taxi arrived. Savita threw an arm around Michael and pulled him close. James let go of his hand and took his wife's. The driver, well versed in manhandling the intoxicated, helped them into the car. Michael and James exchanged a glance as he sat into the back seat. Savita looked into her husband's face. 'What was that?' she asked.

'Man stuff,' he laughed, turning her back towards the door. She was about to speak again, to ask another question. 'Ssh!' he said in a whisper. 'You don't need to know everything.'

Chapter 42

The rain drumming on the tin roof sounded like an army of military drummers. I had my head thrown back and was staring up at the roof with my eyes shut tight, trying to recall days like this when I worked here alone. Michael gave me a start when he charged through the door, his shirt was soaking wet and pasted onto his back. He shook himself like a shaggy dog would to shake himself dry, then he turned away from me and looked back towards the house. I walked up to his side and joined him, the house was barely visible through the deluge. Great pools of water began to form in the gravel, and then it stopped raining just as suddenly as it began – as if someone had just turned off a tap. Michael popped his head out and looked to the night sky. I followed his gaze.

The light that had been on in the kitchen went out. Moments later a light went on in the bedroom, a dull light, like the faint glow of a candle.

He stood for a long time watching the house. I surmised from his posture that he was upset, or down. I cursed the powers that brought me back to see this as a witness.

Michael turned on his heels and faced me, to my surprise he was smiling. He was grinning openly as he walked back to the car. I watched him close his eyes and inhale. 'Mmm, that smells good,' he said, as he threw open a door.

The interior was fitted. The seats were finished in a rich burgundy leather. Matching deep pile carpets filled the footwells and surrounds. The roof was finished in a flesh coloured lining. I was speechless. I had seen none of this being done, it was a total surprise, but I totally approved. If I had an active hand in choosing colours and materials I could not have chosen better. I just wish I'd had the chance to see it being done, or had a chance to eavesdrop on the discussions beforehand.

Michael hummed something while he walked around. I thought I recognised the tune but my head was fogged up, it felt like it was filled with cotton wool. I couldn't think, this too was another form of torture. Was there no end to the levels of this agony?

He ran his hand longingly over her body. She was stunning. It was a wonderful piece of work. I was so proud of him, I should have felt a lump in my throat, but I was an empty vessel.

'This weekend we're going to fire you up and see how you run. Everything is in place, Dad. I've been over everything several times, she's ready.' He took three long steps back from the car. 'She's done. The old girl is finished.'

The words rang in my head. He did it. He had finished what myself and my own father had failed to do.

'Please let me be here when he starts the old girl, please,' I beg. 'I want to hear that sweet six-cylinder fire to life. I want to hear the throaty rumble from that exhaust. I want to be here to see her move off that spot under her own steam,' I point to the place on the floor where she has sat for decades. I raised my head to the heavens and pleaded with whoever was toying with me. Even if they were trying to hurt me they had to throw me this one bone.

For some reason, I lingered alone in the garage for a long time after Michael left. I was suspicious. I hadn't slipped away after his visit. I looked around carefully, waiting to be blindsided by some new surprise. I knew from the amount of work that had been done on the car that he had come and gone an awful lot without a visit from me, and yet here I was alone.

I pondered this and wondered if there was a formula I could find to control how I was called back here, something I could do to trigger this. Was there a common denominator I was missing? Did Michael mention my name in passing and somehow, I was summoned? My head was clearer than it had been in a long time. I could think, to consider these things and question my being here. So many times, I had come and gone in a fog of confusion, something akin to a groggy sleepwalk.

The lights in the house popped on and then off again. My mind wandered to thoughts of Mary and of the many nights she had pleaded with me to join her, to come in and leave that cursed car alone for a change. The car I thought, it had been the curse of my life. Why didn't I see it before? All that precious time spent moulding and forging sheets of steel to form this mechanical lump, this soul-less, lifeless thing that I was so stupidly driven to finish – and for what? Vanity? So, that I could get the praise and recognition of a stranger for this wonderful achievement. Even as these thoughts raced through my head I knew this was not true. Whatever wicked thing that was tempting me to abandon my beliefs, my interests, my passions, would not break me. I would not cave that easy.

I walked over to her. 'It's okay baby, it's almost done. You can go soon.' Even if no-one could hear me, I was happy to speak the words aloud. It was how I felt. This lump of metal was formed and forged out of a love for beautiful things, art, proportions, lines, colours; those things we look on and admire, even though we can't put into words what it is about them that makes them a joy to behold.

The crunch of feet on the gravel made me turn around. Michael was walking towards the garage. Savita was following closely behind him. He had a serious expression on his face, and Savita looked decidedly uncomfortable. There was someone else coming too. It took me a moment to recognise James when he wasn't in his work clothes. There was an attractive woman by his side, his wife I assumed. She stepped tentatively into the garage on her high heels, as if she was stepping onto an ice rink. A boy stepped from behind her as if he had been hiding in the folds of her flowery skirt. Eight, maybe nine years old, I guessed. Wide-eyed, he looked around him. The garage probably looked like an Aladdin's cave to him, full of wonderful shiny bits and bobs. A great place to have an adventure.

Michael crouched over the car and mumbled something that none but me heard. 'Don't let me down now old girl, not when we have an audience.'

James stepped away from the others to join him.

Savita and the young woman exchanged a glance.

'Deirdre, watch John,' James called to her. 'Don't let him touch the tools. There is stuff laying around that could fall over on him.'

Deirdre took her son by the hand and pulled him close.

'We all set, James?' Michael asked, smiling at his newfound friend.

'Fingers crossed,' James replied.

Michael struggled into the driver's seat. He turned on the ignition, heard the fuel pump prime the system and paused for a moment. He squeezed his eyes shut as he turned the key all the way. I moved to join him in the passenger seat. The boy stirred when I passed close to him. I thought I saw him track my path to the car, saw him clutch his mother's skirt ever tighter as he did, but I knew this could not be.

I held my hand over Michael's as he turned the key all the way. I wanted to be part of this. This was an iconic moment for me, for Michael and for my father, if he was watching somewhere.

The great cast iron lump turned slowly at first but gathered speed. There were a few splutters as the pistons rushing up the cylinders got the first tastes of raw fuel. A single bark followed by another and another until the cacophony of noises gelled into a great symphony.

Michael glanced in my direction, but he was looking through me not at me. James was peering through the passenger window, a broad grin on his face. He gave Michael the thumbs up.

Savita and Deirdre covered their ears but tried to look excited. First gear was engaged with a loud mechanical clunk. The car lurched forward, rolled across the garage floor and into the courtyard. It was the first time she had seen the light of day in a very long time. Her lustrous paint gleamed even brighter under direct sunlight. I had no idea what to expect when he came as far as the end of the courtyard, what would happen to me? I had tested the extent of my boundary on several occasions, hoping that maybe somebody might take their eye off the ball and forget to shut the gate and I, the prisoner, would be allowed to slip away, but that had never been the case. The pillars at the end of the courtyard were the extent of my world. The car eased closer, I braced myself in the seat. And then we were out of the courtyard, through the pillars and moving into the driveway. Her long elegant bonnet pointed to the horizon. Michael blipped the throttle a few times as he changed gear and we were off. He stopped abruptly at the end of the lane. The refurbished brakes were sharper than he had anticipated. The car skidded a car length or more on the loose gravel.

'Oops!' he said and smiled, pleased that they worked so well.

'Go left,' I whispered and so he did.

The loud throaty bark of the exhaust reverberated through the rows of trees that lined the road away from the estate. I listened with Michael. We noted every sound, anxious that there would not be a breakdown because of a bolt he had forgotten to tighten or the tell-tale smell of oil or fluid from something that had begun to leak.

Once we were both content that there were no nasty surprises we settled into our seats and enjoyed the ride. His grin was almost as wide as mine. It would have been great to be able to talk right then. To discuss the handling, the feel of the car. To share a comment on the readings from the gauges. I turned to face the countryside that sped past my window. The landscape was vaguely familiar, yet so much had changed. There were grand houses where once there were none, and there were derelict buildings where I remembered farmhouses with families I knew. We rounded the corner that led onto the bridge. I swallowed. 'Oh shit!' I exclaimed. I forgot about the bridge. The '69 had not passed over this bridge since that fateful evening when she met her doom there. Michael pointed her to the entrance to the bridge. It had not been improved or widened. It was the same nasty narrow stone bridge it always was.

'Steady son, steady,' I encouraged, stiffening in the seat. In response, he pressed on the throttle even harder. The rear tyres squirmed on the wet road, fighting for grip. I looked across at him, he looked stern and focused.

'No, no, no, Michael. Don't do it. This is not the time. You don't know how she handles yet!' My voice was raised to a shout, but even if he could hear me it would have been barely audible above the roar of the engine. 'Michael!' I screamed again. 'Are you mad? Not today son, it's too risky.' I wanted to cover my eyes, but I also wanted to see what happened next.

The corner of her shiny chrome bumper passed within a whisper of the stone wall on entering the bridge. The tail of the car stepped out. Michael fought to control her, to check the slide. I watched him, he was a picture of concentration as he wrestled with the steering wheel. Yet he didn't look frightened, not like I did. The car straightened up momentarily and then swerved violently to the left as

Michael pulled the steering hard to the right. I froze, my eyes never left the narrow exit of the bridge to our left. He was going the wrong way and we were going much too fast. If he braked hard now, he would just lock the wheels and we would skid straight into the same stone wall that had taken her off the road for decades. At the last minute, Michael pulled hard on the handbrake then gunned the throttle. His swerve in the wrong direction had thrown her weight in the right direction. The '69 responded immediately. Her rear stepped out wildly. The tyres shrieked on the wet cobbles of the bridge. To my shame, I closed my eyes and braced for the impact. But it didn't come. I opened one eye to see us sliding broadside through the narrow exit. I looked across at Michael. He was laughing out loud.

'Yeah!' he yelled. 'You beauty, you bloody beauty.'

'You fucking lunatic!' I yelled at him, then laughed wildly with him, like the mad hysterical relieved laugh of a man given a reprieve from death row. 'You bloody brilliant lunatic!'

I reached over and ruffled his hair. It would have been nice if he'd turned and smiled back like he did as a boy, but I was being greedy. This was perfect, it felt like heaven, even though I had been so sure I had been trapped in hell.

We had a quarter tank of fuel when we started. She was a thirsty brute. The fuel gauge flashed red, Michael slowed down and did a three sixty degree turn in the road. The journey back to the farm was more sedate. Michael had made his point. I don't know if he intended to do this all along and had waited patiently for that epic moment or if it had just occurred to him when he caught sight of the bridge, but it was inspirational.

He gave the stone wall of the bridge the finger as we passed over it again. I laughed, this was the side of the boy a father never gets to see. He was a lot like me, the thought made me blush with pride.

We came in sight of the house again, but I didn't want to go back, back to that prison. I was staring out the window taking a long last look at the countryside when I saw him. It was the same man, tall and lean, standing in the shade of a row of poplars, close to where I last saw him. He had his head bowed, almost as if he was dozing off. Michael slowed down to negotiate the narrow gate into the estate. I looked over at Michael, but he either didn't notice the man or just plain could not see him. He changed gears abruptly, the exhaust emitted a sweet bark that echoed through the trees. The strange figure snapped his head upright and stared at us, at me. His mouth twisted into a smirk, not a smile but a look of approval. He nodded his head and doffed his cap to me. The Jag went out of sight, scurrying up the loose gravel, the rear of the car slipping and squirming as Michael gunned the throttle.

I couldn't think straight, the others were standing in the courtyard waiting for us, I barely noticed them. We were back in the courtyard when we stopped. I stepped out and rushed back to see if he was still there but I got no farther than the end of the courtyard when I was whisked back to my default starting position, the chair.

'Well?' James asked anxiously, then dropped onto one knee to take a quick look under and around the car. 'Any surprises?'

'I'm not sure how to answer that,' Michael replied, he ran both hands through his hair. 'I never drove anything that old. I thought it would be, well, I suppose old and boring, but oh my God, James!' He grabbed his friend by both shoulders and shook him. 'She is an absolute cracker,' he said, nodding his head in disbelief. 'I wasn't ready for that. Here, see for yourself.' He said, opening the driver's door.

James considered being polite, 'I probably shouldn't. I mean it's your car and it's worth an absolute fortune... but I just can't say no.' It was understandable, there was no way he could decline the offer.

'Forget anything?' Deirdre asked. Her arms folded across her chest, a scornful look on her face.

'Sorry, love. Want to jump in?' James leaned across and popped open the passenger door.

'No thanks,' she said sharply. 'But I know someone who will.' she said, gesturing with a nod of her head to the little boy still holding her hand and staring at the car with eyes like saucers.

Deirdre had no interest in squeezing into the tight little passenger seat. But the boy was awestruck by this shiny growling beast.

'You better close your mouth or you'll catch all the flies,' Savita said laughing, she tucked his mouth shut with a press of her fingers under his chin.

'Well what are you waiting for, son?' James called to him. In two swift skips, he was in the seat. 'Is it really fast, Daddy?' he asked, as his father buckled up his safety belt.

'Too fast for Mammy,' James leaned over and whispered to the boy.

'You'll have to throw in a bit of petrol, before you go too far, the old girl is thirsty!'

'No worries, when something looks really good it's okay if it's hard to run.' He smiled at his wife.

She shook her head and laughed. 'Will you just go.'

I watched as Savita, Michael and Deirdre step back to allow them to turn. The boy gave us two thumbs up as they moved off.

That could have been my father and I, or Michael and me. I wondered if this was the first time a father and son got to take her for a spin?

Twenty minutes later they returned, both grinning from ear to ear. I envied the boy, it was an experience he would hold onto forever. A story he would be able to recount to his own kids someday. The time he and his father went for a drive in an E-Type Jag.

Deirdre smiled at Savita, who was clearly not as excited as her husband but was doing a pretty good job at masking her boredom. Deirdre noticed something else; Savita had gained a little weight, not a lot. She had always felt Savita was a little too skinny and peaky anyway, but there was a healthier look about her now, a glow. She sidled over to her side. 'Are those boys nearly done yet?' she whispered.

Savita held her smile but answered through clenched teeth like a ventriloquist mouthing the words for his dummy. 'I really hope so. I can't stand the fumes. My eyes are watering and I think my make-up is starting to run.'

Deirdre turned to face her, 'We could slip into the house for a cuppa?' she glanced back at the boys.' I don't think they will even notice.'

'It's okay. I'm good.' Savita replied. She wanted them all gone so she and Michael could retire to the comfort of a fire for the evening.

'You know you really are good. I mean you look great, in fact better than I've seen you in ages,' Deirdre answered, a sarcastic edge to her voice. She had an annoying ability to infer so much in a single statement.

'That's very kind of you,' Savita spoke quickly, eager to change the subject and clearly uncomfortable. She had no interest is discussing anything personal.

Deirdre leaned closer and whispered, 'Does Michael know yet?'

Savita snapped her head around and stared hard into her face.

'It's okay, I'm not prying. I won't say anything.' Deirdre retreated, her hands held in the air apologetically.

Savita took Deirdre by the arm and turned towards the house. She called back over her shoulder, 'Kettle's on whenever you boys are done playing here.'

All three boys were engrossed in the car. James had his son by the hand and was hunkered down to his level, telling him all about the car and how old it was. The boy stared in awe at the bright shiny chrome pieces.

Chapter 43

The whistle of the kettle filled the awkward silence. Deirdre took a seat by the window, she pulled back the curtain and looked out at the boys drooling over this new toy. Savita plucked the kettle of the stove to silence it and filled Mary's old crockery teapot to the brim, overfilling it, her mind elsewhere.

'They're just like little boys,' Savita said, passing Deirdre a cup of tea. 'They never really grow up, do they?'

Deirdre smiled back at her, 'No, they never do. Maybe that's why we love them.'

Savita took a seat across from Deirdre at the table, she took several long sips from her cup before she spoke.

'Michael doesn't know yet. I'm afraid to tell him,' she said, setting down her cup and staring straight at Deirdre.

'I'm sure he'll be delighted, Savita,' Deirdre replied. She had brought up the subject, had broken the ice by venturing to say more than she should have, given that they were not close friends.

'I've seen the way he looks at our John. I'll bet he would love a son.' Deirdre continued. Her tone could almost have been considered patronizing, but Savita missed it.

'Yes,' Savita said, suddenly cheery. 'You are so right, there is nothing more on this earth he would love than a son,' she paused, debating whether she should say any more. She didn't know Deirdre that well, their husbands had become close, but she and Deirdre were not exactly close. 'It's not that simple. We've had our problems.' she continued.

'I'm so sorry,' Deirdre put down her cup. 'I shouldn't have said anything,' She realised the topic was a little too sensitive for their burgeoning friendship. 'James is always telling me I interfere too much. I apologise Savita. I didn't mean to pry.' Those who knew Deirdre would have laughed if they heard her say this, she was harmless, but she did like to gossip. She rose from her seat, but Savita raised a hand and urged her to stay where she was. She was willing to talk, she wanted to talk, and needed Deirdre to stay. Without a female friend to confide in, all her concerns had been building up. She was like a pressure cooker she needed a release, needed to speak her fears aloud before the pressure became too great and she exploded.

'It's okay Deirdre, I don't mind. Nobody here knows what happened. I see the curious looks. I come from a small town myself, I know how it is. People talk, they speculate, they're curious.'

Savita picked up both their cups, took them to the sink and emptied them. 'This is going to call for something a little stronger,' she said. She pulled out a stool and set in in front of an old cupboard. Even with the help of the stool she was at full stretch to reach the upper shelf. She withdrew two large glass tumblers, raised them in both hands and smiled. 'Only glasses I have to hand, sorry,' she said and set them on the table. She opened a bottle of chardonnay that had been chilling in the refrigerator and topped up both glasses to the brim.

'Hope you don't mind the glasses, the fancy stuff is still packed away.' It was more of a statement than a question, as she did not wait for Deirdre's reply.

Deirdre shook her head and smiled through clenched teeth, 'Of course not, a glass is a glass.' Of course, she did mind, she was horrified, she would never dream of serving wine in a plain tumbler. She raised the glass to her lips, took a tiny sip and tried to look composed. She looked hesitant to swallow, as if the wine from an almost industrial container would taste foul. She perked herself up and readied herself for what she was sure would be a juicy morsel of gossip. News, either good or bad, was always welcome with the ladies from the women's group. Michael and Savita had been a mystery to them all and as a result had become the source of wild speculation. Michael had returned to his family home with this exotic new partner, but made no effort to mix with the community. There was an element of resentment among them. Did he think she was better than them, when he would not introduce her to their neighbours? Why had they retired so young? Were they incredibly wealthy? Had he made a fortune in the Middle East? And yet they lived simple and not extravagant lives.

'We were happy,' Savita's words gave Deidre a start, she was already basking in the glory of the elevated ranking this news would raise her to within the group.

'We had everything we wanted, except a family,' Savita looked up at Deirdre. 'We did try, but it just wasn't happening. The stress and frustration tested us both.'

Deirdre felt compelled to contribute something, 'I can only imagine, it must have been awful for you.'

'We had all but given up hope when out of the blue I discovered I was pregnant. Michael was over the moon. He went online and bought just about every book written on how to be a father,' Savita smiled as she recalled what must have been an incredibly happy time for them both.

'Michael's like that you know. Everything should be researched. Preparation is his thing. Anyway, two months in I got a call to get to the hospital. There was an accident, Michael had fallen at work. The girl from his office assured me he was okay, there was nothing to be worried about, they were taking care of everything.'

Savita turned away and stared out the window into the distance as if she could still see herself in that moment. 'There was something in her tone that unnerved me. She spoke to me slowly, as if I was a child. Reassuring me that there was nothing to worry about, the company were doing all they could, all that was required of them. I remember I got angry,' Savita looked at Deirdre. She was listening intently. 'You know what I mean, her polite smarmy tone drove me mad, made me even angrier. My husband was hurt and in hospital and all she seemed to care about was that I understood and accepted that the company were doing all they could to take care of things.'

Deirdre smiled back, a reassuring smile that made Savita feel she understood what she meant, but Deirdre was lost, she had no idea what it was Savita was trying to say.

'Not at all reassured, I leaped into our company car and tore off. It was stupid of me. My imagination was working overtime. With every mile that passed, I imagined Michael in a hospital bed, bandaged from head to toe and tubes sticking out of him. By the time, I got to the intersection I was nearly hysterical. I wasn't paying attention. The truck driver did all he could to avoid me. I didn't see him coming. He swerved hard to his left to try and get around me, but the truck had just too much momentum. He hit me broadside. The impact threw me across into the passenger seat.' Savita looked apologetically at Deirdre, 'I wasn't wearing my safety belt. I was in too much of a hurry. I mean, I was rushing off to see my husband in hospital, I wasn't expecting to get hit myself!' Savita was babbling, upset by the memory of it all.

'Of course,' Deirdre assured her in her most soothing tone, one she'd used time and time again to console some of her friends from a husband that cheated, or one that might have slapped one of them in a fit of rage, or even some who had financial worries, but never anything like this. She had to summon all her sympathetic energies to be convincing here, and yet she found it easy. She could genuinely empathise with Savita, this frail young woman who sat slouched at the table across from her.

'Don't beat yourself up over this, I mean what are the odds? Who could be in their senses with that kind of news, rushing to the hospital to see your man and no idea if he was alive or near dead!'

Savita looked at her, mildly reassured. She did not know this woman and wondered why she was confiding in her; why her and why now?

'Anyway, I was alright, not a scratch,' she continued. 'The police officer at the scene was able to make some sense of my story through my snivelling and tears. He took my name, but insisted I go by ambulance, even thought there was hardly a scratch on me. He followed behind. I was brought to the same hospital that Michael was in. I felt fine but the doctors insisted on giving me a thorough examination, you know, since I was pregnant.' Deirdre nodded her head, but said nothing. She did not want to interrupt the flow of the story.

'A very nice nurse wheeled me in to see Michael, in my wheelchair – hospital policy they explained despite my protests. He was laying back in bed his head bandaged like he'd been in the war. I felt so sorry for him and for coming to visit him in that bloody wheelchair. Can you imagine his shock? He was waiting for me to call, and then I arrive in a bloody wheelchair!'

'Was he okay, what happened to him?' Deirdre asked, trying to keep Savita on track.

'It was nothing, a simple fall. A nasty gash and a couple of stitches. He was released that evening.'

Deirdre listened intently, both elbows on the table and leaning ever closer to Savita. 'That must have been awful, but you were both so lucky, it could have been so much worse.'

Savita smiled, a cold and forced smile. 'I miscarried the next day. The doctors said they couldn't say for sure if the accident had anything to do with it. I'm sure it had, they were just being nice. It's just too much of a coincidence. I sometimes think Michael was angry with me, that he blamed me.' Savita wiped the window that had fogged up to look out on her man.

'That's just being silly, of course he couldn't blame you. Why it's as much his fault. If you weren't rushing to the hospital to see him, there wouldn't have been an accident.'

Savita drew a long sigh, she contemplated going on, saying more, telling this woman – who she had no doubt would not be able to hold all this gossip on them to herself.

'There's where the irony lies. A week later Michael was called back to the hospital. The routine scans after his injury showed a growth, a tumour.'

'Jesus!' Deirdre exclaimed, unable to contain her shock.

'They didn't know how long it had been growing. They couldn't even tell for sure if he had fallen because of it. We were both surprised something hadn't shown up in all the tests he had done when we were trying for a child. Our lives were torn apart, shattered, prospects of a family gone and the worrying prospect that Michael might not survive.'

Deirdre laid her hand on Savita's. It was a genuine act of compassion, understanding and sympathy. It was a compelling story and would take a long evening with the ladies to get it all told, every juicy morsel. But she was shocked and saddened by this twist in the story and her heart went out to Savita.

Savita just smiled back at her. 'And so here we are, waiting to see how his condition progresses. Patiently waiting and now a child, when he may become ill and not recover. How could he watch a child grow inside of me while he is slowly dying? I don't know if I can tell him just yet.'

There was a long silence.

Deirdre could offer no words of advice. She would like to have offered her some words of hope but she was wise enough to know that her platitudes would sound so flat and empty.

Chapter 44

'My grandfather, my own father, now finally me. It's done.'
Michael said with a sigh.

'And very well done too,' James added.

Michael rambled on about how long it had taken from start to finish, but James was not listening, he was distracted, admiring his own handiwork. It was indeed a fine paint job, especially given the limited conditions. He dropped onto one knee to look along her lines where the light caught the sides of the car. He ran a hand lightly over the panels feeling for any flaws or tiny pieces of grit that might have settled on the paint before it set. He closed his eyes as he did this so as not to be distracted by anything around him. His son wrestled to free himself from his father's grip. He broke free and rushed to the workbench to all the shiny tools. James should have called him to hand. It wasn't safe to let a boy his age run free through a workshop, but his father was lost in concentration, nodding his head as he listened to Michael while he beamed with pride at his own work.

The boy stopped in front of the tin poster of the Alfa Romeo. He reached out and placed his tiny hand in the imprint of my grandfather's handprint. He drew it back quickly, as if he'd touched something hot, the blood drained from his cheeks and he turned ashen white.

I saw him flinch when he touched the metal I watched him look around the garage, wide-eyed and scared. It looked like he needed help, wanted someone to come to him. His gaze settled on me, or at least on where I stood.

I knew he couldn't be looking at me, but he was staring at where I stood, staring through where I stood. It unnerved me. I deliberately moved to one side, his eyes followed me to where I moved. I knew he couldn't see me, but I also knew he was aware of something, a movement, a stir of air or energy within the garage. How could this be? Was there something in the innocence of a child that allowed them to see, to understand, primeval things that would become lost to them when they were forced to comply with what society considered acceptable?

'John, come over here, son,' his father called.

The boy didn't move, I could see he was straining to see what was there. Looking so hard at me, I almost felt it.

'John,' his father called in a firmer voice. The boy ran to his father's side, clasping onto his trouser leg and searching the garage wildly with open wide eyes. James sat into the driver's seat and beckoned to the boy to join him in the passenger seat. The boy sat in quickly and pulled the door shut, his eyes scanning the garage for where I was. The child was petrified.

Michael looked on. I saw him swallow and draw a deep breath before he exhaled very slowly. I saw it too. I knew what he was thinking. Father and son behind the wheel. Was he thinking of me? Did he imagine himself in the passenger seat beside me, or was he dreaming of a son of his own by his side. Nobody spoke for a long time, both men lost in their own dreams, and the boy stunned into a fearful silence.

The girls returned, arms linked together, decidedly cosier than they were when they left their men. Michael gave Savita a second glance, he suspected they may have had a few glasses of wine. He could always tell when she was a little tipsy, she would grin uncontrollable like a Cheshire cat. She winked at him. He smiled and shook his head.

'James! Little John! We should be getting home.' Deirdre called, louder than she intended, making it sound like a command. James gave her a look, then glanced to Michael. They both shrugged and smiled.

'Will you stop calling him that!' James replied, as he struggled from the car. 'People will think I'm Robin Hood and you're Maid Marion.'

Savita moved closer to Michael, slipped her hand into his and laughed.

James took the boy's hand and helped him out. The boy was unusually quiet.

'Are you okay, John?' she asked.

He just smiled back. James ruffled his hair and ushered him along. He ran to his mother, grabbed a fistful of her skirt and from this position of security he looked around, panning the garage. He'd lost sight of me, he was straining to see where I had gone, I could see his little mind was struggling to understand what he had seen.

Savita pressed herself closer to Michael. He stared at her, noting she was in an unusual mood. He threw both arms around her and pulled her to him.

Deirdre put a hand on her shoulder, leaned in and gave her a peck on the cheek, 'Good luck, Savita.' she said as she took her boys by the hands and led them away.

'What have you two been up to?' Michael asked, pushing Savita an arm's length away so he could look into her face.

'Oh nothing, just some girls talk,' she shrugged, and squeezed him tighter.

'Well, what do you really think?' Michael asked, turning to face the car again.

'I have to admit, it is absolutely beautiful. I don't know anything about cars but that looks fantastic.'

Michael pushed her away again, 'What do you mean...?' he asked, and stared her down. 'She,' he corrected her, 'she is beautiful, this beautiful creation is alive. It is a spectacular living thing. My father and my grandfather tried to finish it but now I have finally breathed life into a lump of metal.'

Savita smiled as she watched him prance around the car. She had not seen him so excited in years. The vitality and energy that she knew was so much a part of the man she loved had been absent for a long time. She opened her mouth to speak then hesitated. She was apprehensive.

'New life is a good thing Michael, it's a wonderful thing. You should be proud that you have created a new life.' She lowered both hands and cupped her tummy, a tummy that was a little plumper than he remembered.

Michael froze where he stood. She could see he was trying to digest what she'd just said. She kept her head bowed, her gaze fixed on her tummy. Her heart was racing. There was a long silence... too long. He was in shock, maybe even angry.

'What are you saying?' his voice was raised. 'You can't be… How? When?'

'I think you know the answer to all those questions,' she replied, her eyes still focused on the little pot shaped bump above her waist.

'I'm going to be a father? Are you sure? Don't joke about this. You can't joke about this.'

Savita raised her eyes to look at him. She needn't have worried. She knew from the look in his eyes and the expression on his face. He was ecstatic. She shook her head to say she was not joking.

Michael let out a loud whoop, swept her off the floor and spun her around.

'I know we didn't plan this but maybe there's still a chance for us to...' she began. He pressed a finger against her lips. 'Don't... don't say anything to jinx this. We deserve this. It's time we got a break.' He threw his head back, and looked upwards. 'Right,' he added. 'You hear me, make this happen. It's time, okay.'

'Michael, please.' she protested.

'Don't worry,' he replied. 'There's nobody up there to listen.'

I couldn't be sure if there was anybody up there or not, but I was listening. I was going to be a grandfather. My son was going to have a family. The old house would echo with the patter of little feet and the sound of laughter again. If there was any emotion left in me, in this empty vessel that I had become, I would have laughed, or cried. I'm not sure which. However, I did feel something stir, a warmth, deep within, it wasn't the euphoria I craved but it was a welcome replacement for the icy chill that occupied my core.

'Can we afford this right now?' he asked, stepping back from Savita he clasped his head between both hands. He was pressing his hands together, his head looked like it was trapped in a vice, his eyes were wide and staring.

'Relax,' she laughed. 'Don't overthink this. It's what we want, what we always wanted. We'll make it work. Okay.'

He lowered his hands and his face grew dark. 'That's not what scares me. What if I leave you alone, with a son to raise?'

She reached up and cupped his cheek in her hand, even though he towered over her he looked like a little boy by her side, frightened and afraid of what would happen next.

'Don't talk like that, you know I don't like it. We agreed to be positive,' she whispered to him.

'Yes, but we have to be realistic now. There's someone else to consider. We have to think about his future.'

'Really,' she laughed out loud. 'His future! You know the sex of my child, already?'

'Yes, I do. It will be a boy, an heir. Someone to take over from me here and someone to look after you.'

'It will be alright. I know it will,' she reassured him. He smiled and kissed the top of her head. He was not reassured, but he would not spoil this moment for her.

Savita pulled her cardigan around her shoulders and shivered. 'It's cold here, I'm going in, are you coming? Or do you have to tuck her in?' she nodded her head towards the car.

'I'll be right up, put the kettle on... Mother,' Michael patted her on the butt as she left.

He watched her all the way to the house, and so did I. She was a treasure, he was a lucky man. Mary would have been proud of him, proud of them both. Oh, if she were here to see this. A newborn in the house.

'Limelight's been stolen from you, old girl,' Michael whispered. I'd been distracted, watching Savita go. I didn't see him climb back into the car.

'We'll get a few trips down the road to do you justice but then I might have to let you go. There are bills to pay,' he looked towards the house when he said this. 'You might have come to our rescue at just the right time.'

I wasn't saddened at the news that the '69 would have to go. The job was done she was back on the road. Job accomplished. She will have been put to good use if she helps my grandson into the world.

Chapter 45

Michael had slipped into my own habit of talking to myself, or was he talking to the ghost of my father, to me and whoever else lingered in the shadows. I had no idea any more, and I was finding it increasingly hard to concentrate or to focus on a memory.

I looked again at the shadows that lingered on the periphery of my vision, in the rafters and just outside the doors, the boundaries to my world. They swirled ever angrier when it was mentioned that the car might be gone. I could not tell if they were angry at the thought of it leaving or was the turmoil a result of some battle that waged therein. A battle to pull me from this world to themselves or to protect me and keep me here and safe. I had no idea, but when I stood on the edge of those shadows I felt a force trying to pull me in and yet another repelling me, forcing me away, as if it was for my own good.

Michael placed both hands firmly on the bonnet, he allowed his head to loll forward and hang limp. 'I am to be a father, if all goes well,' his voice was low, weighed heavy with worry, apprehension and fear. 'I'm afraid I will fail to do the one thing expected of a father, to raise, guide and provide for my son. If the doctors are right, I may not see out the year.' He raised his head and stared into the car.

I would have liked to think he was talking to me, coming to me for advice. I too felt the pains of failure. I was not there for him, for my own son. To guide and provide for him. He was thinking aloud, speaking his concerns. The garage door was shut tight, he was alone, isolated from the world in this little cocoon we, the men of this house, had made for ourselves. In here we felt in control.

I felt inadequate, my son was struggling, his faith in himself was waning. It would have been my place if I were alive to offer him hope, to encourage him to go on. I placed my hands where his rested on the car, I closed my eyes and willed myself to summon something, a spark of life, a few pathetic watts of energy to act as a conduit between us.

'You have done me proud son. Your mother would have loved to see you and your family together. I thought it was wrong of me to have placed this foolish burden on you, to finish this, a car, nothing more. But son, it has given you focus, distracted you from your worries and now it has filled you with pride and satisfaction. It was a good thing, one you didn't expect it to be. I had no idea why it should be important, but the universe is wiser than us both. The '69 has saved you. I've watched you. You came back home with your tail between your legs, you were a broken man. Look at you now, you have another chance at a family. This hope should help you overcome almost anything. Don't give up son. Fight to live, fight to be by your newborn son's side.'

He remained there for a time, a part of me thought I had succeeded, he'd heard me and was considering my words. I waited.

He stood up slowly, exhaled loudly and turned to leave. I watched him go, he strolled towards the house. I thought he stood a little taller, reassured by my words. Could he subconsciously hear me, be aware of my words as thoughts in his own head like some kind telepathic communication?

I knew I was clutching at straws, hoping the advice I offered would get through. Why else was I here?

I saw them as a single silhouette, wrapped in each other against the light of the kitchen, standing by the window. They were good for each other and would fight together to overcome whatever obstacles came their way. But his illness – determination and prayers would not be enough to fend off the ravages of a cancer, if that was what he had. I could only assume from the way they tiptoed around the word that my son had been smitten with a cancer of some sort, something serious given his comment that the doctors had only given him a year or so.

It was at times like this that I yearned for herself, her advice. Mary had a way of cutting to the core of the problem, laying it bare before me and making me face what was to come.

Time, who would have thought it could be used as a weapon of torture. And yet here I was suffering at its hands, wincing at the tick of every second that passed, not knowing how many hours, days or years had passed since my beloved had left this plane for another and left me in this god-forsaken no-man's land. Waiting for, I had no idea what to happen.

Chapter 46

A dry creaking noise startled me. Something needed a drop of oil, the mechanic in me was always thinking of a quick fix for the problem. There was a little boy going around and around in circles on the garage floor, his little feet pedalling like mad. The fire engine red tricycle he sat on was much too small for him, his knees barely cleared the handlebars, the little boy had outgrown it. I watched him for a long time. He couldn't have been more than four or five, a fine sturdy boy. The garage door was open just enough to allow him and his bike in, had he sneaked in here? Was he allowed here alone?

I watched him, he was pedalling with such purpose. Then I realised what he was doing, he was making ever-decreasing circles in the thick film of dust on the floor. I smiled to myself, I remembered doing just that myself once, a long, long time ago. The axles continued to creak as he went; it was an incredibly irritating noise. The tricycle looked quite old. In fact, it looked very old, not old enough to have been mine but it looked just like one Michael had. I peeled myself from the chair and crossed the floor to have a closer look. I stood as close as I dared without stepping into his path.

'Jesus!' I exclaimed. I staggered backwards as if I was dealt a physical blow. It was Michael, I was sure of it. His face, that hair and that little dimple in the centre of his chin. What cruel game was this? Had I been dragged back to his childhood? Would I be forced to watch him grow again, powerless to speak, to call out to him or worse to hold him?

This time I felt it, an almost forgotten feeling, anguish, worry. Though they are painful I welcomed them. To feel was to be alive, or at least closer to being alive.

'Michael!' a raised voice called, full of concern. 'Michael, are you in there?'

I didn't recognise the voice. Could it be Mary, his mother? It was so long ago; her voice would have sounded different when she was younger. I swallowed as the door pushed open. I felt it, something different, a new sensation. I felt lighter than before, of less substance. I began to sink into the floor. I had lost all concept of time, how long had it been, how long had I lingered in the shadows in the garage? I had no idea, but the thought of seeing her face again, even if I couldn't embrace her, excited me.

The sunlight of a rare bright and sunny day filled the garage with an unnatural light, momentarily blinded, I panicked. Her silhouette stood out, a black shape against this light.

'Michael, you know your father doesn't allow you down here,' she stepped out of the light and into the shade of the garage. Confusion, disappointment, joy, sadness – I couldn't tell which won over. I stood and watched Savita pick up the boy.

'Michael?' I spoke his name as a question.

Wrapped in his mother's arms, he snapped his head around. Had he heard me, heard something? There was no doubt that he'd reacted to my voice. He was looking to where the sound came from. He didn't look frightened, but then he was too young to know that a voice from out of nowhere was something to be concerned about.

Savita turned to go, but paused as she pulled the door shut and took a long look back at the covered shape in the corner.

My eyes followed her gaze. 'Why are you still here?' I asked. They should have let you go, sold you for the money they would need to raise the boy. That familiar shape lay still, back again to its resting place in the shadows at the back of the garage. The boy must be three, maybe four years old. She spoke about his father, Michael must be okay, he must still be here. What of his illness? I walked around the car again. The '69. How many times had I stood over her? And here she was again, finished, ready for a new owner and yet back under cover. I yanked off the cover with one swift motion. She still looked good, too good to waste away in the shadows. The old girl needed sunlight and the open road. This was not right. Michael should have known better. He did all the hard work to put her back together but it was time to let go, to move on. This was wrong, it was like locking a leopard or a powerful predator into a dark room. The beast needed light, freedom, the open countryside.

When I threw open the doors again it was pitch black outside. I looked to the night sky, a wonderful starry sky. I could not see the top of the hills anymore. The trees in the courtyard had grown so tall they blocked out the view. The kitchen light was still on, I saw figures moving inside. The back door opened and he stepped out. He was a little stooped, but not much. In the dim light, I tried to make out his age from the lines on his face, but it was impossible. Life can etch so many lines on a man's face that don't match his age, experience is a much greater sculptor.

Michael didn't come into the garage right away, he stood in the moonlight looking in for a long time, he seemed apprehensive about entering.

When he did he walked slowly towards her. 'Easy girl, it's just me.' He spoke softly. I had seen cowboys do this in the movies, walk carefully towards a wild stallion they were afraid they would spook. 'It's been a while hasn't it,' he set his hand gently onto her roof. 'A lot has happened,' he took his hand back. There was something he was struggling to say.

'I would so have loved to get to know you, to spend time along the country roads. None of us got the chance to enjoy you, old girl,' Michael turned and looked to the rafters, to where he felt my presence would linger and my father's too.

'It's time, old girl. I have to let you go,' Michael whispered. 'My son and I will go for a drive tomorrow. I've waited as long as I could. He's just a child but I think he is old enough to remember and I want him to remember. I want him to remember the experience, to remember this garage and what was done here. Remember all the men that went before me. I want him to tell his children about this place.' He turned on his heels and marched back towards the house.

I watched him go. He was right, it was time. The '69 had served her purpose well. She was instrumental in bonding two generations of fathers and sons together and would play a part in helping a third make a start in life.

I patted her on the bonnet like one would a faithful hound. Easy girl, it's not over for you yet. You still have a part to play and you might have the chance to change even more lives before you are done.

Chapter 47

The first of the prospective buyers appeared, since I had no yardstick to measure the passing of time I didn't know if this was a day a week or a month later.

He was young gentleman, younger than one I thought would have an interest in the car. I withheld my judgment until he had a look around the car – and I had a look at him.

'How old did you say it was?' he asked, in an unfamiliar accent.

Obviously not an enthusiast or he would have had an idea of the age.

'1969,' Michael replied. 'It's the Series II, a four point two litre, six-cylinder engine with the four-speed manual gearbox. It is, of course, the two-seater, the more sought after model and not the two plus two.' My son fed him all this information, but it was apparent from the blank expression on his face that he had no idea what any of it meant.

'I love the curves,' was all he could add. 'Do you have a service history with the car?'

Michael exhaled loudly. I watched the colour drain from his face and braced myself for the outburst I expected would come. I was sure I heard him counting to ten like his mother had warned him to do.

'I'm sorry, young man,' he replied, in a low calm voice. 'I think you're mistaking this for a Ford Focus. If you're after a family saloon you should try the dealership down the road.'

'I beg your pardon?' he exclaimed.

'Beg away,' Michael raised his voice an octave, not enough that the young man would notice, but I did, I saw him struggling to suppress his anger.

'Go!' I shouted at the young man. 'Go now!' I laughed. Michael did not suffer fools lightly

The young man thought about responding to the rebuke, but thought better of it and stormed off.

'Time-wasters.' Michael said, under his breath as he watched him leave.

I saw a few more groups of men come and go. They came to the farmhouse, met Michael and stood in the yard talking. None were invited to the garage to view the car. Voices became raised, car doors were slammed and they left, spitting up gravel as they went.

'Wise move,' I muttered. Vet them there, don't waste their time and yours if they are not genuine buyers.

'Tyre-kickers.' I heard him say.

Savita stood behind him, arms firmly folded across her chest.

'What?' he asked, defensively.

'Are you going to ask them for a C.V. next? Interview them, ask for their medical history?' She was scolding him but fought back a smile as she did. He was incorrigible, but she loved him.

'They're just wasting my time, I know who they are. The locals have been talking about this, my grandfather's car, finally finished after three generations. They're making a great big joke of it, think it's funny that it took us all this time to get one car finished.'

'Calm down, love. I'm only joking. I know what it means to you. I know what it means to have to part with the car, sorry... with her.'

Michael flashed her a look. Savita smiled back at him, and as was always the case his anger dissolved.

'That car has been a part of everything that has happened to this family, from my grandfather until this day, to the day she vanishes down that road,' he pointed towards the gate at the end of the driveway as if anything that passed through that gate would be gone forever.

'I'm glad we don't have a daughter,' she said. 'I would hate to be a boy calling to pick her up for her first date!' She turned for the house laughing as she went.

A group of middle-aged men stood together in the garage. I leaped from my chair, like a host that had been remiss in greeting his guests. I was on my feet and dusting myself off when they walked past me. 'The invisible man,' I snorted.

They stood in near silence all three of them. Michael explained the cars history, described in great detail the work that was done and how it was done. A few heads nodded, knowledgeable nods I thought. This is more like it. It looked like they came prepared to make a thorough examination of the car. I tried to keep track of them all but while I watched one lying under the car with a torch there was another poking and prodding under the hood and a third behind the wheel running a hand over the upholstery.

Michael stepped back and let them be. Like myself, he had every confidence in the work. There was nothing to hide, the more they examined the better they would understand the extent of the work that was done.

'Car looks the business,' the tallest of the trio spoke. I assumed he was the oldest of the group, the others seemed happy to let him do the talking.

'Yes indeed, she is exactly as I described. You can bring along a Jaguar specialist if you like. I have nothing to hide.'

He turned to the others, they exchanged a few smirks and smiles.

'Do you mind if we discuss this for a minute?

'By all means, take all the time you need.' Michael stepped back to give them privacy.

A new spokesperson came forward. 'We saw her advertised at the end of last summer, had you no luck selling back then?'

'I took her off the market,' Michael replied, frustrated at the direction he saw the negotiations were heading. 'I got tired of entertaining fools and time-wasters.'

'Easy son, easy!' I urged.

'Really?' the second man replied, in a tone of disbelief.

'What about the price, how much movement is there on the asking price?' The third man, and it would appear the actual buyer asked.

'None!' Michael replied sharply. 'She is exactly what I said she was, and the price is exactly as I said it would be. Why would you think anything else?'

All three glanced at each other.

'Surely the advertised price was an asking price, you have to have allowed for some compromise?'

And there it was, the change. Michael bristled, his posture changed and so did his attitude, his tone, and his impatience.

'I'm sorry if you thought this would be an auction,' he said. 'I made no compromises in the work, I will make no compromises on the price.' He was already turning away from them towards the door.

Again, they looked at each other, mystified.

'I'm sorry but are you sure you really want to sell the car?' the buyer asked.

I applauded him, he was quick to see what I had missed. Michael just did not want to sell the car. He was going to examine each buyer even more stringently than they would examine the car. I laughed out loud, comfortable in the knowledge no-one could hear me. I was going to enjoy this. He would make each potential buyer prove he was worthy of the car. He would make them cringe if he had to, but they would have to earn the right to buy the car.

None of them spoke to Savita as she met them crossing the courtyard to their car. She had a tray of teas in her hand, she smiled at them as they passed but none returned her smile.

'What happened?' she asked. 'What's wrong with them, they look upset?'

'Time-wasters, the lot of them,' Michael replied. 'Bloody time-wasters! They think they can come in here and toss out a few reservations about the car, it's history or the work we've done and I'll just knock thousands off the price!'

All I heard from this conversation was, the work we've done. He was acknowledging the work that went into the car before he took up the challenge at the last hurdle and completed the task. He was crediting myself and my father with the work.

'It's frustrating,' she said, holding his arm and rubbing his back with her other hand, 'But you do know we'll need the money very soon.'

'I'll go hungry before I let those tossers drive off in her.'

'And will you watch your wife and son go hungry too?' she smiled at him, but there was a serious edge to her voice. She saw the dilemma he was facing. The car had to go. They needed the money. He was just so reluctant to part with her. She suspected he still hoped some miracle would come along and save them from this. Savita already knew they had used up more than their fair share of miracles, her husband was alive and well and they had a son, they were a family. There would always be sacrifices, and it looked like the '69 was going to have to be his.

He wanted to stay angry. He hated to part with the car, the last physical link to me and a shared past, but the reality was they did need the money. He wanted to vent his anger at someone, kick something, shout out loud. Savita standing there with her wonderful warm, winning smile made him even angrier. He wished she would go and let him cool down in his own good time. Savita would not leave him when he was like this, she wanted to be here to be with him, unaware that her presence was robbing him of a chance to curse and shout and maybe throw a few tools around. So, he smiled and let her hug him and hold him, and while she held onto him his anger slowly melted away.

'Now,' she said, as she stepped away from him, content that she'd soaked up his anger as if it was some great mystical power she possessed. 'Come on and I'll make some tea.'

There was a steady stream of phone calls for the next few weeks from home, the UK and some from America. Some were genuine inquiries, but many were from fools and dreamers, hoping the owner might be desperate, under some unknown financial pressure and the car would be snapped up for a fraction of the asking price. Speculators, hoping a bargain could be squeezed from some poor sod down on his luck. Michael was reluctant to accept that he was, in fact, that poor sod.

Savita noted the interest with excitement, but she waited. She knew Michael would accept the inevitable. He would do the right thing, the wise thing; for a change he was thinking with his heart. This would ordinarily be a simple calculated transaction. The best deal would be wrestled from the strongest buyer. Sentiment would have no part in the sale. But that was not so, she knew it, but she also knew she had said enough on the matter. Her views were clear. He knew what she wanted and he would do the right thing in the end, but it was important that he be allowed to make that decision alone. She would not insist that he sell the '69. It could come back to haunt her if things turned bad between them, though she doubted that would happen.

Chapter 48

The sun was barely up, but I was already up and about, pacing the garage alone. I rarely appeared here so early in the day. The doors were shut, the lights were out and there was no sign of Michael – the catalyst that brought me back here.

I had a sensation I couldn't quite describe, something like a feeling of apprehension, butterflies in my stomach; it was not fear, it was more like excitement.

Hours later I heard the footfall of two or three people and the sound of hushed conversations. Michael was the first to come in. The gentleman that followed stopped abruptly at the doorway. He wore a flat cap; his head was bowed so I could not see his face. He took off his cap and gripped it nervously in his hands as he stood with the tips of his shoes against the concrete edge of the floor. He craned his neck and looked around, reluctant to come any further.

'Come on in,' Michael urged. 'Come in.'

'Yes,' I said aloud. 'Now we're talking. A gentleman at last.'

He stood wringing the cloth cap in his hands, like a shy teen on the doorstep of a girlfriend's house, nervous to meet her father. It might have been cute, coy even for a teenager but this man was no teenager, he was too old for such timidity. Michael was busy pulling the cover off the '69, but I did not take my eyes off him. He put one foot into the garage as if he was dipping a toe into a pond to test the water. He eased himself inside and out of the sunlight. Then he did a strange thing, just as he entered under the doorway he nodded his head. It was a slight gesture, barely perceptible. I was sure Michael didn't notice, or if he did he thought nothing of it, and why should he. It looked like nothing, but I knew that was not true. It was the way he kept his eyes fixed on the rafters. He was looking for something, someone. There was intent in that gesture, he had dipped his head in a gesture of respect, an acknowledgment. But of who? He continued slowly, treading ever so carefully. His face showed no sign of emotion, but his eyes were wide and wild looking. I saw his chest rise and fall rapidly under his jacket. He was anxious, nervous or perhaps just excited. Maybe I was reading too much into it, over analysing his every move.

While Michael talked, he paced the floor of the garage. Michael was unusually eager to impress him. He was giving him the five-star tour; every detail of the work done was being explained, every snippet of history detailed. I had seen him give a few time-wasters a couple of short sentences and a business card, as they were ushered to the door. I expect he saw a little of what I saw, a polite dignified man with a knowledge of cars, probably a genuine enthusiast. If he had claimed direct lineage to the queen I would have believed him, such was the presence he exuded.

He looked impressed by the surroundings, pursing his lips and nodding his head in an approving fashion as he walked around. He took in every tiny detail, pausing regularly to take a closer look at some inconsequential item.

Being invisible as I was, I had great freedom to stare, to walk right up to him and look in his face, run a hand over the fabric of his garments, put my nose to his chest and smell his aftershave. His jacket felt coarse and grainy, definitely not something off an assembly line. I took a few steps back to get a better look at the bigger picture. He was dressed differently. He wore a three-piece tweed suit, the cut and styling very dated. The suit may have been tailor-made for him, it was hard to tell. If it was once a snug fit for him, it was no longer so. It hung loosely on shoulders I was sure were once much broader. His shoes were highly polished. I remembered how my father would fuss over the look of his shoes as he readied himself for mass on a Sunday morning. This memory stood out because for the other seven days of the week my father wore the same pair of scuffed working boots. Perfectly polished shoes were from another time.

I may have been a prisoner in my own little garage for, I don't know how long, but I could still tell fashion had not gone into reverse.

He stood perfectly straight, noticeably so for a man his age, almost standing to attention. His hair was cropped short, crew cut style. I suspected he had served in the military at some time in his past, an officer perhaps given his air of confidence and authority. When he was done perusing his surroundings his eyes moved to the '69, as if he was intentionally saving the best for last.

Michael had stopped talking. He had said pretty much all there was to say. The car would have to do the rest if this man was to be impressed. He backed away from the car and leaned against the wall allowing the gentleman room to walk around her. His dignified approach had earned him this measure of respect.

'He'll definitely do, Michael, if he doesn't do or say something to cock it up.' I whispered into Michael's ear.

As I watched him, I thought there was something familiar about him. Was it that he reminded me of someone from an earlier age? Yet there was never anyone as well-dressed in my past, the landed gentry and my friends rarely mixed.

'And this is all the handiwork of yourself and your father?' he asked, and smiled at Michael for the first time.

'Yes sir,' Michael replied.

'You!' I exclaimed, stopping mid-step. 'It's you, I saw you there by the poplars that day Michael and I went for a drive. I recognise that smile.' I had been relaxing, content to let this gentleman wander around our garage, but something was wrong, this was not normal. He had stared at me that day I was sure of it, or had he just stared and nodded at the '69?

'Hey!' I shouted into his face, I was no more than three feet from him. I could count the wrinkles on his forehead, but he did not flinch.

'Are you a Jaguar enthusiast, sir?' Michael asked.

'Sir?' I looked at Michael and frowned, this man was a good few years his senior, but not enough to warrant a title. Yet it was amazing how his manner and his air of authority had required that he be addressed as such.

'You should be proud of yourselves, this is a very well presented motorcar. I'm impressed, and that doesn't happen too often,' he added.

'Thank you, it's been a long road but we're happy with the result.'

He looked around him as if he was expecting someone else to be there, given that Michael acknowledged that it was a we who did the work.

'My father is not with us anymore I'm afraid,' Michael added, acknowledging his reaction to the comment.

Almost immediately the stranger looked to the shadows that had retreated to the back of the garage.

'Oh, I wouldn't be so sure,' he replied. I saw him strain his eyes, trying to look deeper into that inky blackness. The shadows were still. The swishing and swirling that I was sure only I could see, had stopped. The motion had ground to a sudden halt. The way someone playing hide and seek, stops and stays perfectly still so they can't be seen.

Michael fell silent, and followed his gaze to the shadows. Neither spoke for a moment.

He smiled the faintest of smiles, as if this stranger saw something familiar, something that he was happy to see. And then is was gone, the sombre expression rushed back to wipe the smile away.

I had not noticed when, but it had grown quiet. I had always thought it quiet here, but this was a real silence. The hum was gone, the ever-present hum that I did not notice until this silence made me aware of it.

Michael opened his mouth to speak, but no words would come from there. The remark had thrown him.

'Henry,' the stranger said suddenly. 'Call me Henry.' He smiled at Michael, it was an incredibly warm and welcoming smile, not a practiced smile like that of a car salesmen – the kind of smile that's meant to win over customers, to assure them it's okay to trust them. It looked like a smile he had not used in a while but one that was delighted to be aired again. He had very few laugh lines on his face, but there were lots of troubled furrows on his brow. Deep lines I imagined that were put there by stress and hardship. As I watched him I got the feeling he was not a particularly content man, yet today he was genuinely happy.

The metal sign for the old Alfa caught Henry's eye. 'May I?' he asked, pointing to the sign. Michael shrugged his shoulders and nodded to him to go ahead.

'A wonderful time, a golden era in the manufacturing of motorcars,' he said.

'I couldn't agree more,' Michael replied.

'The '69, how soon would you need to be paid for the car?'

A shiver ran through me, nobody referred to it as the '69 other than ourselves.

Michael didn't answer right away, unsure if he had heard him correctly. 'Don't you want to take it for a short drive first?' he asked. He was shaken. I could see it. I don't know if Henry's words had been a coincidence or an inadvertent slip but I didn't like it. There was something going on here that I didn't understand but I was glad that Michael too was perturbed, and he had the power to ask the questions.

Henry was still looking at the poster when he next spoke. 'This garage, these walls, that sign,' he reached out to touch the sign but stopped. He allowed his hand to hover there, inches away from touching the cold metal. He understood it's importance, it's place here.

'I know the commitment it takes to turn out this kind of work, it can only come from a love of the work, a passion for the motorcar and most of all, an artist's hand.'

I thought his description of the process a little too flowery but I agreed with what he was saying.

'You have a passion for old cars, Henry?' Michael asked.

'I suppose I do,' he tilted his head at an unusual angle and considered this for a moment. 'I suppose I have a passion for all things old really. The fifties and sixties were simpler times, better times. Life moved a lot slower, people had time for each other. I don't think I really moved on with the times.' He was looking up into the rafters again, then stopped and turned to Michael, as if he had forgotten he was there and had been talking to himself all this time.

'Elizabeth lectures me on this,' he said with a wry smile.

'Your wife?'

'Yes, but she passed away several years ago.'

'I'm sorry to hear that.'

'There's no need to be, she had a wonderful life. We had a wonderful life.' He fell silent again as if contemplating those days.

'But now I can indulge myself,' he said, his voice suddenly raised as if he was trying to shake off old memories. 'I can throw myself back into an era I love.' He threw his arms open wide and looked down at the clothes he wore, then raised his head and looked at Michael, inviting him to do the same. 'As you can see Michael, I am a man trapped in the past.' Michael looked at his perfectly polished shoes, his baggy tweed trousers and his matching waist coat and jacket.

'Nothing wrong with that, Henry,' Michael said, with a smile.

'Indeed,' he replied, as if he doubted the wisdom of living in the past and was looking for a stronger affirmation from Michael.

'What do you do?' Michael asked.

'Do?' he looked surprised by the question. 'Why nothing Michael, I'm an old man.'

'Of course,' Michael shrugged apologetically, 'But what did you do Henry? You were not always an old man.' Michael persisted.

'Oh, this and that. I dabbled at a lot of things over the years.' He plucked a piece of fluff from the sleeve of his jacket as he spoke. He looked distracted but I suspected it was more that he wanted to move away from this subject.

'Did you ever serve in the army?' Michael's question took him by surprise.

I laughed. Michael was like a terrier when he got hold of an idea or a suspicion. He would not let go. Henry had piqued his curiosity. Michael would have to have answers and would not rest until he did.

'Why do you ask?' Henry snapped, almost defensively, as if he felt the question was an accusation.

'You stand incredibly straight for man of your age, like someone who had spent some time on the parade ground.'

'That is very perceptive of you, young man,' Henry patted Michael on the shoulder and walked back to the '69.

'The army has always played a part in our family. I think I first joined up as an act of protest against my father.' He looked at Michael and shook his head to acknowledge the foolishness of this. 'My father did not approve, he hated the army. We rarely spoke after that. My loss, I'm afraid. He was a great man. But it was too late when I realised that.'

'I'm sorry to hear that Henry, but we all make mistakes. I too had a chance to get to know my father better but wasted it.' Michael looked at the '69.

'Indeed.' Henry followed his eyes to the old car. A silence followed, both lost in thought.

'Am I being vetted here?' Henry asked suddenly

'What do you mean?'

'I feel like a gentleman caller, presenting myself to the potential father -in-law.'

Henry laughed, but considered the analogy for a moment.

'I guess you are,' Michael said, with an air of certainty, pleased that Henry grasped the gravity of the situation.

Henry stared wide-eyed at him, surprised at his candour, then extended a hand. 'If I agree to your price, do we have a deal?'

Michael looked surprised by the sudden change of subject. In fact, Michael, had been on the back foot from the moment Henry walked into the garage. Henry had been quite good at throwing him off guard, sudden changes in the tone and subject of the conversation had unsettled Michael. He was struggling to get a handle on this unusual gentleman that stood before him and I knew it. Michael took a long look at the '69. He reached out to take Henry's hand then stopped. 'I'm sorry Henry, this is just a first date. You've made your introductions and you can call again. Besides you are not the only suitor; there is another gentleman caller coming this afternoon. I promised him I wouldn't sell the car without giving him a chance to see it and make an offer. I can't sell without letting him know, or at least giving him a chance.'

'I understand,' Henry replied, but he could not mask the irritation in his voice. 'She would be going to a good home son, she would be well cared for.'

'I don't doubt it for a minute Henry, but as a matter of honour I think it only fair that I let the other man know,' Michael replied, 'I'm sure you understand.' There it was, that steely tone I remembered. Michael was never one to be bullied, press him too hard on this and he would go into reverse and Henry would be made wait.

He marched off, through the courtyard, an energetic spring in his step for one so old. Michael turned back into the garage, but I watched Henry all the way to the end of the estate. He stopped there and turned to look back. He looked right at where I was standing. He stood there for a long moment. It was there again, that look of longing on his face, longing and sadness. I felt sorry for him though I had no idea why. I could not tell if the mist that hovered over the river had moved out over the meadow and swallowed him up, or did he step back into it, but either way he was gone.

Chapter 49

Savita watched Henry stomp off. She knew from his body language that he was not a happy camper.

Michael was preparing the case for his defence in his head when he entered the kitchen. She stood facing him, her arms folded and an angry scowl on her face.

'It's okay, don't fret. He's still interested,' he explained. 'He's just going off to have a think about it.' He stuttered the words in a less than convincing manner. Savita knew he was not telling her everything.

'And when will he be back?' she asked in a sharp tone

'Ah, he ah, he hopes to call again at the weekend.' Michael sidestepped her and turned his attention to the cupboards. He was opening and closing cupboard doors, then went rifling through the drawers.

She laid a hand on his shoulder to stop him. 'What are you looking for?' she asked in a softer tone.

'The laptop. Where is the bloody laptop?'

Savita took him by the shoulders and turned him to face the kitchen table where the laptop was sitting. He was flustered. She knew she would have to be patient with him, even though she wanted so badly to ask if this potential buyer was gone forever. Too many questions now would result in a fight.

Henry Blackwood. She watched him type the name. Thousands of search results popped up. He looked at the screen, a lost look on his face.

'Here,' she said, 'let me.' She ushered him off the chair

and sat down. He took up position behind her and he began to massage her shoulders, a small gesture of appreciation, for her help, for her understanding and for not flying off the handle and lecturing him.

She smiled and leaned her head to brush her cheek on his hand. 'What else do you know about him?' Her fingers were poised over the keys.

Michael had to think, he regretted not asking more questions.

'He served in the army.'

'When?' the question came back quicker than he would have liked

'Don't know.'

Savita kept her eyes on the keyboard. 'Did he mention a unit, a brigade or anything like that?'

Michael did not answer. She turned around and looked up at him. Michael clenched his teeth, threw his head back, closed his eyes tight and tried to recall their conversation.

Savita suppressed a smile. She knew it wasn't fair to make him suffer, but she was enjoying herself. He was clutching the chair, wringing the life out of it with both hands.

'Okay then. Where is he from?'

'Scotland,' Michael blurted, glad to have an answer. 'His family have estates in Scotland and England, but I think he said he was from Scotland.

'Okay.' She tapped at the keys. More results appeared, about two million results. Michael ran both hands aggressively through his hair. Savita closed the laptop and rose from her chair.

'What?' he stared at her, impatience and frustration written all over his face.

'It's okay, love. Take a minute, write down everything you know and when I have some time tomorrow I'll check it out, okay?'

He laughed. 'You know me too bloody well, love.' He kissed her forehead. They laughed together and held each other.

He exhaled loudly. 'There's something about this guy Savita, something strange, not bad strange… I can't put my finger on it, but I'd like to know a little about him before the weekend.'

Michael junior was having his mid-morning nap. Savita liked to use this time to get some housework done, but today she knew it would be best used to get some information for Michael, to satisfy his curiosity, and get the car sold so they could get their bank account into a healthier state.

She threw herself into the task; it was a welcome distraction from the daily grind of running a house. Armed with a few pathetic scribbles Michael had left for her, she began.

Minutes ran into hours, she glanced at the clock. Michael junior would soon be awake again. A few more hours sleep for herself the night before would have helped. The boy was as demanding as his father. She was about to close the laptop when it caught her attention, an article on Scottish landlords in Ireland and the plantation of Ulster.

Oliver Cromwell had rewarded those loyal to him

by gifting them with tracts of land in Ireland. He was not concerned that there were farmers already working this land, it belonged to England so he felt entitled to do with it as he pleased. This was why protestant landlords appeared and took title to vast lands. Savita was oblivious to Ireland's history and found it fascinating. She did a search on the Morgan family, the previous owners of Michael's home. There were a few brief entries on their time there. Positive stories of how they treated their tenants and then she found it. In the last paragraph, she'd almost missed it as her eyes scan read over the page.

William Moore III arranged to have his only son married. It was an opportunity to join two great families closer together. He needed an heir to continue the line and the Blackwood women had a long tradition of bearing fine strong sons. Hence William Junior wed Elizabeth Blackwood. They took up residency in their newly acquired estate in the west of Ireland and gave William a son, George, to continue the family lineage.

'Michael, Michael!' Savita rushed screaming through the back door; forgetting about her sleeping son, she ran towards the garage. Michael was making so much noise that he could not hear her until she was standing by his side. She gave him a fright when he turned to find her standing there, her hands on her hips gasping for breath.

'What? What's wrong? Where is the baby?' he asked glancing over her shoulder towards the house.

She raised a hand to calm him. 'He's fine,' she said between breaths. 'But you have to come with me and see this.' She took off again for the house, without waiting to see if he was following behind. She led him to the table and spun the laptop around so it was facing him.

'Read the last paragraph.' she said, handing him his glasses. He squinted to focus on the small print and began.

She stood back and watched his face for the reaction. It took him a moment to digest what he was reading. 'Jesus Christ!' he exclaimed, and a few seconds later their baby boy cried out, as if frightened by his father's outburst.

'I'll get him,' Savita rushed down the hall to comfort the boy. A few short seconds later she returned holding the frightened child, yet anxious to see what Michael made of her discovery.

He was staring at the ceiling, both hands clasping his virtually bald head.

'I don't know why, but I knew there was something about him.'

'Surely it can't be a coincidence, can it?' she asked.

He snorted, 'Damn right it's not. He's related to the old landlord, to the Morgan's. And more importantly to the Captain.'

Savita rocked the child back and forth as she paced the floor until he settled. The boy was in shock, yet his tears had not brought them both rushing to his side; they were barely listening to him. Exhausted, his sobs fell away and he dropped off to sleep on his mother's shoulder.

Savita waited for her husband to add more. She knew only a little of their family history, mostly snippets from Mary. She watched Michael rock back and forth on his heels, his mind elsewhere, his eyes roving around the room as if the answer to his questions were floating about above his head.

'Why was the Captain important?' Savita asked, when she could wait no longer.

'It's about the cars. The Captain was always about the cars.' Michael looked through the window into the dark night towards the courtyard and the garage. 'He had no interest in anything else on the farm. That's why it went to ruin under his management.' He paused to consider something. 'The old Alfa,' he said suddenly, as if something new and important had occurred to him. 'Henry was fascinated with the sign for the old Alfa.'

'But who is he?' Savita interrupted. 'What relationship does he have to the Captain – the Blackwood's were his mother's family?'

'I have no idea?' Michael conceded. He returned to the computer screen again.

'Where has this man been? Why has he waited until now to come here? I mean he's an old man. What does he really want?' Savita asked.

Neither of them spoke, they watched the screen as Savita scrolled down the search results for anything more.

Savita turned her attention to the warm body that was snuggling into her neck. She looked at him and smiled. 'I'll pop him back to bed,' she said, as she crept out of the kitchen and into the hall.

Michael was still staring at the computer screen when she returned. 'Was there anything left behind when they left the house, any old documents, something that might tell us more about the family?' she asked.

'Nothing I can think of, besides it's not that family we need to find out about, it's the Blackwood's. The Captain's mother's people. Their roots were in Scotland. We need to find out if they have any connections here.'

Chapter 50

The clang of metal on metal woke me. Michael was standing on a steel drum, stretching up into the rafters when I rose from the chair.

'What do you want with that?' I asked.

He plucked the old steering wheel from a nail above the rafters where it had hung undisturbed for years. A cloud of dust followed him to the ground when he jumped off the drum onto the floor. He gave it a rough wipe with the sleeve of his overall.

'It's not in great condition, son,' I looked over his shoulder at the remains of the wheel he held in his hand. The wood was faded and cracked, the once polished and shining metal spokes had long since lost their lustre.

Michael stared at it for a long time. 'Why was this of so much interest to you?' he asked.

'What?' I shouted, forgetting that he could not hear me and would not be answering. 'Who are you talking about Michael?'

He climbed up on the drum and set the steering wheel back exactly where he got it. He looked around the rafters. I followed his gaze. 'What the hell are you looking for?' I shouted.

He crossed the floor to the pressed tin poster of the Alfa Romeo. He allowed his hand to hover over the sign for a moment, as if he could sense or detect something from the metal, a magnetism, or an energy.

'The stranger, that gentleman – Henry, you called

him. This is about him, isn't it? We both knew there was something about him. What is it son, shout it out in anger so that I can know.' I was so tired of second guessing what was going in his world. I just wanted somebody to say the words.

Michael crossed to the '69. 'I'm not entirely sure he was genuinely interested in you, old girl,' he said. 'I think he just wanted a chance to look around the place.' He pulled out the stepladder and set it against the wall. He climbed to the top of the ladder and looked up over the rafters.

I remembered putting some old stuff up there occasionally. Mostly old tat that I wanted out of the way, but I could honestly say I had no idea what was in half of the old boxes and chests that were pressed far into the centre of the roof and out of reach.

Michael struggled to reach most of the boxes, but persisted none-the-less. An hour later he had everything pulled onto the floor. A lot of the boxes disintegrated once they were manhandled. He rifled through these quickly and threw the contents, all sorts of rubbish, outside the door and onto the gravel of the courtyard. I saw that it was going to take a while to go through so much so I made myself comfortable in the chair.

Savita came to see what the racket was. She tiptoed over the debris at the garage door and stood arms outstretched palms upward in a gesture of confusion. 'Have you lost your mind?' she asked.

'Look,' he explained, in an exasperated tone, 'if there is anything that will tell us more about the house and this man, it's going to be in here somewhere.'

'What has the house got to do with him?' I exclaimed, rising suddenly from my chair.

I stood waiting for them to say something more, something that would tell me what it was they were looking for and what the hell it was they were talking about. But they sifted through box after box together in silence.

'What about that big wooden chest?' she asked.

'Murphy's law,' he replied. 'I'm hoping it has something and I'm leaving it to last.'

'Who is Murphy?' Savita stopped and stood upright. Michael was on his knees pulling open a shallow cardboard box, he turned and looked at her mouth agape and about to speak but no words came out. I guessed he was considering how he would explain the expression, but closed his mouth and reconsidered. 'Later,' he said. 'I'll explain later. For now, just humour me and leave that box to last.'

I walked around as they worked, fingering items I had packed away that brought back memories and items I had never seen before and had no idea they were hiding up there.

Then Michael stopped, 'Phew,' he exhaled, tired and more than a little sweaty. It was carnage all around him. Breathless, Savita stood up and took stock of the mess they'd made. 'Michael, it's going to take forever to clean this up.'

'Don't fret, most of this is for the scrap heap,' he said, edging his way ever closer towards the chest, it sat untouched in the heap of ripped cardboard. He mopped the sheen of sweat that glistened on his brow with his sleeve and plucked a nail bar from the workbench.

'Fingers crossed, love.' he said, as he pressed the pointed edge into a space on the cover. It was stuck fast.

It barely moved with his first effort. He raised his foot and stood on the bar for leverage and with a sharp crack it gave way. When the dust settled, they leaned in and looked all the way to the bottom of an empty chest.

'Guess it doesn't always go like it does in the movies,' Savita smiled at him and shook her head as she walked away.

'I'm not done here yet,' he called after her.

'I know you're not,' she laughed, 'but you might be by the time you get that mess sorted.'

Michael looked again at the carnage on the floor. 'Shit!'

I looked and listened as they'd worked, but neither of them said a single word that would help me understand what it was they were looking for.

It took Michael a lot longer than he expected it would but he had the place looking spic and span again. He walked towards the chair where I sat. I jumped out of it smartly. I had no intention of sitting there while he sat in me or on me.

He mumbled something incoherent to himself and his eyes darted wildly around the walls.

'What is it, son? What are you looking for?' I asked, following his gaze.

'He was looking for something that day.' Michael said in a suddenly raised voice. I never knew when he did this if he could hear me, or sense me. There were so many times that these uncanny coincidences occurred that I became convinced he could feel my questions.

I was still pondering this when he sped past me and stopped in front of the sign. Like everyone else that faced it, he too was reluctant to lay a hand on it. Then in one swift move he whisked it off the wall and set it onto the workbench. He gave it a gentle wipe of a rag, careful not to touch my father's handprint. I knew from his expression it offered him no new information. Turning it over, careful not to scratch the paint, he set it onto a rag. There, in the pressed indentation of the poster, was a mouldy leather pouch. Michael hurriedly prised the pouch from its hiding place, he unbuckled the strap that held it together and opened the pouch. He laid the contents carefully onto the workbench. There was a faded owner's manual, some receipts for work done and some brochures advertising motor racing events in England and a few for the Phoenix Park races here in Dublin. There was a log book tucked into the pages of the owner manual, an original logbook for an Alfa Romeo 6C. It was in the name of George Moore. He thumbed through the pages of the manual hoping there might be something more. It was fascinating to find such interesting old trivia, but there were no revelations there. I was still hovering over the papers, reading the words aloud when he shouted, 'Savita!' at the top of his lungs and gave me a start. He did not take his eyes off the page as he shouted her name again with even more urgency.

I heard her scurrying across the gravel, then she dashed through the door, breathless.

'What is it, what's wrong?' she gasped.

Michael held a single piece of paper in his hand, he held it out to her but offered no explanation. She took it from him gently, quick to realise it was fragile. I watched her eyes dart back and forth as she read the text.

'Jesus! Michael, are you serious?' she exclaimed.

'It's hard to believe,' he said, setting the page back on top of the other papers.

I rushed past them to read it. It was a motor racing license, issued by the Royal Irish Automobile Club. It allowed the owner of the license to compete in events in the UK and the Republic of Ireland. Nothing unusual in that, I thought he would have to have had a license. And then I saw it, the signature, it was hard to read, but it was printed again in bold lettering. It was the license holder's name; George Blackwood.

I spun around to find Michael and Savita locked in debate.

'Did he have a cousin that would have raced the car with him?' Savita asked.

'You know exactly what it means, Michael,' I said, standing between them, but directing my remark only at Michael. I knew the boy would be quick to come to the same conclusion I had come to. I watched his expression change as the realisation struck him, and I spoke the words with him. 'He changed his name.'

'What?' she asked, 'Why would he do that?'

'I have no idea,' Michael replied. 'But I'm sure that is what he did. He changed his name to his mother's maiden name, and became George Blackwood.'

Chapter 51

It was the only hotel in the village. It was built in nineteen seventy-five and had one pathetic low budget refurbishment since then, and it showed. The stairs creaked with every step. Henry smiled as he went. The place was old and tired, just like he was. The receptionist had gone for the night, and he doubted there was anyone else staying there that night – at least it felt that way. There were photos along the top of the landing showing images of the town in better times. He gave them a passing glance as he made his way upstairs to his room. From his second-floor window, he could tell those times were long since gone. He looked at his watch, it had stopped at six thirty. He'd forgotten to wind it. He sat onto the end of the bed and dialled her number. It rang out several times. His heart sank, she was not home. Tonight, of all nights he needd to hear her voice, any voice. He rang one more time before he gave up.

'Hello,' her voice chirped on the other end of the phone, youthful and full of hope. 'Dad, is that you?'

He felt the lump in his throat and paused before he spoke. 'Yes honey, it's me,' he answered. 'Are you alright?'

'We're good Dad, and you?' It was a loaded question. She was asking him an awful lot in that one sentence.

'I'm okay,' he replied, after a long pause. 'I was there. I saw her. I saw the house and the grounds, but they have other buyers. They won't commit to selling until everyone has had a chance to view the car.'

She didn't answer right way. She was waiting, hoping

he had more to add. But there was only silence.

'Do you think it's the money, Dad? Are they being clever, are they trying to hold out for more, because I can help you out on this. You know I can.'

'That's sweet of you, but it's not the money. They are good people. I can feel it. It's something else, Maria. I can't explain it but it was like walking into the past. The atmosphere, the presence. I could almost taste it.'

'Be patient Dad, it may work out yet.'

He laughed into the phone. 'I have waited a very long time, honey, a few days more will not be a problem.'

She relaxed. She took comfort from the calmness of his voice, then she changed the subject.

'Are you comfortable? Did you find somewhere nice to stay?'

He looked around his room, 'I found a room in a nice little two-star hotel close by.'

'Two-star?' she said, in an exasperated tone. 'What is that like?'

He laughed, 'Well let me put it like this, honey – there is no such thing as a no star hotel.'

'Jesus, Dad! Why didn't you find somewhere nice for yourself?'

'I'm not a big one for creature comforts, honey. I don't sleep anyway. It's fine. I'll call you in a day or so and let you know how it went.'

'Good luck, Dad. We all have our fingers and toes crossed for you. Love you.'

'Goodnight, honey,' he said, feeling a lot cheerier for having spoken to her. He set the phone aside and tipped the contents of a timeworn folder onto the bed. The letters and photos spilled out over the floral-patterned bedspread. He sifted through them, as he had done so many times over the years. Personal letters, the ink long since faded and illegible, photographs and postcards worn from years of handling. Just like every other time he searched through this collection, his fingers sought out the same black and white photo. Two men, arms folded boldly in front of their chests, each covered in dust and grime, were leaning against a car. One of them looked much older than the other. The car they leaned on was scratched and covered in spatters of oil. It was an Alfa Romeo 6C, and they leaned against it like it was a mistress they shared. Henry fingered the photo between finger and thumb as he looked out the window of his hotel bedroom. He stared hard, as if he could see all the way to the house and beyond, into the mists of time if he stared hard enough.

Chapter 52

The '69 had been pushed into the centre of the garage for the viewing. With great effort Michael pushed her back into the garage, back into the shadows. It took much more effort than it took to push her out.

'I should have taken you out more often,' he gasped with the effort. 'Either your brakes are binding,' he paused. 'Or you're reluctant to go back there.' He looked into the shadows and shivered involuntarily. 'Don't blame you, old girl. It's not a fitting place for you. Hopefully you will be in the limelight soon.' He patted her roof and walked to the door. I stood by his side in the doorway. I was back to the old routine, I did not appear unless Michael was here. I took the opportunity to scan the treeline by the river. I was straining to see if he was there lurking in the mist, or under the shadow of a tree. I was convinced this stranger was him, Henry Blackwood. Call it intuition, a dead man's newfound understanding of the things that the living cannot see, or whatever you like, but I could feel it in my bones. There was something about the way he looked around him, not just looking at the garage and its paraphernalia, I knew he was looking for something. What it was, I could not tell. I was not able to decide if the vibe I got from him was something I should be worried about. My instinct was to like the man, but maybe that was just a nostalgic thing, I liked him because he was from my time, and seemed to share my values.

No matter how hard I strained I saw nothing, there was no-one there. Or at least I could see no-one. Yet I had an ever-growing sense that there was someone near, either in or around the garage. I turned to the shadows and stared. My eyes could see no farther than a few inches into the inky blackness. Though I had lost all sense of touch and feeling I did still feel a chill somewhere down in my core when I stepped into that darkness, it made me venture there less and less. This angered me, for my world was already small enough, I didn't need anything infringing on it and making it even smaller.

Angrily, I took a few bold steps towards the shadows, my courage waning with each step. A living man fears death, what could I possibly be afraid of, and yet there was a force greater than death. Was there a battle raging in those shadows for my soul, the forces of good and evil clashing head to head? Was that the turmoil I felt when I tried to peer into that darkness? Or was I being vain, was my pathetic insignificant soul of any godly importance? Standing on the boundary of the light of the garage and the darkness of the shadows I stopped. I looked down at my feet, the shadow crept over the tips of my shoes. I shuffled backwards.

'Dad, are you there?' I asked the question softly and waited, but there was nothing but silence.

I closed my eyes, inhaled and leaned my head back. 'You are, I know you are.' I opened my eyes and looked around the garage where he toiled. 'Where else in heaven or earth would you be?' The wind rose outside, it rattled the tin on the roof.

'You're not on your own though, are you?'

There it was, that sensation I could not put into words, but I felt it – anger, disappointment, regret. So many negative emotions coiled into one. An overpowering weight that gave density to the blackness of the shadows.

'Who are you?' I demanded in a raised voice. I summoned the courage to ask, aware that I was part of their world now, a world of those who had passed away. Were there more like me, men and women who were trapped between life and death, perhaps trapped in those shadows.

'What is it about this guy?' Michael muttered. His voice gave me a start, I had forgotten he was still there. He was talking to himself of course, but I could not help but answer. 'Don't know son, but there is something.' If my head wasn't filled with cotton wool I might have been able to concentrate, to think. His face was not familiar, and though I was always bad with names, I never forgot a face, and yet I felt like I knew him.

Chapter 53

'I'm going for a walk. There's nothing more to discuss, unless he comes clean and tells me what he's up to. I won't part with the car.' Michael struggled into his jacket and was already half way out the door.

'He's going to be here in a few hours. Why don't you phone his hotel and have it out with him, save him coming all the way out if you feel like this?' Savita pleaded.

Michael paused and looked at her, clearly pondering the wisdom of her words.

'No, let him come. I'll see what he has to say and decide then.'

'I thought we would decide these things together,' Savita called after him. He ignored her and stomped off at a pace, his feet matched the speed of the wheels that were spinning around in his head.

'No sense trying to talk to your father when he's like this,' Savita said to the little boy playing with a toy car at the table.

Michael had not made it to the end of the lane when he met him. Henry was early. Michael turned his wrist to look at his watch. Henry saw him. 'I'm sorry. I know I'm early, but I'm a bad sleeper.'

Michael hesitated for a moment. He would have liked to lecture Henry for coming too early, for not being honest, but he was willing to wait, to give him a chance to explain. He extended a hand. 'It's not a problem Henry, we've been expecting you. I was just going for a walk to kill the time, but it's best you're here. We can get this dealt with.'

Henry turned his head slowly and looked at him. Michael was calm, he was giving nothing away but the old man took no comfort from his cold emotionless greeting. He continued slightly behind Michael, his head bowed a little more than it had been.

Savita heard their voices as they approached. She sent the boy into the playroom and followed them as they passed the house on their way to the garage. Henry heard her quick step in the gravel, trying to catch up.

'Good morning,' he said in a neutral voice. The corners of his mouth tried but failed to turn upward into a smile.

'Nice to see you again, Mr Blackwood.' Savita quipped as she passed him and entered the garage ahead of him.

Michael snapped his head around, and scowled in her direction.

Henry drew a deep breath. This was going to be contentious. He could feel it coming.

'Henry, I have to tell you that the other buyer hasn't come yet and...'

'Please,' Henry interrupted. 'I don't want to play games. I am old and tired but I am seriously interested in the car. I know I should play the part of the reluctant buyer, but I have no energy for such games. I am prepared to pay your asking price. I won't haggle.'

Michael and Savita stared at each other. Savita gave him her, eyes wide open 'don't do anything stupid' look, that he knew all too well.

Michael held her gaze when he spoke. 'Blackwood? That isn't an Irish name, is it Henry?'

'What?' Henry replied, surprised by the question. A long silence followed. Tension mounted. I saw Savita swallow and Michael ready himself for whatever was to come, truth or lies. The next few words from Henry would make or break the deal.

I watched Henry closely. I could tell there was an inner turmoil he was battling to contain; and then he surprised me, he smiled. He took the cloth cap he had been passing from hand to hand and mopped his brow with it.

'Nothing is ever easy,' he said with a light chuckle as he stared into the rafters. He turned his eyes to the sign that lay upside down on the bench. I saw him flinch, he must have known something of the signs hidden secret. I could almost hear the whirr of the gears and cogs in his head spinning as he put two and two together.

Savita moved to Michael's side, she put an arm around his waist and pressed herself against her husband.

'I barely knew the man,' Henry said, his voice distant and detached. 'I was just ten when my father first left us. He came in and out of our lives so many times after that, I'd lost count. I do remember sitting on his knee once, I was so terribly young it surprises me that I can remember the moment,' Henry looked to Michael and Savita, his eyes had grown soft and he looked tired. He smiled a simple and apologetic smile. 'I listened carefully as he described this place, this haven. It is exactly as I imagined it would be.' He looked directly at Savita. 'I have to say, my dear, so many things in life are a disappointment, it is wonderfully refreshing to know that this, at least, has lived up to my expectations. I recall my father saying he felt safe here.' He turned his attention to Michael as he continued. 'He had a horrid time during the war.'

Henry stumbled suddenly, his legs looked like they were no longer able to hold him upright. Savita rushed to his side. She took him by the arm. She was much smaller than the old man but Henry was fragile; she had no difficulty supporting his weight. Michael didn't move. She shot him a disapproving glance, but Michael did not move. He stared solemnly at Henry, awaiting the remainder of his story, his explanation.

'Thank you, my dear,' Henry mumble. 'I felt a little lightheaded, skipped breakfast I'm afraid. I just wasn't in the mood to eat.'

'Sit,' she ushered him into my chair. 'I'll get you a cup of tea.'

Henry made himself comfortable in my chair. It was not easy; the chair had gone even more knobbly than it had been; the springs had surrendered their tension and the cloth was frayed to the point it looked like it would scatter at any moment.

Savita dashed off to make a pot of tea, glancing at Michael as she left. I could tell he was being reprimanded in that glance but he ignored her gaze. Henry looked his way.

'My father said the locals always spoke fondly of the Captain,' Michael broke his silence.

'That is very kind of you to say,' Henry replied. 'But he did not like being called the Captain, even though it was how he was best known. He wanted to forget all about the war. The last thing he wanted was a title that reminded him of that every day. That's why he changed his name.'

Savita returned with a tray, three cups and a few cupcakes. 'Here,' she encouraged Henry, 'get something sweet into you to get your blood sugars back up.'

He took the cup and bit into the sweet cake. 'Mmm, you're too kind, my dear,' he mumbled, his mouth full, 'these are excellent.'

Michael stood firm, frustrated at her interruption and eager to get some answers from Henry. Savita hovered over the old man like a mothering hen, concern written on her face. I could not help but pace back and forth as I listened to every word.

'These walls, that sign, it's like stepping into my past.' Henry dusted the crumbs from his lap. He looked at the couple who stared back at him. He knew they expected him to continue. He took a deep breath and exhaled slowly before he began.

'He met my mother when he came back from the war. He said she was the only one who tried to understand him. She said she fell in love with him the moment he stepped into the courtyard; his brass buttons shining in the sun, rows of medals across his broad chest. He was a sight to behold, she said.'

'Were they happy together?' Savita asked. Michael scowled again at her interruption, he didn't want her to go off the subject and get distracted with tales of Henry's life as a boy.

'My father, it turned out, was hard work, but they courted off and on for the next ten years before they eventually married; but to answer your question, yes ma'am, they were very happy – for a while.' Henry smiled at her, grateful for her consideration. 'My father never really came home from the war, not all of him anyway. My mother tried her best to hold us together but it was never easy.'

I listened to Henry and remembered how my father talked about the Captain, and his exploits on the racetrack. He said the other drivers were a little afraid of him. He took reckless chances, as if he was not afraid of dying. From what Henry was now saying it sounds like that may have been true.

'How did he get hooked on the cars?' Michael had to ask. He knew Savita and before long she would have the old man recounting the story of his life, forgetting why they were all gathered here.

'The war,' Henry replied. 'It began during the war. He was driven to and from the front a few times in some old jalopy. It fascinated him, he marvelled at this invention, and I guess he was hooked from then on.'

Michael walked to the workbench and picked up the old sign. I saw Henry flinch, then he turned and handed him the sign. 'Do you remember this?' Michael asked.

'I'm not sure,' Henry stammered in a less than convincing tone. His word-perfect eloquence deserted him when he had to tell a bold-faced lie. He pondered the question for a moment longer. 'I think I remember the car being here, but then my father had told me about it so many times, I can't be sure the memory is my own.' He looked at Michael to see if he understood what he was trying to say. 'Maybe I just remember being told about it?'

I understood how he felt. My father told me so much about the Alfa Romeo. I sometimes thought I was there and had seen it for myself.'

'Anyway,' Henry continued. 'The cars soon lost their shine. His head went down, he just was not able to shake off the effects of the war. He became morbidly depressed, he took to gambling. It has been said that those who come close to death and escape, are fond of taking risks forever after. Maybe that's how it was with my father too.' Henry sat forward, resting his elbows on his knees he clasped his head in his hands. Savita moved to go to him. Michael caught her arm and shook his head, urging her to wait, to give him time. The mother in her wanted to help him to ease his pain, to mother him. Henry was old enough to be her father. I could see she empathised with his suffering. And I too could not help but feel sorry for him, this tired old gentleman that was coming apart before all our eyes.

'Been a long road for you, Henry,' I said, kneeling to his level. I looked into his face. It was an honest face, but a troubled one. I looked at Michael and Savita, I could see they too felt for the old man.

'He'd lost most of his inheritance by the time they married.' Henry was looking at the floor, his head still clasped in his hands. 'These walls were never my home. He'd lost the estate by the time I came along. My mother had to work, to scrimp and save to get us by. And yet I never heard her say a bad word about him. Our fortunes went up and down depending on the roll of his dice or the turn of a card. Then one day luck dealt him a good hand, he fell in with a better crowd. Upper class, more money to spend and careless with the cards. He won a bit of property and some valuable items. He was transformed, his self-esteem returned. He thought he could get out of the game, make a few investments and straighten himself out. He was almost there. He had almost made it, almost made his escape when he lost her.' Henry raised his head and pointed to the '69.

I jolted to attention as if I'd been slapped in the face. The '69? Had Henry just pointed to the '69?

Michael took a step forward, away from Savita and towards the car. His head snapped back and forth between the old man and the car several times as he tried to accept what he just heard. He opened his mouth to speak but Henry interrupted him.

'That's right son, it was once my father's car. He won her in a card game. She came along with a house and a sizeable piece of land.'

I had been hunkered down in front of Henry where he sat, almost at eye level with him when he dropped this bomb. I fell back onto my ass on the floor in front of him. I looked to the shadows, they were static, as if they too had frozen in shock.

'She was red and shiny, reminded him of his Alfa Romeo. The car drew him back into the real world for a while. He took stock of what he was missing. He talked about starting up a specialist car dealership. My mother was excited too, but also a little apprehensive. She knew it was the ramblings of a man, desperate to salvage something from a wasted life. He was seventy-three, too old for pipe dreams. Unlike me, she'd seen all of this before, the highs and lows of a gambler, an addict. She didn't get her hopes up, she remained cautious, watched him closely, tried to keep him away from his old buddies until he was well free of the addiction. But she was not diligent enough. An American appeared, flashing money. A sure thing, a soft touch his friends told him. Easy money.'

I walked over the car. Put both hands on her bonnet and looked around me. 'So, you were his mistress too. You've been around, old girl.' The others were still listening intently to Henry, he was pouring out his heart, laying his life bare before them. I knew he wasn't doing this to gain their favour, it was like a great purge, all the emotions that he'd bottled up inside that were eating at him were bursting free, he could not contain them any longer. It seems he had no-one to share these thoughts with.

When I wandered back to sit between them he was still talking about his father's gambling.

'He didn't see it coming. He'd taken the American for an amateur – a chump was the word he used. But he'd been played. He wasn't expecting the ace, was sure the American was bluffing.' Henry's voice grew faint as he told this last bit. Savita topped up his cup with some fresh tea, as if he was a machine that needed to be lubricated, oiled so that he could continue.

'He lost the house and lands that he'd won. This didn't bother him.' Henry pointed again at the '69. 'But her, it broke his heart to part with her. That was the last straw. Something in him broke when she was taken from him. He lived, no that's not fair to describe his existence as living; he survived for another three years as a hollow shell.'

Henry supped loudly from his tea.

'Do you remember her?' Michael asked. He was trying to get the chronology right in his head. It was nigh impossible to keep track of it all. The Captain, my father, me, Michael and somewhere in between, Henry had played a small part.

'Vaguely,' Henry replied, shaking his head. 'My mother and I were in and out of his life. But she remains the last physical thing in this world that he owned, that he possessed. The '69 reminded him of his true love, the motor car, the love he abandoned when he gave himself up to the addiction. I hope you understand?'

Savita was quick to nod her head, Michael was slower to respond. I knew him well. He would have to have it all worked out in his head. He would have to understand the how's and why's of Henry's case.

Henry looked at him blankly, he looked spent. He had poured out his heart and it left him defenceless. He'd held nothing back, had no leverage, no bargaining point.

'I am at your mercy, Michael. Only you can decide what to do. I hope I have showed you that I have a history with the car; that we are in some small way bound together.'

'So, this was why the American had so little regard for the car,' I said. 'It was an easy win at the cards. My father could never understand how he parted with it so easily.'

Michael stared at Henry for a long time. They held each other's gaze without a word.

'Oh, give him the car, for Christ's sake, Michael. I don't care what he can pay!' Savita exploded, she took Michael's hand and looked up into his face.

Michael looked down at her, a hint of a smile on his face. 'What about all the costs, the boy's education, security? You said they were critical.'

'Oh, to hell with what I said. He has to have the car. It's like karma or fate or destiny or whatever you want to call it, but there is no way anybody other than Henry can be allowed to drive off in that.' She pointed an accusing finger at the car.

Michael rubbed his chin, exhaled loudly and was about to speak when Savita interrupted him again.

'Don't be an ass, Michael. We both know you're going to sell him the car. I know you. You won't let it go anybody else.'

'Jesus, woman!' Michael sniggered, 'We're supposed to be making a sale here. You've shown our hand.' he said laughing loudly.

'Yeah, right!' she exclaimed, 'There are no more secrets here. Everyone has laid their cards on this table.' She was standing in front of the car, still lecturing. When she turned Michael and Henry were vigorously shaking hands. Then they took each other and embraced. Savita's eyes filled with tears. Mine would have too, if I were capable of such a living human act.

And there it was, the end – the '69 was leaving, going to a new home. My father's work, my work, my son's work. It was finally done.

'You'd be proud of them both, Mary,' I said looking upwards first, then turned to face the shadows. They were still darker than the shadows in the back of a garage should have been in daylight hours, but they didn't exude that same aura of peril. Make no mistake, they still scared me, scared me enough to stay clear until I knew what lay there. I turned at the sound of the garage door closing as they left.

The threesome made towards the house making happy mumbling noises. And still I remained. Now I thought, now is a good time to go, to take me. It's done. Mary is gone. My son is well. He has a happy family around him. And the '69 is sold. I spun around in a circle, arms outstretched and eyes shut tight, like a mad whirling dervish. No dizziness overcame me. I felt if I wanted I could spin around in circles forever, no-one would stop me. Was that it, there was no-one up there? Was I condemned to these walls for eternity. To watch generation after generation come and go.

'What the fuck did I do to deserve this?' I screamed.

The shadows swirled violently again. Were they trying to tell me something? Like a frustrated dog barking at its owner, neither having the language to communicate to the other.

I moved closer, put my face against the darkness, felt its coldness, my first physical sensation in a long time. I pulled away. 'Tell me what you want?' I leaned closer as if to whisper into the ear of the shadows. Still nothing. Muted voices in the distance caught my attention. They were at the back door of the house, shaking hands and hugging. Henry took off, a brisk lively step that told his mood. He paused to glance my way, tipped his cap to me, or to the car, and was on his way again.

I felt myself grow thin as he went. Was this it, would I go for good this time? To where I had no idea, but I needed to be gone from the garage. Too many long nights working here and too many long, lonely nights standing here as a ghost.

Chapter 54

The tin on the roof reverberated at the sound of the engine. Michael revved the throttle sharply a few times and the car rocked where she sat. The garage door was wide open, beyond the courtyard at the corner of the house a car transporter was lowering its ramps. The sound of her engine drew me back. Reluctantly I opened my eyes on another day. It was not over yet.

Michael eased the '69 out of the garage. The low burble from the exhaust sounded so sweet as she passed me. I was sitting in my chair, struggling to motivate myself to get up.

Henry stood by the truck with Savita. Both were distracted. Savita was trying to pay attention to what he was saying, but she wanted to be at her husband's side to hold his hand when Henry took the car. They all stood still as the '69 rolled out of the garage and passed through the courtyard for the last time. This had been her home, had been Henry's father's home. Henry explained to Michael and Savita what his plans were for the car. I was fortunate to be close enough to hear the conversation; maybe it was more than good fortune, maybe I was being allowed this important piece of information?

Henry intended to introduce the car to his grandson. It was to be the boy's inheritance. A parting gift from him. He was an old man; his health was failing. It had taken him a long time to get to this moment. It meant everything to him.

'I imagine you will be glad to see the car gone,' Henry said flippantly, casually laying a hand on Savita's arm. 'Your husband admitted it took up too much of his precious time, especially given his poor health.'

His words stung her, she had no idea he would know so much. She snapped her head around, her mouth open about to speak when he continued. 'I think your husband told me more than you would be comfortable for me to know,' he looked to Michael who was engrossed in his task of preparing the car to go. 'I think he needed me to understand the circumstances that made him let her go. He was afraid I was judging him, questioning why he would sell such an important piece of family history.'

'It's been a hard few years for us both, but more so for him,' Savita gestured to her husband with a nod of her head. 'Letting the car go has been tough, but it seems he's told you pretty much everything?'

'He did indeed, my dear. I was delighted to hear, delighted for you both.'

Savita smiled at him. 'The doctors were confounded, there was no rational explanation for his recovery. Total remission, the doctor said,' Savita laughed. 'The doctor was almost disappointed, annoyed that he couldn't explain it. He went on the defensive to explain how they had arrived at their original prognosis.'

'I don't care, how or why, I told him. I have my husband home and well.'

Little Michael circled his mother and Henry on his little tricycle as they chatted.

'Michael,' she scolded. 'Get away from the truck. The man is trying to get the car loaded.'

The boy pushed his tricycle aside and stood to watch. His father smiled at him as he eased past, lining the car up for the loading ramp. The '69 climbed the steep ramp effortlessly, ticking over smoothly. I felt a pang of regret that such a wonderful machine would be lost to us forever.

The driver folded up the ramps and strapped her down, my heart was breaking as I watched. Michael leaped to the ground.

'I expect you'll want to be paid?' Henry joked, he reached into the inside pocket of his jacket and withdrew a thick envelope. Michael smiled faintly at him. 'Savita will take that,' he said, his eyes still on the car, visibly reluctant to touch the money.

I walked to the edge of the courtyard. I put a foot outside, farther than I had been able to, and nothing happened. I wasn't whisked back to the chair. I took another and another and kept going until I was right by the truck. I reached out a hand to her and looked to the heavens. 'Thank you for this.' I whispered, 'I needed to say goodbye to the old girl properly.'

Michael, Savita and Henry were deep in conversation. I walked around the truck and surveyed the wonderfully curved lines of the '69 for the last time. I was unaware that young Michael had stepped away from the corner of the house to follow me. Yet again he was staring straight at where I stood and yet not at me.

'What do you see, son?' I stared back at him. 'Can you see me? Can you hear me?' I asked, my voice raised to a shout. But the boy didn't stir.

The truck started up, Savita moved to her husband's side and sidled up close to him. He threw an arm around her and pulled her even closer.

'Come here Michael,' she called to the boy. 'Wave goodbye to the car. This was Daddy's car, the '69.'

The boy did as he is told, 'I thought you said it was granddad's car?' he asks.

'It was son, it was.' Michael said, his voice breaking.

The '69 disappeared down the driveway for the last time. Yet it wasn't entirely a sad moment. My son was well, he had a family, the house would come to life again and hopefully now I would find closure to whatever it was that had me suspended here.

Savita stood on her tip-toes and reached up to kiss her husband. Michael still held his son's hand. The boy strained to break free, then paused. 'Who are those men, Daddy?' he asked. He was staring in my direction. I raised a hand and waved to him. He turned to his father who was paying him no attention, then he waved back. 'Who are they Daddy? Daddy? Daddy who are they?' The boy shouted, frightened and yet excited.

I felt a familiar hand grip on my shoulder. Emotions denied to me these past years washed over me in a tidal wave. I turned to face him, he was still wearing those same old greasy overalls, a smear of grease on his cheek just under his eye, as if he'd just stepped away from a project in the garage. He looked younger than I last remembered him, maybe around the age he would have been when he first brought me here.

I hugged him, overjoyed to be able to feel flesh and bone again. He ruffled my hair, like he did when I was a boy, and with an arm around me, he turned me back into the garage. The shadows faded away as light from the open door filtered in, all the way to the back, leaving a figure exposed. A tall thin man. 'Henry?' I asked, 'Is that you?' I stepped away from my father. This stranger, this ghostly figure was much younger than Henry, though they shared the same features. I looked again. 'Captain?' I asked, reaching out to shake his hand. He considered me for a moment, then with one hand he twisted the corner of his moustache, the other he extended to take mine.

'What's wrong with you? What's all the shouting about?' Michael took his son by the shoulder and turned him around to face him. 'What is it son?' he asked. The boy pointed to the garage, but there was no longer anyone there. His father ruffled his hair, a gesture that was in our family genes, then turned him towards the house. All three entered the kitchen, Michael, my wonderful son, the last to go in. He paused and took a long look back towards the garage. I saw him strain to look inside. He smiled a knowing and satisfied smile before he went inside to join his family.

The End

Dear Reader,

I hope you enjoyed 'The Shadows of Time'.

As an author I love feedback. We are living in a wonderfully technological age, where you, the reader, have the power to influence discourse and have a say in how future books are written. Please do take the opportunity to let your voice be heard by contacting me directly or by following my blog via the links below.

Email: josephmccloskey99@gmail.com

If I could ask for one thing, I would really appreciate if you could leave an honest review of my book on Amazon. You can do this by going to amazon.com/author/josephmccloskey. You will see my book here, and my other books too. By clicking on my book you will be taken directly to the page where you purchased it from. At the end of the page click on the Write A Customer Review. Many thanks - Joseph McCloskey

Other Books By The Author

Chasing Dragons

The untimely death of his father gives Joe the opportunity to make his escape. He takes off on a quest to trace his grandfathers footsteps through WW1 France; hoping that somewhere along the way he'll stumble on his own purpose in life.

But he unsettles a past that draws him in, setting off a chain of events that binds him to his grandfathers past, and seals his own future.

Available from Amazon.

Anna

The antique shop Paul works in is burgled, Benjamin the owner is missing, and the only thing taken is an unassuming portrait of a young girl.

Alice, an insurance investigator, turns up with tales of masterpieces stolen by the Nazis. She's been on the trail of the painting, Anna, for some time. As she outlines it's past it becomes apparent that the painting is linked to his own past and to Benjamin's.

They set off to find Benjamin and find out if the painting is just a family portrait, of nothing but sentimental value, or a masterpiece lost in the ravages of the war.

Their investigation draws the attention of some unsavory characters. A Nazi war criminal and art collector, set on getting his hands on Anna at any cost, and an assassin for the Russian Mafia.

Paul struggles to come to terms with the ruthlessness of the people he encounters in this alien world of murderers and gangsters...and then there's Alice. The experiences they share serves to bond them to each other, but like the missing painting, Alice is not all she appears to be.

All the parties involved are drawn to where it all began. Prague, a boundary between East and West where both sides are pitted against each other one last time in a climatic showdown.

Available from Amazon.

Printed in Great Britain
by Amazon

69218768R00184